THE TWO GATES

THE TWO GATES

a novel

Ken Davenport

The Two Gates
©2017 Ken Davenport

The Two Gates is a work of fiction. All characters and their dialogue, with the exception of some well-known historical and public figures, are the product of the author's imagination. Where real-life historical figures appear, the incidents, situations and dialogue concerning those persons are entirely fictional unless footnoted or detailed in the Author's Note at the back of this book. In all other respects any resemblance to actual persons is entirely coincidental.

———

This book was designed by THE FRONTISPIECE. The text face is Minion Pro, designed by Robert Slimbach in 1990, with other elements set in Vanguard CF, & Lucida Sans Typewriter Std.

DEDICATION

To the 2.7 million American service men and
women who served in Vietnam from 1961 to 1975.
This nation owes you a debt of gratitude.

AND IN MEMORY OF:

1Lt. (Ranger) Donald R. Judd, USA

Killed in action in the Central Highlands of
Vietnam on June 22, 1967.

Aged 24 years.

A soldier once, now forever young.

ACKNOWLEDGMENTS

This book would never have been written without the encouragement of my good friend, author Eliot Peper. I had written the first 80 pages of The Two Gates almost 10 years ago and then dropped it. Eliot encouraged me to "just finish it." I'm glad I did. Thanks, Eliot!

Writing is a solitary endeavor, but it can't be done without support. My wife Juliet, a paralegal in a past life, read the manuscript several times and provided great feedback on the writing, story and characters. In addition, I received helpful edits from Maya Rock at Writer's Ink and Bethany Sullivan. Thanks also to my son's 5th grade writing teacher, Dennice Rousey, for reading an early draft and providing encouragement and some very helpful comments.

And finally, I am grateful to have the chance to work with veterans, young and old. Decorated Vietnam veteran and author Karl Marlantes is a personal hero of mine, and his raw and honest writing on war inspires me daily. And to Elizabeth Washburn and the many Iraq and Afghanistan combat veterans at Combat Arts San Diego, thank you for teaching me how art can be a powerful tool for healing.

Herbert Hoover once said, "Older men declare war. But it is the youth that must fight and die." May we always remember the human costs of war.

More than 58,000 Americans died in the Vietnam War, but only 200 had been killed as of November 22, 1963— the day John F. Kennedy was shot in Dallas, Texas...

NEWS FLASH ALERT
November 22, 1963
1:40 p.m. EST
United Press International

Dallas, Texas – Three shots were fired at President Kennedy's motorcade. It is unclear at this hour if any member of the President's motorcade was hurt in the shooting, though there are unconfirmed reports of injuries.

More information to follow as it becomes available.

CHAPTER 1

The Robert F. Kennedy Residence
Hickory Hill, Virginia
1:55 p.m., November 22, 1963

I wish the damn telephone would stop ringing.

United States Attorney General Robert Kennedy was trying his best to ignore the phone. He was just finishing a working lunch with U.S. Attorney Robert Morgenthau, and was in the middle of an intense discussion on the Justice Department's—as yet unsuccessful—strategy to take down the New York mafia. It was an issue that the Attorney General cared deeply about and had staked much of his professional career on. It was no time for interruptions.

Whomever was calling was persistent, and the phone continued to ring with an urgent rhythm: five rings and then a pause of precisely five seconds, followed by five more rings and another pause.

Finally, Kennedy gave in. "Can someone please answer the telephone?" he yelled.

Kennedy's wife, who knew the phone was obviously for her husband, picked up the receiver. "Kennedy residence."

A hiss followed by a metallic voice came on the line. "The Director is calling for the Attorney General. It's urgent."

Ethel Kennedy didn't have to ask which director the operator was talking about. Holding out the receiver, she said, "Bobby, J. Edgar Hoover is calling."

Bobby Kennedy instantly knew something was wrong. The Director of the F.B.I. and Bobby hated each other, and Hoover never called him at home.

He took the phone from his wife, "This is the Attorney General."

"Hold for the Director, please." After a series of clicks, Hoover came on the line. "I have news for you," Hoover said, his voice flat and without emotion. "The president's been shot."

"Oh my God!" Bobby blurted. He paused to try and gather himself, wanting to be in control of his emotions in front of Hoover. "Is it serious?"

"I think it's serious. I'm trying to get details. I'll call you back when I know more."

Hoover abruptly disconnected the line, leaving Bobby Kennedy holding the phone in silence. Trying to make sense of what he had heard, he called out to his wife.

"Jack's been shot," he said, putting a hand up to his mouth, as if he didn't believe the words had actually left his lips.

Ethel cried out. "Oh, Bobby! What's happened?"

"I don't know. I'm calling the White House switchboard now."

President John F. Kennedy lay on a metal gurney in Trauma Room One as a frenzy of activity took place around him. His eyes were open but unfocused. His gray suit had been cut away, the pieces of which now littered the bloodstained floor. A quick visual search of the president's body identified a dime-sized entrance wound to the back of the neck; the bullet had exited his throat just above the trachea, miraculously missing any vital organs. After the first shot from the 6th floor of the Texas School Book Depository struck, Kennedy had grasped his neck, slumping forward and then to the left toward his wife, who reacted instinctively, pulling him toward her in a protective embrace.

Now, every surgeon at Parkland Hospital flooded the trauma bays to try and save the president. In Unit One, doctors cleared the president's airway, gave him an IV and a blood transfusion. His pulse was regular and steady, and his blood pressure stable. It had quickly become clear to the surgeon attending him, Dr. Mac Perry, that the president would survive this wound.

Unfortunately, the same could not be said for the patient in Trauma Room Two. There, Dr. William Kemp Clark, Parkland's Chief of Neurosurgery was attending to the First Lady. Jackie Kennedy's protective embrace had placed her directly in the path of what would become known as the "kill shot"—the assassin's third and final bullet. Clark took one look at Jackie and knew that the situation was hopeless; the damage to her brain was catastrophic. All Clark could do was piece the flap of her skull back together to protect her brain matter from prying eyes. He ordered Trauma Unit Two cleared of all non-medical personnel. He wanted to give the First Lady some privacy. It was the least he could do for a woman who had suffered a gruesome death in the most public of ways.

When Secretary of Defense Robert S. McNamara heard about the shooting in Dallas, he had gone immediately into the conference room known as "The Tank"—a protected bunker with secure, global communication capabilities. Seeking confirmation of whether or not the president had died, McNamara had instructed his staff to speed dial Parkland Hospital until they reached someone who could verify the president's condition. In the meantime, McNamara sprung into action on his own accord. His first move had been to call the U.S. Ambassador to Moscow, Foy Kohler, asking him to immediately send a message through channels to Chairman Nikita Khrushchev. This request reflected two convictions McNamara had about what had transpired in Dallas. First, he believed that it was of vital importance to make a clear and unambiguous statement to the Soviets that the president was in complete control of the government. Second, he feared that in the absence of such a clear statement the Soviets would immediately move to press their positions around the world. His next step had been to call an emergency meeting of the Joint Chiefs of Staff, to be held later that day at the Pentagon, while simultaneously putting on alert the Commander in Chief of NATO, the Commander of the Strategic Air Command and all other theater commanders to await further instructions as to the disposition and movement of their forces.

He then called Bobby Kennedy, who was also trying to find out about his brother's condition.

"Bobby, since we don't know the president's condition and Vice President Johnson is still at Parkland, I'm going to raise the DEFCON level one notch to DEFCON 4." The American Defense Condition Level reflected the state of readiness of the U.S. military. Normal conditions were Level Five.

"Wouldn't that create unnecessary tension with the Soviets? They tend to overreact, and that's not something we want right now."

"I think it's worth the risk," McNamara said. "Raising the DEFCON level will signal to the Soviet Union that the U.S. military is still under clear control, and that we won't tolerate the Soviets taking advantage of the assassination attempt."

Bobby, who was already lost in thought, said simply, "Ok."

"Thanks. And one other thing. Do you know where the nuclear football is?"

Bobby momentarily didn't respond. The nuclear football was the last thing on his mind at that moment. "How the hell should I know? I imagine it's at the hospital in Dallas."

"Find out where it is and please secure it. We don't want the press seeing the officer carrying the football aimlessly wandering the halls of Parkland Hospital."

Bobby Kennedy looked at his watch. "I'm leaving in fifteen minutes to go down there. They've laid on a C-135 that's been fully converted to a flying hospital. We are going to bring the president back as soon as possible."

Intensive Care Unit – Parkland Memorial Hospital
Dallas, Texas
7:45 p.m., November 22, 1963

After a nerve-wracking four-hour flight from Washington, Bobby Kennedy entered the ICU in Parkland Memorial Hospital's surgical ward. He was immediately surprised by the number of people surrounding the bed of his older brother, the 35th President of the United States.

"Who the hell is in charge here?" he barked.

Bobby knew that in the interest of security it was necessary that the president be protected from non-essential visitors. Consequently, his first order was to "clear the room," followed by a single question: "Where's the guy with the football?"

After some frenetic searching, the Air Force officer carrying the nuclear football was located, and escorted into the president's room and shown to a seat in the corner. The "football" referred to the leather satchel that carried the nuclear launch codes and that accompanied the president whenever he was out of the White House. It was to be carried by a uniformed military officer within reach of the president at all times. In the event of a nuclear attack, the president would be able to access a 3 x 5 card with the nuclear launch codes as well as a black book of retaliatory options and target packages. It was, in the president's hands, akin to a mobile nuclear arsenal.

Kennedy then turned to the head of the Secret Service detail at the hospital and told him that he wanted Dallas Police placed at all external hospital entrances, and for visitors to be limited to essential medical personnel only. A phalanx of security was to be posted outside the entrance to the room, and an agent was to be seated inside the room at all times.

* * *

Vice President Lyndon Johnson and his wife Lady Bird had been sequestered in the bowels of Parkland Hospital for the past five hours. With the president's condition still unknown, and with security concerns paramount, Johnson was not allowed to leave the hospital. He was like a caged animal, pacing back and forth in the small confines of the Minor Medicine department on the hospital's ground floor. Johnson's Secret Service detail had found sandwiches and sodas for them, and done their best to relay information to Johnson and his wife as soon as it became available. But information was scant, and Johnson was unable to even make a phone call. Already he was worried.

Why the hell did this have to happen in Texas of all places? Johnson asked himself.

When Bobby Kennedy walked into Minor Medicine, Johnson stood up to greet him. "Bobby, I'm glad you are here. Any news about the president?"

Bobby immediately went to Lady Bird Johnson and took her hand. "I'm glad you are ok, Mrs. Johnson," he said.

"Thank you, Mr. Kennedy." Choking back tears she said, "I'm very, very sorry about Jackie."

"Thank you." Turning to the Vice President he said, "President Kennedy is in the ICU. He's expected to make a full recovery."

"Thank God almighty!" Johnson exclaimed, sounding a like a Baptist preacher.

"Lyndon, I need you to stay here until we are ready to transport the president back to Washington—hopefully by tomorrow morning. I've made arrangements for Lady Bird to fly back to Washington tonight."

"Bobby, I want to get the hell out of this hospital. I've been cooped up here for five hours!"

"I'm aware of that, Lyndon. But until the president is on the plane back to Washington, the Secret Service is asking that you stay here. And I agree with them."

"Bobby, I…"

"Goddamnit! Did you hear what I said? You are to stay here in the hospital until I tell you its time to go. Are we clear?"

Johnson, who very much wanted to punch the Attorney General of the United States in the nose, instead smiled and said, with dripping sarcasm, "As clear as day, Bobby."

* * *

Bobby Kennedy stood before a gurney in the refrigerated room that served as Parkland Hospital's morgue. Next to him stood Dallas County

Medical Examiner Earl Rose, the man responsible for certifying deaths and conducting autopsies. Behind them, standing like a sentinel in the shadows at the back of the room, was Secret Service Agent Clint Hill. Hill who had been close to Jackie and had run her security detail, now looked completely shattered, his suit coat stained with a dark substance that looked black, but that Bobby knew was blood.

"I want to see her," Bobby said to Rose in a soft, almost inaudible voice.

Rose stepped forward and gently pulled back the sheet, exposing only her body above the shoulders. Lying on the cold steel slab was the First Lady of the United States, Jacqueline Bouvier Kennedy. Her face was a ghostly white, her lips had a light blue hue. Her dark black hair, which had been perfectly coiffed under her pink pillbox hat, was now soaked in dried blood and tangled in a bunch behind her neck. She would have hated anyone seeing her this way, even in death. It was a further ignominy for her, and it made Bobby scream inside.

Bobby, a devout Catholic, made the sign of the cross and started to pray quietly. "God our Father, your power brings us to birth, your providence guides our lives, and by your command we return to dust..." After a moment, he again crossed himself and turned suddenly and walked toward the door, passing Agent Hill with barely a nod. Out in the corridor, he waited for Rose to appear.

"I want the First Lady ready to travel by tomorrow morning. Is that clear?"

Dr. Rose blanched. "Mr. Kennedy, ah, I can't permit that to happen. Mrs. Kennedy was killed in Dallas County. Texas and state law requires that we perform an autopsy here before she is transported out of the state."

"I don't care what state law says, doctor. You are to ensure that Mrs. Kennedy can be transported with the president when we leave Texas tomorrow morning. In the meantime, I've instructed the Secret Service to guard the First Lady's body until it is time to leave. Do I make myself clear?"

"Yes, quite clear. However—"

Bobby turned on his heels before Rose had a chance to finish his sentence.

* * *

"Mr. Attorney General!"

Secret Service Agent Roy Kellerman ran up to Bobby Kennedy who was talking on the phone to Robert McNamara from the office of the hospital's chief administrator. Bobby stared at Hill and waited for him to speak.

"Sir, I've been asked to tell you that the president is awake."

"Bob, I'll call you back," Bobby said promptly hanging up on the Secretary of Defense. Knowing that he was about to have a painful conversation with his brother, he walked slowly toward the ICU.

John Kennedy was lying not quite flat on a standard hospital bed, a pillow propped under his back, designed to help alleviate some of the chronic spinal pain he had suffered since an injury he had received when his motor torpedo boat was sunk by a Japanese cruiser in the Pacific during World War II. A series of tubes hooked into the president's arms provided fluids and medication, and a heart monitor above the bed beeped with a steady rhythm. The president's eyes were open and alert. A bandage covered his chest and neck area; though his voice wasn't permanently damaged, he had been told not to talk.

But it can be difficult telling the president of the United States what to do.

"Bobby..." he rasped in a voice that was difficult at first to understand. "What happened...?"

Bobby cut him off. "Jack," he said. "Shhh. Don't speak—you must save your voice." He paused, looking into his brother's eyes. "I'm afraid I've got bad news, Jack. There was a shooting in Dallas. You were shot once through the neck. The doctors have assured me you are going to make a full recovery." He paused again, taking his brother's hand, overwhelmed himself by the emotion he was feeling at that moment. "Governor Connolly was also wounded, but he's going to be ok," he continued, trying to steel himself for what came next.

The Lord is my shepherd...

"Where's Jackie?" the president asked, in a ragged whisper. Bobby met his brother's eyes and in an instant realized that John Kennedy already knew what was coming next.

Three simple words followed: "She's dead, Jack."

The president moaned softly, a single tear tracking along his left cheek as he closed his eyes tightly.

CHAPTER 2

Office of the Vice President
Room 274, Old Executive Office Building (OEOB)
Washington, D.C.
4:30 p.m., November 23, 1963

Lyndon Johnson sat alone in his office. It was a far cry from the massive corner suite he had occupied as the majority leader of the United States Senate, when he had arguably been the second most powerful man in the country. As Senate Majority Leader, Johnson had a staff of ten and virtually unparalleled influence in the United States Congress. That was then, before he had agreed to join the Kennedy ticket as vice president, a heartbeat away from the presidency but an empty suit in the corridors of power in Washington. It was before yesterday in Dallas. Dallas, of course, would change everything.

Since arriving at his office that morning after a sleepless night, the light on his telephone had been blinking steadily, but Johnson—a man rarely at a loss for words—didn't feel much like talking. The vice president knew that press speculation about him was running rampant and that every friend he'd ever had was fielding calls from reporters. He hadn't been surprised when his longtime aide Walter Jenkins had called him at home earlier that morning to say that a reporter from *The Washington Post* had called him at 4 a.m., wanting to know if Jenkins had any comments to make about the vice president's "situation." Jenkins, one of Johnson's oldest friends, could be trusted not to comment. But he wasn't naïve enough to think that others would be so careful or restrained; Johnson knew well that people generally had a hard time resisting the urge to comment to the press, and that some would want to assuage their sorrow by verbally processing the tragedy—even to a reporter.

Johnson had been in Washington for 25 years. He knew how the game was played. The press, the public—everyone would be looking for someone to blame for this horror. And he was a logical choice. After all, *he* was from Texas—the president had been shot in *his* backyard. The president's trip was necessary in part because *he* had failed to ensure that Texas was solidly behind the Democratic ticket in the lead up to the 1964 election. *He* was on the ticket to help Kennedy, the epitome of Harvard-educated, Eastern "blue blood" carry the rural, unsophisticated, beer-drinking Southern states of which Texas was the main prize. And just the fact that Kennedy had to go there at all, let alone a full year out from the 1964 election, meant that Johnson had failed.

The vice president swiveled around in his high-backed leather chair and looked out his second floor window onto the White House below. It was a gray day, a gloom that befitted his—and the nation's—mood. The country was in mourning for Jackie Kennedy. The reaction to her death had been immediate and universal; from virtually every corner of the world, telegrams of condolence had been streaming into the White House. Correspondents from every European, South American and Asian nation were in Washington to cover the elaborate memorial planned for her at the National Cathedral. The White House was expecting representatives from more than 45 nations to attend, including 22 heads of state. This, the vice president knew, was testament to the star power of Jackie Kennedy, and the degree to which she had made a deep impression on the world in the thousand days she spent as First Lady.

And they're all gonna think that I got her killed, thought Johnson.

Johnson suddenly turned back to his large oak desk and reached for the switch on his intercom. There was one person he did very much want to talk to.

"Yes sir?" came the metallic reply from his secretary, Juanita Roberts.

"Juanita, see if you can get Clark Clifford on the phone as soon as you can. He may not be in his office, but see if you can find him."

"Right away. Anything else, sir?"

"Not now, honey. Thank you."

He had known Clark Clifford since the late 1940s when, as a junior Congressman from Texas, Johnson had become an occasional member of President Harry Truman's regular poker games on the presidential yacht *Williamsburg*. Clifford, who was then the Naval Aide to President Truman, was responsible for organizing the games, which were strictly stag affairs that included some of the most powerful members of the government. Clifford had immediately taken a liking to Johnson, and they had remained friends through Johnson's rise to power in congress.

Clifford was one of Washington's classic insiders. He had become one of Truman's principal advisors, eventually rising to the position of "Counsel to the President." With Truman, Clifford had dealt with every type of issue one could imagine, from political scandal to serious issues of foreign policy. In 1960, he had been tapped by newly elected John Kennedy to head his transition team, and was now the Chair of the President's Foreign Intelligence Advisory Board. Most importantly, Clifford knew Kennedy quite well. He was the best person to help deal with the political fallout Johnson knew was coming.

The last time Johnson had spoken to Clifford about his role as vice president was in the wake of the Cuban Missile Crisis the previous year. Clifford had given him some sound advice about how to improve his role in the Kennedy White House without appearing to usurp the president or overstep his bounds. Johnson had found the Cuban crisis to be an exercise in extreme frustration; as vice president, he had attended most of the Executive Committee of the National Security Council—EXCOMM—meetings that dealt with the crisis, where the United States had come alarmingly close to a nuclear confrontation with the Soviet Union. Despite his consistent attendance, he had been only a fringe player, saying virtually nothing and sitting at the table only as an observer. He was there to be seen but not heard. Meanwhile, the president's brother, who Johnson despised, had played a major role in running the EXCOMM and in helping his brother through a very dangerous time. Johnson had ended that episode particularly depressed, realizing that his decision to join the ticket had neutered him.

"Mr. Johnson, I have Clark Clifford on line two."

Johnson quickly snatched up the phone. "Thanks for taking my call, Clark."

"Mr. Vice President," began Clifford, with practiced formality. Clifford, part of the old Washington establishment was a stickler for protocol and felt strongly that titles had important symbolic power. "Let me first say how sorry I am about what happened in Dallas—to the president, Mrs. Kennedy and the governor."

"That poor, sweet woman," said Johnson with real emotion in his voice. "You know, of all the Kennedys she was always the nicest to me, always treated me with respect and kindness—"

Clifford cut in, trying to shift the subject. Johnson's problems with the Kennedy clan—with Robert Kennedy in particular—were well known to Clifford. It was not an area he felt comfortable discussing with the Vice President. These kinds of conversations had a way of getting back to people and Clifford knew that Johnson had a habit of taping his personal conversations, ostensibly for the "historical record." Clifford, an experienced attorney, didn't want his voice on the record discussing the Johnson-Kennedy friction

"I spoke to Ted Sorenson this morning," Clifford said softly, his voice betraying his own fatigue. Sorenson was the President's Special Counsel, and a close friend of Clifford. "He says the president is now at Bethesda and is stable and improving."

Johnson grunted. "They won't let me see him. Apparently the Secret Service doesn't want us both in the same place. Personally, I think that's horse manure. I can't imagine I'd be in much danger at Bethesda. The real reason is that Bobby blames me for the whole damn thing. I'm already—what is the Latin term? *Persona non grata*."

"I guess since the president has been conscious and alert since coming out of surgery, the Attorney General didn't think it necessary."

"Hell, they won't even let me near the Oval Office. I've been holed up here at the OEOB all day. I'm afraid to show my face around the White House."

"Again, I suspect that's just for security reasons. Everyone is on edge and trying to ensure that this isn't some kind of conspiracy against the entire United States government."

Johnson knew what Clifford had deliberately omitted. They both knew it would be a cold day in hell before the Attorney General and the rest of Kennedy's staff—Kenny O'Donnell, Larry O'Brien and the other members of the "Irish mafia" as the VP derisively referred to them in private—allowed him to spend one minute in the Oval Office as Acting Chief Executive. Even if the president were in a coma, Bobby Kennedy would insist that the president be able to issue orders by fluttering his eyelids or altering the cadence of his breathing.

"Clark, I know this would seem callous to some, but I trust you to understand," Johnson said softly. "I know that things for me here will never be the same," he continued, referring to his position in the Kennedy Administration. "I was on shaky ground prior to Dallas—I know that

O'Donnell and O'Brien thought it was my fault that we even needed to go to Dallas in the first place. I was supposed to make Texas a safe state for the president." Johnson paused, collecting his thoughts. "I guess now I'll be blamed by them—and the president himself—for what's happened."

"Mr. Vice President, I can only tell you that what's done is done. You can't control their reactions. You can only control what happens from here on out. Be strong. Take your medicine, but hang on to your dignity. In the end, you'll have only that to take home to Texas when your time is up in Washington. And we all go home at some point."

It was good advice and Johnson knew it.

"Well, I'm glad the president is going to recover," said Johnson, with genuine sincerity in his voice. He knew the tragedy Kennedy's death would have been for the country.

Clifford said, "I heard from Kenny O'Donnell this morning that the president is awake. I asked him if he knew about Jackie. O'Donnell said that he did. It's a devastating loss for the man."

And a big loss for me, too, Johnson thought as he hung up the phone.

Office of the Attorney General
Department of Justice
Washington, D.C.
5:25 p.m., November 23, 1963

Bobby Kennedy sat slumped low in his desk chair smoking a cigarette. It was a Carlton Menthol that he had "borrowed" from his secretary earlier in the day, and that he had kept in his desk drawer for just this kind of moment. Bobby was a closet smoker—he never smoked in public and didn't buy his own. As he saw it, if he didn't buy the cigarettes or smoke in front of others he didn't really "smoke" per se, and managed to avoid having that nasty habit that the Surgeon General was just starting to issue report after report on. He took a long drag and savored it.

The exhaustion from the long day was settling in. He had shuttled between the Bethesda Naval Hospital, the White House, and the Georgetown home of W. Averell Harriman where Jackie Kennedy's parents and family were staying. Harriman, the Undersecretary of State for Political Affairs, was a long-time friend of Jackie and her family. Jackie's mother, Janet Norton Lee, had been so distraught since her daughter's death that she had been unable to talk to Bobby. Jackie's sister, Caroline Lee, had done most of the work helping Bobby make decisions regarding the funeral arrangements and ceremonies, the timing of which was complicated by the president's condition. At present, the funeral was to be in four days time. Bobby knew that Jack being there was imperative—both for the president's children, and the nation as a whole.

The funeral itself had proved to be a sticky issue. There was no precedent for a sitting First Lady dying in public at the hands of an assassin, especially one who had died taking a bullet meant for her husband who happened to be the leader of the free world. While it seemed entirely natural that she be treated with the respect of a state funeral, there had been some question as to whether that would be acceptable to her family, who initially had preferred a more intimate service at the family plot in upstate New York. In the end, it was the president who had made clear his desire that she should be buried with full honors, lying in state in the Capitol Rotunda, followed by burial at Arlington National Cemetery. She was the wife of a decorated naval officer, and was, herself, a national figure and now a national hero, having saved the life of the president. It was hard to argue against that logic, and Bobby was relieved to have the issue settled.

Bobby wondered how his brother would ultimately react to the death of his wife. It was a complex relationship. The public saw John and Jackie as a glamorous young couple in love, a fairy-tale prince and princess. This was a theme reinforced at every turn by the Kennedy public relations team.

The reality was more nuanced. Yes, John and Jackie loved each other but they also led busy, separate lives. Each had interests and needs that excluded the other. For the president it was primarily an insatiable sexual appetite and an endless stream of affairs. For Jackie it was frequent international travel and love of designer fashion, along with a country estate where she rode her beloved horses. They accepted each other's peccadilloes even if they didn't always approve of them. It was a relationship that worked, bound together by a mutual love of their children.

Now that she was gone, Bobby knew his brother would be wracked with guilt—not just because of his womanizing. It was the president who suggested that Jackie accompany him to Texas. Just a few months before they had lost their newborn son Patrick after just 40 hours of life, and the president thought the trip would do her good. Jackie rarely traveled with her husband on domestic political trips; in the ultimate of cruel ironies, she had died for it. Bobby knew this would be a very heavy burden for his brother to bear.

Even with the sadness he was feeling about Jackie, Bobby knew that fate had twisted in their favor. His brother had come within a whisper of being assassinated. That would have been the end of all their team had worked for since the early days of the 1960 campaign—the end of the campaign against organized crime and the end of their agenda on civil rights. It would have been the end of carrying the torch of the "new generation" forward, replaced as it would have been, so starkly, by the administration of one Lyndon Baines Johnson.

For the first time in two days Bobby allowed a slight smile to creep across his face. Not only was Johnson not going to be president of the United States, Bobby was going to do his level best to exile him, sending him back to the desolate backwoods of the Texas Hill Country where he came from.

CHAPTER 3

Lt. Col. Patrick O'Shea, dressed in civilian attire—black gabardine slacks and a dark gray sport coat—held a mug of piping hot coffee as he looked over cable traffic from Vietnam. He normally didn't work Saturdays, but with conditions in Saigon unstable he felt it important to keep abreast of the latest news. Though Kennedy was working a reduced schedule as he recuperated from the shooting in Dallas, he was still the president and required a constant stream of information and analysis.

O'Shea was serving as President Kennedy's military representative—essentially the president's personal military advisor. His route to this high visibility position in the White House was unconventional: he had been plucked from a staff job at the Pentagon and assigned to take over for Kennedy's previous military advisor, retired General

Maxwell Davenport Taylor, when Taylor was ordered back into uniform to chair the Joint Chiefs of Staff. In a controversial move for the rank-conscious Pentagon, Taylor himself had recommended O'Shea as his replacement. Kennedy was pushing a new defense strategy that emphasized flexibility and support for irregular forces fighting communism, and O'Shea, a decorated Green Beret, was an expert in counterinsurgency strategies and tactics. In 1961, O'Shea had spent almost a year in Vietnam as an advisor to the South Vietnamese army, all the while learning Vietnamese and putting the finishing touches on his master's thesis at the Army War College. With Vietnam looming as a major foreign policy issue, Kennedy saw O'Shea as a perfect choice to be his military aide.

And it didn't hurt that O'Shea was a fellow Irishman with a biting, acerbic sense of humor. Simply put, O'Shea and Kennedy had hit it off.

"Oh, shit!" O'Shea said to himself, louder than he intended.

All eyes were suddenly on O'Shea, including those of McGeorge Bundy, the president's national security advisor. Tall, thin and balding, Bundy now stood over O'Shea, casting a shadow over the cable O'Shea had just read. Without a word, O'Shea handed the cable to Bundy.

```
OUTGOING TELEGRAM

UNITED STATES EMBASSY, SAIGON

REPUBLIC OF SOUTH VIETNAM


JANUARY 30, 1963

FROM: AMBASSADOR LODGE

EYES ONLY FOR SECRETARY OF STATE, BUNDY, NSC


GEN MINH HAS BEEN DEPOSED IN BLOODLESS COUP TODAY.
NEW LEADER IS GEN NGUYEN KHANH. SITUATION IN SAIGON
IS EXTREMELY CHAOTIC.

AS PRECAUTION HAVE ASKED GEN HARKINS TO MOVE TO
REINFORCE THE EMBASSY COMPOUND AND TO ENSURE THE SECURITY
OF TAN SUN NHUT AIR BASE. HAVE REQUESTED AUDIENCE WITH
KHANH ASAP.

RECOMMEND A HIGH-LEVEL WORKING GROUP TO REASSESS THE
STRATEGIC AND TACTICAL ISSUES THAT WE NOW FACE AND AS
SOON AS CAN BE PRACTICALLY ARRANGED. LODGE
```

"Shit is right," Bundy said. "Let's go see the president."

The Residence
The White House
Washington, D.C.
8:45 a.m., January 30, 1964

When Bundy and O'Shea entered the residence on the third floor of the White House they found the president sitting in an easy chair reading *The New York Times*. Kennedy routinely read three newspapers a day, a habit he had taken up when he first ran for office. He quickly learned that information was the currency politicians trade in, and the more you knew the less often you got yourself into trouble by saying something stupid.

The president had been officially back at work with a light public schedule since mid-December, but the truth was that he hadn't regained enough strength to work at his desk for prolonged periods until mid-January. His neck wound was virtually healed, with only a small discoloration from two scars—an entrance wound in back and an exit wound in front—that were at the precise angle of the bullet's path from the Texas School Book Depository building.

Looking up, the president removed his reading glasses and asked, "What's happening, Mac? Sounded urgent on the phone."

"Mr. President, sorry to interrupt your Saturday. An urgent cable just came in from Lodge in Saigon," Bundy said, handing the cable to Kennedy.

Kennedy quickly read the cable. "Jesus! It's a revolving door. We should never have removed Diem."

Kennedy was referring to the coup that toppled long-time South Vietnamese President Ngo Dinh Diem just a few weeks before Jackie was killed in Dallas. Diem and his brother Nhu had been overthrown and killed by forces loyal to General Duong Van Minh, all with the explicit support of Ambassador Lodge and the CIA. In recent years

Diem had become increasingly difficult for the U.S. to control, and the hope was that new leadership would create a more stable partner for the American effort in Vietnam. The result turned out to be just the opposite: Minh was never able to consolidate his support inside the military, and was thus vulnerable to a counter-coup.

"What do we know about this General Khanh?"

"Sir, Khanh is a consummate opportunist," offered O'Shea. "He was a loyal supporter of Diem before it became clear that U.S. support for the regime was wavering. Khanh then shifted his loyalty to Minh. But Minh felt threatened by Khanh, and so he banished him as far from Saigon as possible. Khanh obviously didn't take too kindly to that."

Kennedy shook his head. "So is this Khanh going to be able to stabilize things? Is he someone we can work with?"

"Hard to say, sir. He has a reputation as a good fighter. But he's mercurial and…" O'Shea didn't finish his sentence. He was trying to find the right words.

"And what?" pressed Bundy.

"And impulsive and unstable," O'Shea said.

Kennedy looked at O'Shea and started to laugh. "Of course he is! I would expect nothing less at this point!"

Both Bundy and O'Shea tried to hide their smiles.

"Ok," Kennedy said with a sigh. "Please monitor the situation closely and let me know when Lodge makes contact with Khanh."

Presidential Palace
Saigon, Republic of South Vietnam
10:20 a.m., February 1, 1964

General Nguyen Khanh took a long drag on his celebratory cigar. He triumphantly blew the smoke into the morning air, and watched it float off the balcony overlooking the Palace's vast front lawn. He could barely contain himself. After a quixotic 20-year career in the Army of the Republic of Vietnam (ARVN), he was now in charge. Taking another big pull on the cigar, Khanh let out an audible laugh. It had been so easy! Without a shot being fired, he had become the president of the Republic of Vietnam!

As Khanh stood on the balcony, he contemplated his next move. As he did he absentmindedly slapped his "swagger stick" against the balcony railing. Khanh had seen pictures of the famed World War II British general Bernard Law Montgomery carrying one, and he decided to copy it. Made of bamboo and with a leather tip, the stick gave the diminutive Khanh what he hoped would become his signature style. After all, every great leader had a distinctive style: General George Patton had his pearl handled revolvers Winston Churchill had his cigars. Now Khanh, who saw himself the equal of Patton and Churchill, would have his swagger stick.

Slapping the stick a final time on the balcony railing, Khanh yelled to his aide, "Call the Turks in for a meeting."

"Now, sir?"

"Right now!"

Khanh knew that his first order of business was to consolidate his power. And that meant figuring out quickly who was a threat to him. This was not easy in the chaotic politics of South Vietnam, where allegiances were fleeting. He himself had been a supporter of President Diem until it became clear that he was impossibly corrupt and had lost his will to prosecute the war against the communist North Vietnam and the Viet Cong insurgency. Once it was apparent that the Americans were supportive of a move against Diem, Khanh threw his lot in with General Duong Van Minh. The coup that deposed and killed Diem and his brother Ngo Dinh Nhu had promised to put Khanh in a better position to influence the fight against the North, and also increase his access to the vast wealth being created by the Diem regime's rackets—opium, gambling, prostitution and extortion.

But General Minh had other ideas; seeing him a threat to the consolidation of his power, Khanh was banished to the far north of the country, assigned to command the I Corps of the ARVN. Rather than becoming an essential part of the new government, Khanh found himself frozen out, unable to influence military strategy and unable to take part in the lucrative lifestyle that Minh and his leadership were now enjoying. In exile, Khanh's response was to immediately begin laying the groundwork for a counter-coup.

For his part, Minh made it easy for Khanh. Enamored with the trappings of power, Minh showed little interest in running the country or fighting the VC. As a result, the situation in Saigon began to rapidly deteriorate, and infighting increased inside the government. By late January, the conditions were ripe for Khanh to take control. Rallying many of the younger generation of ARVN officers to his side, Khanh was able to overthrow Minh's government without a shot being fired. These young officers—nicknamed the "Young Turks"—were unquestionably loyal to Khanh and would now become the foundation of his new government.

"Sir, the Turks are ready for you," said Khanh's aide.

"Good." Khanh turned on his heels and followed his aide to the conference room off the presidential office. When he entered, the Young Turks—six junior ARVN generals—stood at attention.

"At ease." Khanh then waited for his aide to pull out his chair at the head of the table. Once he was seated, the Young Turks took their seats.

"Gentlemen, time is of the essence. We must move quickly to squash our opponents. Here's what we are going to do…" For the next thirty minutes, Khanh dictated his plans for systematically demoting senior generals in the ARVN who might be against him, and for co-opting all of the political patronage systems that Diem and Minh had used to curry support throughout the country. It was a plan that would take several months to complete, but it was fully baked and focused on creating a South Vietnamese government totally beholden to Khanh, and establishing a security scheme that would ensure he would remain in power. When he finished, Khanh opened up the floor for questions.

"Sir, what do we do with the opium trade? Nhu had been using it to fund his secret police."

Khanh slammed his swagger stick down on the mahogany table. "The opium trade is a program of the Americans, one they use to manipulate and control us! The CIA is not our friend. They worked to overthrow Diem and they could do the same to me."

"So, you want us to kill it?"

Khanh was silent for a moment. He relished this moment, he was in charge and the men around this table waited for his next utterance. "I don't want to kill it. I want to squeeze it. Hard. I want to make the CIA hurt, and to ensure that all those profiting from it feel a great deal of pain. They need to know who is in charge. Understood?"

One by one, the six Young Turks nodded. But Khanh had unwittingly opened up a can of worms; by telling them he wanted to squeeze the lucrative opium trade, he had given the Turks the green light to exploit it for their own purposes.

In his myopic quest for control, Khanh had created problems for himself he'd come to regret.

CHAPTER 4

The O'Shea Residence
2234 Scranton Place
Alexandria, Virginia
2:00 p.m., March 11, 1964

Liz O'Shea, at the wheel of her mother's red 1962 Mercury Comet, took the left turn onto Scranton Place at a speed that proved once again Newton's first law of motion: an object in motion tends to stay in motion unless an external force is applied to it. In this case the object was Patrick O'Shea sliding rapidly along the red vinyl bench seat, and the external force was the passenger door or, more specifically, a very shiny, very sharp door handle. He was just about to yell "slow down" when Elizabeth stepped hard on the brake pedal, bringing the car roughly to a stop in front of the family's two-story red brick colonial. O'Shea was sure that he now had a mild case of whiplash added to the bruise on his thigh from the door handle, but he was nonetheless relieved to have not hit another car or run over a little old lady out walking her dog. And fortunately, the weather had been mild for the past week and the roads were both dry and free of snow and ice.

It hadn't been this difficult teaching his son Kevin to drive, but his daughter Elizabeth was another story altogether. She seemed to lack hand-eye coordination and an ability to anticipate distances before turning the wheel or applying the brakes. O'Shea couldn't imagine what would have happened if the Comet had been equipped with a manual transmission, instead of the three-speed automatic. Worse yet, the girl had a lead foot. It was going to take a lot of practice between now and her driving test in March. Maybe O'Shea could get his wife to take over these duties and he would wash the clothes and do the dishes. For the rest of his life. That seemed like a decent trade at the moment.

O'Shea took a deep breath and was just about to go over Newton's law with his daughter when his wife Maddie approached the passenger side of the car. She leaned in with her arms folded on the doorframe, and O'Shea caught a glimpse of the fullness of her breasts under her white blouse and the freckles on her chest. Even at the age of 42, Maddie O'Shea could still turn heads. He was incredibly proud of his wife and looked forward to White House events during the year when he could show her off. He'd noticed both the president and his brother admiring her on more than one occasion; his private joke with Maddie was that he had vowed never to leave her alone at the White House lest she end up in the the coat closet with one of them. Maddie thought he was being silly—but she did love the attention from two of the most powerful men in the world.

"I was about to ask 'How did it go?' but I can tell from the look on your dad's face that's a silly question."

"Very funny, mom," his daughter answered. Elizabeth was a month shy of her 16th birthday and though she still had some of the awkwardness of puberty, she was becoming more of a young woman every day. "I think I did just fine. Daddy hardly had to correct me at all."

O'Shea wanted to tell his wife and daughter that his silence had been more from shock than it had been because her driving required little or no correction. But he tried to be delicate.

"Well, Liz, the thing is that I was trying to observe you—much as a license examiner would do. I think you need more practice. But I'm sure it's nothing you can't handle. When I learned to drive they only had standard transmissions and you had to learn to steer, shift, and work the clutch at the same time. If I could do it, you can certainly handle the Comet here," he said, slapping a hand on the dash of the car to reinforce his point.

"That's right, isn't it? The Model T's they had when you were her age only had stick shifts," Maddie said, smiling broadly.

"Ha, ha. And you could get any color you wanted, as long as it was black," said O'Shea. "Ok, let's call it a day. Maddie, I forgot to tell you that Ed Summers is in town. I asked him to stop by this evening."

"Patrick how in the world could you forget to tell me *that*?" Maddie said, her voice suddenly an octave or two higher than normal. Colonel Ed Summers had been two years ahead of O'Shea at The Citadel and had been the best man at their wedding 19 years ago. He was Patrick O'Shea's best friend. They had served together in Korea and, more importantly, had shared a week of terror as young officers when the Chinese had streamed across the North Korean border in a blinding, overwhelming counterattack. O'Shea's company had nearly been decimated and he and a few dozen of his men had been trapped for days in a small gulch about twenty miles south of the Yalu River. It was Summer's company that had managed to double-back against the enemy's flank to rescue O'Shea and his men from what would have been certain death. This had bonded them like brothers.

"Honey, this really was last minute. He's delivering a report at the Pentagon tomorrow morning."

"Well, ok," she said, disappointed. "Can he at least stay for dinner?" Summers was a life-long bachelor and Maddie was, in a very sweet way, protective of him. O'Shea understood it completely and, rather than be threatened by it, found it endearing.

"I'm sure if you were to cook your famous pot roast for him he'd find a way to stay for dinner."

"Then I'd best get myself over to Food Fair," she said, already coming around the front of the car to take Liz's place behind the wheel.

* * *

After dinner, Ed Summers sat comfortably on the leather couch in O'Shea's study. It was a warm, comfortable room that was dominated on one end by a massive mahogany desk, and on the other by floor-to-ceiling bookshelves. The shelves held an impressive collection of classics, from Plato to Cicero to the collected work of John Stuart Mill. O'Shea had studied philosophy at the Citadel and had quickly picked up the nickname "The Thinker." Upon graduation, some of his classmates chipped in to buy him a miniature version of the Rodin sculpture. That sculpture sat now on that big desk, a continuous reminder to him that effective military leadership was a thinking man's game. In that same vein, on the wall next to the fireplace O'Shea had hung a quote from Virgil's *The Aenid*:

Two gates the silent house of sleep adorn;
Of polished ivory this, that of transparent horn:
True visions through transparent horn arise;
Through polished ivory pass deluding lies.

Delusions had cost O'Shea a great deal in Korea. American commanders had convinced themselves that China would never enter the war, and even when Chinese soldiers were being captured on the battlefield, they continued to deny it. These delusions turned into lies that killed many of his men. After Korea, O'Shea vowed to always take the gate that led to truth, no matter the consequence.

Summers cradled a tumbler of Famous Grouse Scotch whisky in one hand and a Churchill-sized cigar in the other. There was an ashtray on his knee and a bucket of ice cubes on the coffee table before him. He was dressed in gray gabardine slacks, tasseled loafers and a multi-colored wool sweater that O'Shea had happily told him was just about the most hideous piece of civilian clothing he had ever seen. It was something of an inside joke between them, as Summers' sartorial ineptitude was one of the reasons he had joined the army to begin with: the government gladly tells you what uniform to wear and when to wear it, down to even the socks and underwear. Making matters worse, he was barely 5' 8" tall and quite muscular. Clothes never seemed to fit him quite right, and his uniforms had to be specially altered, making it impossible for him to buy them off the rack. He looked more like a drill instructor than he did a field-grade officer—a fact that actually helped him enormously with the men under his command.

Colonel Ed Summers was currently based at Fort Bragg outside of Fayetteville, North Carolina as the Commander of the Special Warfare School at the Special Warfare Center (SWCS)—the home of the Green Berets. Summers was specifically in charge of the Special Forces Training Group which taught counterinsurgency tactics and prepared men for operational assignments working with indigenous forces all over the world. He and O'Shea had last seen each other when O'Shea had come to the SWCS to provide specialized instruction to the School's staff on counterinsurgency tactics. It was just before O'Shea started his job at the White House.

"How are things with Kennedy?" asked Summers, looking thoughtfully at the ashes as the cigar burned with perfect symmetry.

"With the president? Or with the job? I imagine things are pretty rough for the president, but I'm not sure. I've only seen him once since Dallas. We're not exactly buddies, you know."

"That's not what I hear," Summers said with a grin. "The scuttlebutt around Bragg is that you and the president are like this," Summers said, holding up his hand with his index and middle fingers crossed.

O'Shea grunted. "Shit, I never wanted this damn job. It's a political minefield. I see the man once a week at most, and usually it's in the company of ten other people trying desperately to impress him with their intellectual heft."

Summers smiled. He knew that O'Shea was downplaying the truth—that he and the president often met one-on-one and talked as much about history and politics as they did military tactics and strategy. Summers guessed that O'Shea was downplaying it because he didn't want to make him feel badly. They both could see that O'Shea's career was on the fast track to becoming a general officer. That much was clear. Less clear, except to those who understood the opaque career paths of the military, was that Ed Summers had likely reached the end of his career—he and O'Shea both knew it.

"Ok, ok. Whatever you say," Summers said, laughing. The scotch had begun to do more than warm his belly. "Anyhow, I trust that you have been schooling our Commander in Chief on counterinsurgency strategy in a manner that would make the Special Warfare School proud."

"Teaching the president about counterinsurgency is easy," O'Shea said. "Kennedy truly believes that it's the future of warfare—small regional skirmishes against fast moving guerilla forces. He's been like a sponge, wanting to know everything he can about the tactics that can work in a place like Vietnam."

"On those rare occasions when you see each other, of course," Summers said with a straight face.

O'Shea laughed. "Exactly."

"It sure seems to me like getting rid of Diem really screwed the pooch and we're looking at a major increase in force levels this year. Any truth to that?" Summers knew that O'Shea would only tell him what he was authorized to. They both held Top Secret security clearances, and both understood the security issues involved.

"Honestly, I'm not sure…and I'm not just saying that. The all these coups have really changed things—that's for damn sure. Everything I've been hearing is telling me that things are getting worse, not better. Diem was far from perfect, but..."

"Sometimes the devil you know is better than the one you don't know," Summers said.

"Bingo. First Minh and then Khanh. Who knows what's next? Taking out Diem was a bad move, and an example of how easy it is for things to get out of control. Kennedy was shocked when word came that the coup had taken place and that Diem and his brother were dead. I was actually with the President and General Taylor when he found out. The president got white as a sheet and left the room without saying a word."

"Leaving you and the Chairman of the Joint Chiefs to have tea?"

"Tea and cookies," O'Shea said with a laugh. "Taylor really opposed any move to take out Diem. He's a 'devil you know' proponent. I could see in his eyes that he was furious at the news."

"I'm surprised that Kennedy was so shocked."

"I am, too. It was clear from the meetings I'd been in with the president since mid-summer of last year that coup planning was taking place. I have a feeling he imagined a much more dignified exile for Diem somewhere in the South of France."

"Did they ever figure out exactly what happened to them?" Summers asked.

"Not officially. The initial reports from the coup planners tried to paint it as a double suicide. That was laughable. Lucien Conein at the CIA reported that they were shot and stabbed in the back of that Armored Personnel Carrier."

"I've heard about Conein," said Summers. "He has a reputation is as a ruthless son of a bitch."

"Ruthless and suave," O'Shea said. "He started out at the Office of Strategic Services during World War II and then was a star in the CIA's 'Department of Dirty Tricks' if that tells you anything. I met him once at an Embassy dinner. He brought his third wife along—a very beautiful

Eurasian woman in a very low-cut strapless gown. I couldn't keep my eyes off her. Conein didn't seem the least bit concerned—he spent most of the evening at the bar drinking Cognac and smoking Gitanes."

"Exactly the kind of practiced nonchalance that you'd expect from a heroic former OSS agent," Summers said with a chuckle, "especially one named Lucien."

O'Shea grunted. "At our last meeting, right before he went to Dallas, Kennedy told me privately he was going to look to me to provide an unfiltered and unvarnished opinion on our current ops plan for Vietnam. He also instructed me to prepare for a trip there in January. Obviously, that's now been delayed. But my bag is packed."

Summers made a slight whistling sound. "You have any idea the shitstorm you are about to unleash on yourself?"

O'Shea was quiet for a long moment. He knew Summers was about to give him a big dose of reality.

"If you are going to provide Kennedy with unfiltered analysis and opinion on Vietnam, you really need to watch your back. The Pentagon is thoroughly invested in fighting this war, under the belief—mistaken in my view—that the little yellow man will never be able to withstand the awesome power of our modern military. You know damn well that going against the brass is going to endanger your future in the army. Look at what happened to Vann."

Both Summers and O'Shea had known Lt. Colonel John Paul Vann since Korea, and their paths had crossed in many assignments since. Vann had publicly criticized the South Vietnamese army and the U.S. advisory effort in Vietnam, and tried to convince the Pentagon that the war couldn't be won. For that he was forcibly separated from the military. "Vann got screwed, that's for sure."

Summers sighed. "I'll say he did. Poor guy's living in Denver now, riding a desk for Martin Marietta. Must be bored stiff there, after living in a hooch in the jungle for a year."

"That's something I've always been scared to death of," said O'Shea.

"It's pretty hard to go from riding to work in a Huey every morning with your blood pumping to being the night manager at some factory making paper clips."

Summers laughed. "Vann's not making paper clips, but it must feel just as trivial to him."

O'Shea looked at Summers but said nothing. He understood what Summers was telling him. The Pentagon would broker no dissent.

"Look," said Summers. "you have an incredible opportunity to do something important with your career. I just don't want you to screw it up the way Vann did."

"You know, I'd rather screw it up by telling the truth than put in a quiet thirty and retire. There's no honor in that."

"All very noble, my friend, but you have a lot to lose. You are in an incredible position now, within earshot of the President of the United States. Now, I know he sees the importance of counterinsurgency, and I suspect he will protect you from the vipers in the Pentagon. But, as we saw in Dallas, who knows if Kennedy will be around to finish out this term, let alone the next one?"

O'Shea looked at Summers for a long moment before replying. "I've thought a lot lately about that very question. What if Kennedy had been killed in Dallas? What if Lyndon Johnson suddenly found himself with the keys to the kingdom? Do you have any idea what Johnson would do with Vietnam, Ed?"

"Not a clue."

"Well, I have an idea. During the Missile Crisis, Johnson said very little. But when he did speak he was about as bellicose as can be. Johnson basically labeled Kennedy's decision not to launch a military strike against the Soviets in Cuba 'chickenshit.' Apparently he was bedazzled by Max Taylor and the other generals."

"So the V.P. is a starfucker?"

O'Shea laughed at the derisive term for those in the military who were sycophants to flag officers. "And since he never served in the military, he'd likely never know when he was being bullshitted."

Summers simply shrugged. "My point is that unless you come back and tout the company line that supports MACV, General Harkins and our efforts there, you are going to find yourself shit-canned. Only Kennedy will be there to protect you."

"So, if that happens I'll just go back to an operational command. Someone will need me somewhere."

"Gee, how about Nome, Alaska? You see, it's not that simple. The brass already hates the fact that you have the president's ear. They won't be shy about crushing you the first chance they get."

"Look, Ed, I know what I'm dealing with here," O'Shea said more forcefully than he intended. "I really have no illusions about it. But in the end, if we're going to be sending kids to Vietnam, it's more important for me to be on the right side of the issue than the right side of my career."

"Ok, *Thinker*. I get it. You're a big boy."

O'Shea took another sip of scotch. He didn't feel like a big boy at that moment. In fact, he was much more worried about his career than he would admit.

* * *

Later that night after Summers had left, O'Shea sat alone in his study. He was slightly drunk, listening to Vivaldi's *The Four Seasons* on his stereo; Concerto No. 1 in E Major was playing. It was a lovely piece, especially the beginning Allegro movement, dominated by strings. O'Shea loved the violin.

As the music wafted over him, O'Shea thought about his life. He'd been taught to suck it up, to not cry or complain. His father had been a policeman in Charlotte, North Carolina. He was a man of principle, strict but measured, a hard man who drank hard liquor and in large quantities. His mother was a saint, kind and sweet. But she was also weak, and in the face of his father, had little influence on how O'Shea and his brother had been raised. His father wasn't a mean drunk, and didn't hit them. But he was firm to the point of steel. There was no crying in the O'Shea house. You said "yes, sir" and got on with your work.

The phone rang one night and his mother answered. From his bed in the room above the kitchen, Patrick heard his mother shriek. He was fifteen then and just starting high school. He opened his door and stood at the top of the stairs. He could just make out the words "Is he dead?" between his mother's sobs. He didn't hear the answer, but then again he didn't have to. Patrick's father had been killed in his patrol car when it went off the road as he chased a suspect in a stolen car.

Patrick sat down on the top step and listened to his mother cry. He wasn't sure what to do, so for a long time he did nothing. Finally, he went downstairs. His mother was sitting at the kitchen table, unable to even hang up the phone. Patrick took the receiver and replaced it on the wall. He then sat down at the table with his mother. They didn't talk—there was nothing to say. Patrick was now the man of the house and he would be strong. Just like his father.

With the childhood he had, joining the army had seemed the most natural thing in the world to O'Shea; he thrived on the discipline and structure. He was at the top of his class at the Citadel, and had been the "honor man" at Ranger school. He was a natural. It was the only job he'd ever wanted and the only job he'd ever had. So the prospect of getting cashiered for a job he hadn't asked for made him angry. He never imagined himself doing anything else with his life, and wouldn't know what to do as a civilian. How would he make money?

And O'Shea needed money. He was barely making ends meet on his army pay, and his kids were both going to be in college soon. Maddie hadn't worked in 20 years, and her parents were both ill and in need of increasing financial assistance. Maddie's father, in particular, had been diagnosed with dementia a year prior and would eventually need around-the-clock care. It was a big nut to cover and would only get bigger.

O'Shea drained the last bit of scotch in his glass and stood up on unsteady legs. His den felt like a boat rocking in the waves. Shutting off the stereo, he managed to climb the stairs to bed.

Maybe things would look better in the morning, he thought, heading up to bed.

CHAPTER 5

The Oval Office
The White House
Washington, D.C.
8:45 a.m., March 21, 1964

The president's secretary, Evelyn Lincoln, picked up another batch of the condolence cards and letters that continued to stream into the White House. They had come in daily by the thousands at first, and even now, some four months after what was being simply referred to around the White House as "Dallas," they still amounted to dozens per day. They had come in from all over the world and from all walks of life: children in Afghanistan and China, dock workers in Norway, bankers in Switzerland, even a set of hand-drawn cards sent by some Kikuyu tribesman in Kenya. It was an overwhelming show of remorse and sorrow, and the White House had struggled for several weeks to figure out how to handle it all. Under normal circumstances the president would have personally responded to many of the cards, but the sheer volume had made that impossible. Ted Sorenson, one of Kennedy's principal aides, decided to hire a staff of secretaries to sort and answer each of the cards with a message of appreciation on behalf of the president. But it was left to Evelyn to bring to the president what she felt were the most personal and profound tributes to the late First Lady. She knew that, however painful, it was an important part of the healing process for Kennedy.

Lincoln rapped on the door to the Oval Office and entered without waiting for a reply. She had been Kennedy's secretary since he first entered the United States Senate in 1953, and while officially Kennedy served as his own Chief of Staff, Evelyn Lincoln could rightfully argue that she should have that title as well. She was the keeper of the president's schedule and the guardian at the door, gating access to the president and keeping him on track throughout the day. Kennedy, for his part, was grateful for the structure and protection she provided, particularly in the wake of Dallas.

The president stood behind his desk looking out the window onto the Rose Garden. The weather was blustery and gray, and the grass and trees on the White House grounds were brown and bare. It was an ugly time of year.

"Mr. President, when you have time you should take a look at a few of these cards," Evelyn said, putting them on the edge of the *Resolute* desk that dominated the back portion of the room. The desk itself, like so many of the White House furnishings, was a piece of history; it was made from timbers of the *H.M.S. Resolute*, a British ship that had been abandoned at sea and returned to England by the U.S. Navy as a token of friendship and goodwill. In 1880, after the ship was retired from service, Queen Victoria had the desk built from the ship's timbers, and personally presented it to President Rutherford B. Hayes. Kennedy, with his naval experience and love of the sea, was particularly enamored with the desk. It was just the kind of connection to history that Kennedy loved.

"Thank you, Mrs. Lincoln," said the president absently, turning to face her. "Just put them there—" pointing to the very spot where Lincoln had placed them a few moments before. Kennedy smiled at his secretary and marveled again at how efficient she was. "What's the schedule this morning?"

"You have the Vice President at 9 a.m. Then you are to meet with the French Ambassador at 9:45. You have lunch scheduled in the residence with the children at 11:30. Then you are free until Colonel O'Shea comes in to discuss his pending trip to Vietnam at 4 p.m. That's it for the formal schedule. I know Bobby wants to see you this afternoon as well. He said he'd try and come by around five o'clock."

"Ok, thank you. Put a call into Bobby and ask him to call first. If you can't reach him, leave a message. I know what he wants to discuss. I'm not sure I'm up to that today." The president knew that Bobby would want to see him today, after his meeting with Johnson. "Is the Vice President here yet?"

"He's in talking to Roger Hilsman, who is here early for his 9 am meeting with Mr. Bundy," Lincoln replied, referring to Roger Hilsman, the long-time advisor to Kennedy and now the Assistant Secretary of State for Far Eastern Affairs. "Mr. Johnson's been here since 7:15 this morning, pacing the halls like a caged tiger." Lincoln paused a moment and gave the president a look that told him she knew that all was not well with the VP. "He seems a bit…on edge."

A razor's edge, thought Kennedy.

The president sighed deeply. He didn't relish this meeting, his first private one-on-one encounter with Johnson since Dallas. While Johnson had attended the briefings the president had received while he recuperated, they had been in the presence of senior members of the White House staff and Cabinet. Kennedy knew that Johnson was both deeply ashamed of what happened in Dallas, but was also scared to death of how it would affect his place within the administration. Kennedy suspected that, though Johnson was aware that the president's brother despised him, he had no idea how hard Robert Kennedy had been working behind the scenes to destroy the vice president's career. Robert was by far the tougher of the two when it came to people – something that the president had come to rely on. It made it possible for him to flash his charm with friends and foes, while his brother did the kind of axe grinding that was invariably necessary in any administration. John Kennedy was a man of immense personal charisma; it had as much an affect on men as it did on women—and his reputation with the ladies was the stuff of legend. John and Robert Kennedy had learned to use their "good cop/bad cop" routine to devastating effectiveness since John Kennedy had become president.

The situation with the vice president, however, was far beyond such tactics. Johnson was being blamed widely within the Administration for the death of the First Lady; among all the Harvard-educated elites that the Kennedy's had brought into the government, Johnson was now unofficially a pariah. He had never fit the Kennedy mold, of course. He was the embodiment of the "old" style of government—a career legislator from the Texas Hill Country, who had begun his government career during the presidency of Franklin Roosevelt and who represented the back slapping deal making of the past. By contrast, the Kennedy government was to be the beginning of the "New Frontier," an age of efficiency and reason. Problems were to be analyzed with economic and scientific techniques and disposed of with cold, clear decision-making. This was the government that brought men like Robert S. McNamara to the Department of Defense—brilliant managers capable of great statistical analysis on the most complex problems of the day. These were men of great confidence, who saw no problem as being too big for their big brains—and even bigger egos.

In this world, Lyndon Johnson was an anachronism. He owed his presence on the 1960 ticket to a combination of skilled negotiation at the convention and a willingness to use whatever ammunition he had—and he had plenty—to coerce the Kennedys into taking him as a running mate. In the end, it had been something of a pyrrhic victory for Johnson, who hated the job and had often found himself day dreaming of his days on the floor of the Senate. Nonetheless, he didn't want to leave the job in disgrace, a possibility which seemed all too likely at the present time.

"Mrs. Lincoln, would you please find the Vice President and tell him that if he can find a few minutes I'd like to see him now." Kennedy sat gently in his rocker as he said this, turning his attention to the stack of memos in front of him.

"Yes, Mr. President." Lincoln left the Oval office by the door next to the president's private study, moving down the hall in the West Wing toward McGeorge Bundy's office.

The first memo on the stack was marked "Top Secret" and had been hand delivered that morning by Robert McNamara's assistant. It was a memo summarizing the findings of the two-day trip McNamara and General Maxwell Taylor took to Saigon the previous month.

Though Taylor didn't yet know it, this memo would be one of his last as the Chairman of the Joint Chiefs. Kennedy had made the decision to move him out of the Pentagon even before the shooting in Dallas. Taylor had lost his objectivity when it came to Vietnam, and he was making it increasingly difficult for Patrick O'Shea to do his job effectively. Kennedy had come to rely on O'Shea for unvarnished views and "cut to the chase" opinions not just on Vietnam, but on other matters pertaining to the military. It was something that Taylor found difficult to accept. Consequently, he had frozen O'Shea out of certain meetings, taken him off the distribution list for critical documents and generally made life difficult for him. Kennedy planned to partly rectify this by promoting O'Shea first to full colonel, then quickly to Brigadier General. This would at least be a sign that he enjoyed the president's full confidence, and would give him a bit more "heft" in the rank-conscious Pentagon. The real solution, Kennedy thought, was to send a message by moving Taylor out, even if the move would be considered something of a promotion as the new U.S. Ambassador to South Vietnam.

It had actually been Bobby's idea to send Taylor to Saigon. Since it was clear that Taylor supported the U.S. mission in Vietnam without reservation, Kennedy felt that Taylor should put his money where his mouth was; the president liked it when those working for him had their own "skin in the game."

The president scanned the memo, which clearly laid out the overall goal of U.S. policy in Vietnam as creating "an independent, non-communist South Vietnam." But it was the next paragraph that caught his eye:

> Unless we can achieve this objective in South Vietnam, almost all of Southeast Asia will probably fall under Communist dominance. Thailand might hold for a period with our help, but would be under grave pressure. Even the Philippines would become shaky, and the threat to India to the west, Australia and New Zealand to the south, and Taiwan, Korea, and Japan to the north and east would be greatly increased.

"Jesus H. Christ," Kennedy said under his breath. The Pentagon was now basing their recommendations on the premise that if we don't succeed in Vietnam, the entire region would be threatened. While Kennedy thought the so-called "domino theory"—if one nation falls to communism, neighboring states will fall in succession—had merit, he didn't think that Sydney or Tokyo would soon be under control of the Reds.

He made a note in the margin, "Discuss with O'Shea," and tossed the memo on his desk.

Just at that moment, Lincoln walked back into the Oval Office with the Vice President on her heels. "Mr. President, The Vice President is here," she was in the process of saying as Johnson strode toward Kennedy's desk. He covered the 20 feet in what seemed, to both Kennedy and Lincoln, about three steps.

"Mr. President, you look just fine, just fine," Johnson said, while pumping Kennedy's hand like a car salesman who has met an easy mark.

"Thank you, Lyndon," Kennedy said. The president stood up somewhat awkwardly from his rocking chair and moved to the executive chair behind the *Resolute* desk. He looked at Johnson and pointed to one of the chairs in front of the desk, indicating that the vice president should take a seat. Ordinarily, Kennedy and Johnson would have sat facing each other on the couches in front of the fireplace, but not this time. This wasn't a social call and the president wanted Johnson to know it. He looked at Lincoln, who by custom, was waiting by the door to see if Kennedy needed anything else. Kennedy smiled and nodded, signaling her that he was fine. Lincoln knew that for the next 30 minutes he didn't want to be disturbed. "Only if the Russians launch their missiles," he liked to say, when letting her know he was doing something that required his full and undivided attention. Lincoln nodded back and quietly closed the door.

Kennedy looked intently at Johnson for a full thirty seconds before speaking. He had mixed feelings about the man. On the one hand, he admired how Johnson had come up from hardscrabble roots to reach the zenith of power in Washington. For Kennedy, who had been born into opportunity and political influence, Johnson represented true grit, and that was something to be respected.

On the other hand, Johnson was also a consummate political animal. Kennedy could see that the Vice President was wearing the lapel pin of the Silver Star on his coat. He knew that this award, the third highest given for valor in combat, was presented to Johnson during World War II, and he wore it proudly. But Kennedy also knew that this award was given for purely political reasons. Johnson, then a congressman from Texas, had joined the military after Pearl Harbor and requested that Franklin Roosevelt send him on a fact-finding tour of the Pacific. While there, he managed to hitch a ride on a B-24 for a single bombing mission over New Guinea. Johnson's plane ended up having engine trouble and turned back to base before ever reaching the target. Johnson, however, claimed that the plane had come under fire. Never missing a chance to gain publicity, Douglas MacArthur saw an opportunity to award a Congressman a medal, and thus Lyndon Johnson became a "decorated combat veteran" with a Silver Star for bravery.

This kind of deceit drove Kennedy crazy, having himself been wounded in the Pacific in World War II. The president saw Johnson's Silver Star as an insult to all the brave men who risked their lives in real combat. It was not something he admired in the man.

"Mr. President, you don't know how sorry Lady Bird and I are about Jackie," Johnson began. "She was a very special woman. I—"

Kennedy cut Johnson off in mid-sentence. "Lyndon, I appreciate your sentiments. I got the card you sent, and the flowers for John Jr. and Caroline. We can dispense with the pleasantries." This came out more stridently than he had intended.

Johnson tightened visibly. He knew at that moment that even without Bobby in the room, this was going to be a very tough conversation.

"We both know what's going on here. We both know that your brother wants my scalp for his belt. I know it, you know it—hell, all of Washington D.C. knows it. He never thought I was quite good enough for all you Harvard-types. Frankly, he's always been a prick toward me, like I was some hick just off the farm. And now he has a solid reason to put me out to pasture. Well, Mr. President, frankly, I couldn't give two shits what he thinks. The only thing that's important to me is what you think," Johnson said, pointing a beefy index finger at the president.

Kennedy smiled thinly. "You're a good man, Lyndon."

Johnson snorted. "I'm a son of a bitch, and you know it. But I've done my part in this administration. I used to run the United States Senate, and now I can't even get my parking validated. But it's ok. It's the deal I made when I pushed for a spot on the ticket in Los Angeles"— referring to the location of the 1960 Democratic National Convention. "I'm truly sick about the First Lady. And you know why? Because Jackie was actually nice to me. She felt sorry for me, no doubt. But she treated me with respect. Which is more than I can say for anyone else around here. In particular your brother."

Kennedy stared at Johnson. "Lyndon, what do you want?"

Johnson took a deep breath. "I want you to publicly embrace me or put me out of my misery. Either you absolve me of blame in Jackie's death and reaffirm your commitment to me as your Vice President, or let me resign and keep what little dignity I have left. Maybe by '68 I'll have a chance to run for a state senate seat in Texas. But at least I won't be a dead man walking."

Kennedy understood what Johnson wanted, but wasn't quite prepared to give it to him. At least not yet. He knew he had leverage and wanted to use it.

"Lyndon, I appreciate what you are asking for, and I'll give it due consideration. I really will. But first I need something from you."

Johnson smiled. He saw an opportunity to get back in the president's good graces. "Just name it, Mr. President."

"With Jackie gone my goal is to protect her memory. Her death can't be in vain—and I need to make sure I win the election in November to ensure this all amounts to something. I want to make sure that John Jr. and Caroline understand that their mother was important to the country…" Kennedy paused, partly for effect, and partly because he felt ashamed of himself, "and important to me."

Johnson wasn't completely sure he understood what Kennedy was saying, so he said nothing.

"You are in possession of certain incriminating material," Kennedy continued, "which would prove damaging to the First Lady's image if it were to get out into the public domain."

Johnson gave a little laugh. "I'm not sure what you are referring to, Mr. President."

Kennedy responded with ice to that deception. "Lyndon, cut the crap, ok? You have known J. Edgar Hoover for more than 25 years. You literally live across the street from him here in Washington. I know that when we were in the Senate together, Hoover was passing you information on my personal life, and that you have compiled a decent dossier on my social activities. Frankly, it's the only reason Bobby agreed not to stand in the way of me nominating you in the first place."

Johnson blanched. "Mr. President, I admit to having used many methods of controlling my caucus, and I may have had to twist a few arms from time-to-time, but I can assure you I don't have anything on you that could cause you embarrassment."

Kennedy sighed. "Lyndon, if you have any chance of staying on the ticket this year, it will depend on your ability to deliver the files that you have on me and my brother. And I expect that you will ensure that your friend Hoover keeps his cache buried deep. Because if I ever see even a whisper of a story that I wasn't completely faithful to my late wife, I will drop you so fast your head will spin. And you will indeed be lucky to get elected dog catcher in Stonewall, Texas."

Johnson smiled. This he understood. And this he could do.

"Are we clear, Mr. Vice President?"

"Crystal, Mr. President."

* * *

After a lunch of hamburgers and French fries with Caroline and John Jr., Kennedy retired to the solarium on the third floor of the residence. He had been going up to this sun-lit room to "nap" most every afternoon since he came back to work. His staff thought it was because he was following doctor's orders, but in fact it was because he needed time to think. His world had been turned upside down, and he was still reeling from it.

In the powder room off the solarium, Kennedy opened the medicine cabinet and took out a basket of pills. Since being injured in combat in World War II he'd been in almost constant pain, and had prescriptions for codeine, methadone and Demerol. Today he chose codeine, taking out two pills and downing them with a large glass of water. He then took out a Ritalin for fatigue and a Librium for anxiety, putting them in his coat pocket for later. Since Dallas he'd been in particular need of relaxation, and the drugs helped immensely.

Closing the medicine cabinet, Kennedy stared at his reflection. He saw a face of death. The shot that killed Jackie had been meant for him; a fact he could never escape. The shear evil of the act that took her life was something he struggled to make sense of. For a reason that only God knew, he had been spared.

Kennedy had slowly come to the conclusion that God had cast his providence over him. Now the question remained: *How would he repay Him?* Everything Kennedy did from here on had to be worthy of the sacrifice his wife had made so he could live. It was a greater burden than being president of the United States. He had been chosen, and he would not shirk from his duty.

Sitting at his writing desk, Kennedy fingered a stack of documents that Patrick O'Shea had prepared for him on Vietnam. On top was a thin folder marked "Personal & Confidential" in O'Shea's handwriting. Putting on his reading glasses, the president opened it up to find a letter. It was typewritten on yellowed paper and dated February 16, 1946. It was from the leader of North Vietnam, Ho Chi Minh, to President Harry Truman. In it, Minh wrote an impassioned plea for the United States to support Vietnam's quest to be a free nation. Its final paragraphs were the most important:

Our Vietnamese people need security and freedom, first
to achieve internal prosperity and welfare, and
later to bring its small contribution to world-reconstruction.

It is with this firm conviction that we request of
the United States as guardians and champions of World
Justice to take a decisive step in support of our
independence.

What we ask has been graciously granted to the Philippines.
Like the Philippines our goal is full independence and
full cooperation with the United States. We will do our
best to make this independence and cooperation profitable
to the whole world.

[signature]

Ho Chi Minh

At the bottom of the letter,[1] O'Shea had attached a note: "Truman never responded." Kennedy removed his reading glasses and pinched his nose. He knew the tradeoffs Truman had faced at the end of World War II, and why he had chosen French support for the containment of the Soviets in Europe in return for allowing France to recolonize Vietnam. Kennedy always thought this was the right move, and with what he'd been through with the Soviets in Berlin and Cuba, it was hard to argue against that logic. But now Vietnam was looming and threatening to push the U.S. into a very serious shooting war. Had Truman misjudged Ho Chi Minh's motives? Was war really inevitable?

Kennedy picked up the phone and spoke to the operator. "Please connect me to President Truman."

At the switchboard in the basement of the White House, operators

---

1 The Pentagon Papers: United States – Vietnam Relations, 1945–1967: A Study Prepared by the Department of Defense, vol. 1, Vietnam and the U.S., 1940-1950, 235.

quickly dialed the number of Harry and Bess Truman's home in Independence, Missouri. After the third ring, a male voice with a slight tremor answered the phone.

"Truman residence."

"President Truman, please."

"This is Harry Truman," the man replied.

"Please hold for the President."

After a click, the connection was made. "Mr. President, Jack Kennedy here."

"Mr. President, mighty fine of you to call. I was sorry that Mrs. Truman and I couldn't make it up to Washington for the First Lady's service. Mrs. Truman hasn't been feeling well. I hope Margaret was able to pay her respects."

"Yes, Margaret did pay her respects and I appreciated her coming."

After a momentary pause, Truman said, "What can I do for you?"

"Well, I wanted to ask you about a letter that I came across today. It was sent to you from Ho Chi Minh, dated February 16, 1946. Do you happen to remember it?"

The 80-year-old Truman laughed. "My memory isn't what it was, that's for sure. But that is one letter I do remember. Why do you ask?"

Kennedy paused. He wanted to be careful not to put Truman on the defensive. "Ho Chi Minh seems to be holding out an olive branch, wanting Vietnam to be free and part of the American post-war order. He's been painted as a diehard communist. It surprised me."

"It surprised me, too. But, you see, I didn't see Vietnam as being important. It was a small nation far from where the real threats at that time were. Remember, we had just defeated Germany and Japan. We were trying to stabilize Europe and protect it from the Soviet menace. And the French…" Truman's voice trailed off.

"The French wanted back into Vietnam to reclaim their colony."

"Yes. And President De Gaulle—he would not budge. He made it clear that France would not participate in the defense of Europe if we didn't give back Vietnam. So, we did."

"Did you believe that Ho Chi Minh's letter was sincere?"

Truman paused. "That's a good question. I believed it at that time. The Vietnamese independence movement was in a vulnerable state and wanted desperately to find a way to keep the French out. I think they would have made peace with us to do so. Would it have lasted? That's harder to say. I can't see the Soviets not exploiting them against us."

"Were you tempted to answer the letter?"

"No. I had the Soviets pressing on Berlin at the time and all of Europe to rebuild. I had bigger fish to fry."

Kennedy understood what Truman was saying. "Thank you for your time, Mr. Truman. And please give my best to Mrs. Truman."

"Anytime, Mr. President."

CHAPTER 6

The Oval Office
The White House
Washington, D.C.
3:45 p.m., March 21, 1964

Patrick O'Shea packed his valise and looked around his cluttered desk for his favorite pen, a Parker Model 51 that his parents had given him when he graduated high school. The pen was black with a sterling silver cap, and though ballpoints had come out a few years prior, O'Shea preferred his trusty fountain pen. Locating the pen under a map of South Vietnam, he quickly put it in his left front breast pocket and headed over to the West Wing to see the president.

As O'Shea rounded the corner toward Evelyn Lincoln's desk he almost knocked over Clint Hill.

"Sorry, Clint, didn't mean to run you over."

"That's ok," Hill said. Hill had the same military style hair as O'Shea, and they could pass for brothers. Hill had also served in the Army as a Counterintelligence Officer. O'Shea liked Hill a lot and felt sorry for him.

"How's Gwen doing," asked O'Shea, referring to Hill's wife. O'Shea tried to make small talk, not really knowing what else to say.

"She's doing fine, thanks." O'Shea and Hill stood awkwardly and looked at each other. Hill's eyes were sunken with deep bags under them. He'd clearly not been sleeping. Based on what O'Shea had heard about the scene in the back of the president's car, it was obvious that Hill had been deeply affected by the trauma he'd witnessed, and the remorse he'd felt in not preventing it. O'Shea understood that kind of guilt: he'd lost men under his command in Korea, many in very violent ways and in very close quarters. O'Shea also knew that what he had experienced was war, and during war people expected men to die. Losing the First Lady in broad daylight on the streets of Dallas was a different matter altogether.

Just at that moment, Evelyn Lincoln peeked out of the Oval Office and said "Colonel, the president is ready for you now." O'Shea grasped Hill's hand and without another word, slid past him, entering the president's office.

The president sat at his desk in his high-backed leather chair. Without looking up from his papers, Kennedy asked O'Shea to take a seat. O'Shea did so, his briefcase in his lap, waiting for the president to give his full attention. O'Shea looked around the room, focusing on the family pictures of Jackie and the kids on the credenza behind the president's desk, sitting astride one of the two wooden sailing ship models that adorned the Oval. Again O'Shea was reminded of the tragedy that had befallen this man.

Finally, Kennedy looked up and without preliminaries said, "Colonel, pack your bags. I want you in Saigon by the end of the month. I need you to sort out what's going on there. I need a clear, honest assessment."

"Yes, sir. I'm ready."

Kennedy smiled. "I'm also promoting you to full colonel, and after that I will be sending your nomination as a brigadier general to the senate for confirmation." Kennedy paused to let that settle in, knowing that it would represent a meteoric rise for O'Shea up the chain of command.

"Brigadier general?"

What the hell? Thought O'Shea.

"It's going to ruffle feathers, I know."

"No doubt about that, Mr. President." O'Shea could only imagine what Ed Summers would say when he found out about this. Talk about putting a neon target on your back!

To his credit, Kennedy wasn't naïve about the implications of this move for O'Shea; he knew it was going to piss off every full colonel currently waiting to be promoted to general officer. And it was going to be like fingers on a chalkboard for the Pentagon brass. But it was something Kennedy felt he needed to do in order to give O'Shea the necessary space to do his job. "I need someone on my team with some clout, and I've decided it will be you. Can I count on your full loyalty and discretion?"

"Yes, sir. You can count on me."

The president nodded. "Good. I want to ask Roger Hilsman to join us to discuss your trip to Vietnam. But before I do, I'd like to have an off the record chat." Kennedy looked at O'Shea to see if he understood what he was asking. When O'Shea nodded, Kennedy continued.

Kennedy pulled a letter out of his coat pocket and handed it to O'Shea. It was a standard-sized blank white envelope sealed with a red wax Great Seal of the United States embossed on it. "I want you to take this letter with you to Saigon and be prepared to deliver it by hand. I don't know who your contact on the other end will be, nor do I know where you will need to go to deliver it."

O'Shea took the envelope and held it in his hands.

"I will get you further instructions on the delivery. I need time to arrange things. I am not going to trust normal lines of communication for this. So it will come by courier and it will be someone you know and trust."

O'Shea gathered it would be someone in the military. It would be easy for the president to assign them to temporary duty and get them to Saigon.

"You are to treat this letter as essential to the national security of the

United States, and you will make sure it doesn't leave your possession. Are we clear, Colonel?"

O'Shea slipped the letter into his valise. He was very curious to know whom it was for, but he figured that if the president wanted him to know, he'd have told him. "Yes, Mr. President."

The president nodded and then picked up his phone and said, "Please send Roger in."

Roger Hilsman was a bookish-looking man with thick-rimmed glasses and a gap in his toothy smile. He was one of Kennedy's best and brightest, an academic from Princeton who had been a soldier once, graduating from West Point in the Class of 1942. He had a career that would have made a great adventure movie: as a young lieutenant, he had joined Merrill's Marauders long-range jungle penetration unit, fighting the Japanese on Burma behind enemy lines. Later, in 1944, he was wounded in combat during the battle for Myitkyina, a brutal engagement that so decimated the Marauders that they literally ceased being a fighting unit. After recuperating in a field hospital, Hilsman joined the Office of Strategic Services, the precursor to the CIA, where he ran guerilla operations against the Japanese for the remainder of the War. After the Japanese surrender, Hilsman had parachuted into Manchuria to liberate American prisoners of war, and later became an intelligence officer with the CIA. Roger Hilsman was no ordinary Washington policy wonk.

O'Shea knew his background and respected the man immensely. He was pleased to have him in the meeting, in part because he knew more about Vietnam than anyone else in the administration, and in part because Hilsman was a realist about the use of military force. In fact, Kennedy valued Hilsman precisely because he thought him to be both a talisman and a skeptic; he had cheated death in the jungles of the Pacific, and yet was sober and measured in his view of what war could accomplish.

Hilsman entered the room and O'Shea rose to shake his hand. Taking the chair next to O'Shea facing Kennedy's desk, he carried no briefcase and would be taking no notes.

The president nodded at Hilsman and then looked directly at O'Shea. "I want to make a complete reassessment of our commitment in Vietnam. I already feel I got railroaded during the Diem fiasco, and I deferred to Lodge and the others who wanted Diem gone. That, I'm afraid, was a very serious mistake. Now we've got what appears to be a vacuum there, and I'm being pressured by the Pentagon and the hawks in Congress to fill it with a more substantial U.S. commitment."

Kennedy paused, collecting his thoughts. O'Shea turned to look at Hilsman, who sat stone-faced.

"Roger, do you want to add anything to that?" the president asked after a moment.

Hilsman took out his trademark pipe and tobacco pouch and began filling the bowl. The aroma of sweet tobacco filled the room, and O'Shea was immediately reminded of his grandfather, a lawyer in a small town who always had a pipe in hand. Hilsman lit the pipe and a bit of ash got on the conservative dark suit that he habitually paired with a white shirt and an ink-blue tie. There was just a hint of color in the socks he wore, visible above the top of his black Church's wingtip shoes. He could have easily passed for an IBM salesman.

"In my view there is a cancer in Saigon, and it's not just with the Vietnamese government. For the past two years, McNamara and Harkins have been blowing sunshine at us about the progress we've supposedly been making. That's understandable to a point. They are protecting their turf. But there has been a concerted effort to destroy dissent and to purge the ranks of those who disagree with their official line. For years we've had to sit and listen to their prognostications for success. Last year I commissioned Lewis Sarris, one of my deputies at Intelligence and Research, to do his own study on whether we were making progress or not. McNamara is always throwing out his statistics to show success, and I figured it was high time to see if we could push back in the language he loves: Numbers."

Hilsman stopped to relight his pipe. "Sarris's report achieved my primary objective of showing that the books are being cooked and anyone who deigns to disagree is out."

"I've seen that first-hand. Some of my close friends in the army have had their careers ruined by going against the party line," said O'Shea.

"So, I gather you understand the position we are putting you in here. Relative to your military career, that is," asked Hilsman.

O'Shea flashed back to his talk with Ed Summers, marveling again at how prescient his friend had been. Then, answering Hilsman's question but addressing Kennedy, O'Shea stated simply, "I'm in, sir."

Kennedy looked at O'Shea and nodded. "Good. As Roger said, I don't trust the advice I'm getting. And now I have this," picking up Taylor's memo. "This amounts to a gradual escalation of U.S. support and gets us deeper into the well. It's telling me that if I don't do it, the world is going to come to an end."

O'Shea said, "May I see that, Mr. President?"

"Keep it," Kennedy said, handing over the memo. The president sighed. "The truth is we have no idea what's really going on in Vietnam, and since Diem there has been a revolving door of leadership. It's a mess. So, I want you to go to Saigon to figure out what's really happening. Tell me about the cadre of power brokers now in charge, and whether the South Vietnamese army can get the job done. Get into the field. I want to know who I'm in bed with, and I want to know whether we really have a chance of stabilizing the South. Leave no stone unturned."

"I'll do my best, sir."

The president reached into his desk and pulled out a note card. It had been laminated to protect it from moisture. He reached out to hand it to O'Shea. It said:

March 21, 1964

Colonol Patrick O'Shea, USA, is acting
as my personal representative. Any
request should be considered an order
from the undersigned.

John F. Kennedy

John F. Kennedy
President of the United States

"This should help in a pinch," Kennedy said. "But I advise you to use it only when necessary. You don't want to put a target on your back."

"Yes, sir." O'Shea stood at attention.

The president smiled. "You are dismissed. God speed, Colonel."

CHAPTER 7

The O'Shea Residence
2234 Scranton Place
Alexandria, Virginia
2:00 p.m., April 3, 1964

Patrick O'Shea sat quietly on the edge of the bed as his wife pinned the eagle insignia of a full "bird" colonel on his uniforms and then packed his bags. After almost twenty years as an army wife, she knew just how to fold his uniforms so they didn't get wrinkled; her trick was to turn the sleeves inside out and fold them back against the tunic. It was a technique she had perfected, and one she enjoyed performing for her husband. She saw her role in their marriage as one of taking care of the miscellaneous details that become huge issues when you move every two or three years: keeping the house ship shape, the kids in school and the bills paid.

Maddie was also Patrick's partner in the truest sense of the word, and the past few days had been filled with discussions about what this mission to Vietnam represented for their life together. Maddie had been around the army long enough to understand how the game was played among the "regular" officers who made the military their career. Politics was as much a part of the army as it was in any other organization, and those who play it well tend to get ahead. Those who don't tend to get passed over for promotion and miss out on the most desirable assignments. She also knew her husband wasn't much interested in political gamesmanship, and that he had ended up in the most political of places—the White House—was an irony not lost on either of them.

Maddie already knew that this assignment represented a fork in the road for his career. She knew that going to Vietnam on behalf of the president on a "fact finding" mission outside of the chain of command would mark him as an interloper, and would forever blackball him in the eyes of an army establishment that controlled his career. While her husband seemed at peace with the decision, she knew deep down it had been a wrenching process. Her husband loved the junior officers and enlisted men he had worked with, taken care of, and led over the better part of twenty years. They represented the Army to him, and that was ultimately where his loyalty lay.

At that moment Maddie loved her husband more than she ever had, and that was saying a lot. She knew the moment they met that she would marry him. She had been a Pi Kappa sorority sister at the College of Charleston when they had held the annual dance for the cadets from the Citadel. Maddie had just broken up with her high school boyfriend, and had to be dragged to the dance by her sorority sisters. Then she laid eyes on this tall, handsome cadet in his dress uniform, with a big smile and piercing blue eyes. Maddie had felt like the cat that caught the mouse that night, and she still did.

"I should be back in three months, if everything goes as planned," he said. "I'll phone you when I can, and try to pop some postcards in the mail." He made it a habit of dropping cards to Maddie and the kids wherever he went, usually scribbled with a short note that let them know that he was thinking of them—and that he was still alive. But he rarely called, overseas phone rates being what they were, and their budget as tight as it was on an army salary. This sent Maddie's well-tuned radar into high gear.

"Phone us?"

Patrick immediately realized that he had inadvertently made his wife worry. He tried to backtrack. "I just figured if I could, I'd call home to check-in. Now that I'm a colonel and all." He tried to smile it off.

Maddie looked at him and nodded. An unspoken word passed between them; she understood that he was going in harm's way, and he understood that she now knew it. There wasn't anything to be done—it was the life that they had chosen.

Patrick stood up and moved over to his wife and pulled her to him. He looked into her blue eyes and kissed her lightly on her nose, moving slowly to her lips, and then to her neck. She whispered "Pat, the kids are going to be home from school soon." He grunted, and she knew that wasn't going to stop him. He reached for her blouse buttons and began slowly undoing them; her breasts swelled against a lacy white bra, and she could feel him grow erect. This was the way that her husband connected with her, and it was how he could show her how much he loved her. She gave in.

Later, as her husband showered, she lay in their bed, thinking about how she needed to get up so Elizabeth didn't come home from school to find her disheveled and gleaming with sweat. Maddie could still feel the weight of him on top of her, and knew it would have to last her awhile. Like always, she would file it away and keep it safe, until he came back home to her.

Office of the Attorney General
Department of Justice
Washington, D.C.
8:20 p.m., April 5, 1964

Bobby Kennedy sat at his desk twirling a football. He wore a short-sleeved white shirt, a thin blue and black striped tie, and scuffed oxford shoes. His hair was in its typical tousled state. His face bore the stubble of a long day of meetings. He was exhausted, but too tired to nap and not in the mood to go home for the night.

Since Dallas, Bobby had thought of only two things. The first was the FBI investigation into Jackie's murder. There had been a frenzy of conspiracy theories since Jack Ruby, a Dallas nightclub owner, killed Jackie's assassin Lee Harvey Oswald in the basement of the Dallas Police Station on November 25th. Ruby, who was now in the Dallas jail himself, wasn't talking—so far at least. If Oswald's killing hadn't been caught on live television in front of millions of people, nobody would have believed it had happened the way it did. The Dallas police had played their 15 minutes of fame in the most obnoxious of ways, allowing the press hoard to overwhelm their meager security, that enabled a gawker like Ruby to get into position to shoot Oswald. The Dallas police were media hounds, and Oswald paid the price. Now it would be difficult to figure out whether Oswald acted alone, or whether it really was a conspiracy.

The second thing that Bobby couldn't get out of his mind was Lyndon Baines Johnson. It had become an unhealthy obsession. Since 1960, when his brother had offered the vice president slot to Johnson, Bobby had been in a state of frustration mixed with disgust. Every single thing about Lyndon Johnson repelled him. Johnson was vulgar, pushy, uneducated, but worst of all he was from Texas. Bobby, who grew up in Boston and London and whose blood ran blue, thought of Texas as a place you flew over on the way to Los Angeles. And the fact that his sister-in-law had been killed there only added to his rage against everything the state of Texas represented.

The blood between Bobby and Johnson began to go bad almost as soon as they met in the early 1950s when Bobby had been a lawyer on the staff of the Senate Permanent Subcommittee on Investigations chaired by Senator Joseph McCarthy. Bobby's frequent contact with Johnson always began with the 6'4" Johnson towering over the diminutive Bobby and saying, "Hi sonny," often in front of other senators. Bobby was so embarrassed by this that he determined he would never again have anything to do with Johnson.

Thus it was particularly ironic that Bobby's own behavior would make that impossible. On the morning after his brother secured the 1960 Democratic nomination, a series of meetings to choose John Kennedy's vice presidential running mate were held at the Biltmore Hotel in downtown Los Angeles. One of those meetings was between Senate Secretary Bobby Baker—one of Johnson's closest friends—and Kennedy aide Kenny O'Donnell. In hushed tones over bottles of Coca Cola, Baker calmly explained that Lyndon Johnson was in possession of incriminating material that showed conclusively that John, Bobby and even their father, Joseph P. Kennedy, were involved in a series of extramarital affairs, and had been implicated in what could be charitably described as "suspect" financial dealings with members of organized crime. When pressed for details about what this "material" consisted of, Baker took an envelope from his inside coat pocket and handed it to O'Donnell. Looking inside, O'Donnell saw a series of images of scantily clad women in the company of two men who could clearly be identified as the 1960 Democratic Party nominee for president and his brother. O'Donnell, a former football player, ripped the envelope in half, reached across the table, picked Baker up by his coat lapels, and propelled him roughly out the door. But the message was clear: Johnson wanted a place on the 1960 presidential ticket, and he was willing to use any means to get it.

Both John and Robert Kennedy instantly realized that the vision of "Camelot" that was being carefully constructed for the campaign—based principally on the fairy-tale love affair between John and Jackie—would be destroyed if Johnson's dirt reached the public.

So they caved to blackmail, and made a very rational calculation: as long as Johnson was on the ticket, and as long as his political interests aligned with theirs, the incriminating information he had would stay buried. So, John Kennedy made the call to Lyndon Johnson, welcoming him to the 1960 Democratic ticket. It was, in the truest sense, a Faustian bargain. But such is the lust for power that one truly will get in bed with people one hates.

Now, three years later, Bobby had to accept the fact that his brother was willing to again cut a deal with Johnson that would keep him on the ticket in 1964. Bobby had been sure that in the wake of Dallas, his brother would have the leverage to send Johnson packing. But John Kennedy never had a stomach for the tough stuff, and since Jackie's murder and his own brush with death, Bobby sensed his brother had softened. If it were up to him, he'd have called Johnson's bluff and used whatever dirt they could find on Johnson—and there was plenty of dirt to be had—to counterpunch. Bobby would have ruined Johnson's reputation and sent him out of Washington on a rail, using the public sympathy for Jackie as a cudgel to beat him over the head. Would the Kennedy's have taken a hit? Absolutely. But with the post-Dallas sympathy factor, Bobby would have bet his eight kids that they'd still have won against whomever the Republicans put up in November.

CHAPTER 8

The American Embassy
Saigon, Republic of Vietnam
2:30 p.m., April 20, 1964

"I appreciate you seeing me on such short notice, Mr. Ambassador."

Henry Cabot Lodge waved away O'Shea's gesture with a hand. "Nonsense, colonel. It isn't every day that the personal military representative of the president comes to town."

O'Shea had no illusions that his identity would remain a secret, but even he was surprised at how quickly word had spread that he was there on behalf of Kennedy. It was a strange sensation: on the one hand the red carpet had been rolled out for him, and yet on the other everyone seemed to be eyeing him with a deep suspicion. He'd thus far managed to avoid MACV headquarters, but he knew eventually he'd have to present himself to General Harkins as well. He was determined to wait as long as he could.

O'Shea and Lodge sat opposite each other in the Ambassador's large office. Lodge wore a cream-colored suit and dark tie, looking more like a southern plantation owner than a diplomat. Reaching into his suit, he pulled out a gold cigarette case, opened it, and held it out to O'Shea, who politely declined. By the time Lodge had pulled out a smoke and returned the case to his coat pocket, O'Shea had pulled out his Zippo lighter, reaching across the table to light Lodge's cigarette. Lodge took a deep drag. Pointing to the lighter he said, "May I see that?"

"Sure," O'Shea said.

Lodge turned the lighter over in his hand. It was marked with the Special Forces logo and an inscription, which Lodge read aloud: "War is hell but actual combat is a son of a bitch." Lodge smiled. "That's true, isn't it?"

"It is."

Lodge looked at O'Shea's ribbons and noticed the Silver Star and the Purple Heart. "You've been in actual combat I see. Korea?"

"Yes, sir. I had the bad luck of being in the path of a whole bunch of angry Chinese."

Lodge looked at O'Shea, sizing him up. He instantly recognized that this was not a man to be trifled with, and that he'd better be very careful about what he said around him. Kennedy didn't pick him as his personal advisor for nothing. "Well, please let me know if there is anything you need while you are here."

"Yes, Mr. Ambassador."

"How long will you be in-country?"

"I'm not sure. A month or two, maybe more."

Lodge whistled. "That's quite a long visit." He paused, thinking of all the trouble O'Shea could cause. "Do keep in touch, Colonel, won't you?"

"I certainly will, sir."

* * *

As O'Shea reached the Embassy exit he sensed someone following him. He stopped on the top steps just outside the door and waited. When no one appeared, he continued down to the street. Crossing the wide boulevard that fronted the Embassy compound, he hailed a cab. At that moment he saw a tall, slender man in a tan suit. He was standing in front of the Embassy on the other side of the street pretending to study a map of Saigon.

When a cab pulled to the curb, O'Shea opened the door to get in but quickly changed his mind. Slamming it shut, he sprinted back across the street. The man had been looking at the map a bit too intently, and didn't notice O'Shea until he was already upon him.

"Ok, buddy, why the hell are you following me?"

The man quickly took two steps back. O'Shea was a big man and was quite intimidating. "Take it easy! I was just tailing you until we could talk—in private."

"What do we have to talk about?" O'Shea said over the noise of traffic.

"Look, I know who you are and why you are here. I also have some very important information for you."

"Do you now. And how is that?"

"Because I work for the CIA. There's little we don't know."

O'Shea was pissed that the list of those who knew his identity was growing by the minute. Nonetheless he was intrigued.

The man looked around nervously. "Let's walk." He gently pulled O'Shea by the arm, and they started back across the boulevard, making their way into the warren of small cobblestone streets that ringed the Embassy.

Finally, O'Shea said, "Listen, I'm not just going to start talking until you prove to me who you are."

"Your name is Patrick O'Shea. You live in Virginia with your wife Maddie and two kids, Kevin and Elizabeth. You went to the Citadel and fought in Korea. You were in Vietnam in '61 on an advisor tour. Your father was a cop killed in the line of duty. You now work for the president of the United States and are here to help him figure out just what the fuck is going on in Vietnam. Shall I go on?"

Wow, thought O'Shea.

They walked together until they came to a small café with tables facing the street. They sat down and each ordered a cold beer. It was only March but the weather was already hot and humid.

After downing half his beer in a few swallows, O'Shea asked, "So, what's this information you have?"

The man looked around. "Not here. Meet me tonight at your hotel."

O'Shea finished the remainder of his beer. He felt safe at his hotel and at this point had nothing to lose. "Ok. I'm in room—"

"325. Yes, I know."

Room 325, The Caravelle Hotel
Saigon, Republic of Vietnam
8:25 p.m., April 20, 1964

If you were an American in Saigon, the Caravelle was the place to be. Every evening, a mix of American officers, diplomats and journalists gathered around the bar, joined by a bevy of beautiful women. It was also the location of the daily press briefings on the war, and was thus a font of information about what was happening in Vietnam. O'Shea had secured a room at the hotel for the duration of his stay in Vietnam. It would serve as his home base.

"So who the hell are you?" O'Shea asked.

"My name is Tucker Gouglemann. Technically, I am the agricultural liaison to the South Vietnamese Government. But you already know that's a lie."

"How long have you been in Vietnam?" O'Shea wanted to know just how deep his connections were.

"Since 1961."

O'Shea nodded. "Did you take part in the coup?"

"Which coup? Against Diem? No, that was Lucien Conein's gig. I've been working on…other things."

O'Shea waited for Gouglemann to continue. When he didn't, he said, "So what's this information you have for me?"

Gouglemann stared at O'Shea through tortoiseshell glasses, his eyes the color of molasses. "I have information that I want to get to the president."

"So why don't you put it in a memo and send it through the proper channels?"

Gouglemann laughed. "God, I don't ever want this in writing. And I don't want anyone in the Agency to know where it came from."

"What makes you think you can trust me?"

Gouglemann was silent for a long minute. "Because we are cut from the same cloth. Like you, I'm a patriot, colonel. I was a Marine in World War II, fought on Guadalcanal. Spent two years in a hospital recovering from wounds." Gouglemann lifted up his pant leg to show a massive chasm where his calf had been, the result of a high-powered bullet fired by a Japanese sniper. "After the war I joined the OSS and did covert missions in Korea. We've stepped on a lot of the same ground."

O'Shea was starting to feel more comfortable with this man. "Go on."

"President Diem's brother Ngo Dinh Nhu ran a huge organized crime operation from inside the presidential palace—numbers running, lottery rackets, extortion, currency manipulation. But Nhu's biggest source of wealth was from opium, which he imported from Laos. When Nhu ended up dead in the coup alongside his brother, the drug business went up for grabs. It's now in the hands of a cadre of junior generals that Khanh has unleashed. They're known as the Young Turks."

Corruption in the South Vietnamese government wasn't new. "Yeah, so?"

"So, this is a very dirty business and it stretches across the globe. All they way to the U.S. in fact."

O'Shea was trying to connect the dots. "I'm sorry. I don't follow."

Gouglemann took off his glasses and began to clean them with his tie. "As you probably know, opium's the basis for heroin. It's a vast global market worth hundreds of millions of dollars, and Nhu and his business partner, a guy named Rock Francisci, were getting rich off it. I actually met Francisci at an Embassy event. He's an elegant bastard. He wore a white silk smoking jacket and had more jewelry on than the Queen of England. I asked around and it turns out he's a holdover from when the French ran Vietnam. Anyhow, Francisci is a Corsican with deep connections to the Laotian opium market. He works for the Union Corse—basically the Corsican Mafia."

O'Shea wondered where all this was going. He was also trying to picture Corsica on a map. "That's in the Med, right? Off the coast of Italy?"

"Exactly...but the Union Corse is all over southern France. They run a huge heroin syndicate in Marseille, which also happens to be the number one source of heroin sold in the United States."

O'Shea was now starting to understand where Gouglemann was going with this.

"The Union Corse has very close ties to the New York and Chicago mob families," Gouglemann continued. "Guys like Sam Giancana, Santos Trafficante, and others. They get their product from Marseille. And most of it comes from Laos via Saigon."

"How's it get from Laos to Marseille?" asked O'Shea.

"That's where the CIA comes in." Gouglemann paused. "The CIA backs Francisci, who runs an air transport business that moves the opium from Laos to Saigon. It then ends up on ships bound for Marseille."

"Goddamn. Who knows about this?"

"I suspect it must go all the way to the top of the CIA. But Lucien Conein is running it locally. He's helping Francisci."

"What's Conein's angle in this? Money? Leverage?"

"My guess is that it's both. And this is big money. The kind that buys you lots of leverage, especially in a place like Vietnam."

O'Shea was trying to process what he was hearing. If this were true, it meant the rot in Saigon was even deeper than he imagined. "Does Harkins or Lodge know about this?"

"I can't be sure. It's hard to imagine how they wouldn't."

"So what am I supposed to do with this information?" asked O'Shea.

"I want you to tell Kennedy. Look, I'm no boy scout, but I draw the line when the CIA is helping to bring heroin into the United States. I've tried to stop it—Conein and I came to blows over it. But he's in too deep. He's probably profiting personally from it. The CIA's goal is to ensure the flow of opium continues. I want it stopped."

O'Shea looked at Gouglemann. "I'll tell the president. But what he does with the information is out of my hands."

Gouglemann nodded. That was enough for him. "Thank you," he said.

Over Long Dinh, Long An Province
Republic of South Vietnam
2:10 p.m., May 9, 1964

Patrick O'Shea found himself pinned against the door of the single engine Cessna O-1 Bird Dog as the pilot, a young U.S. Air Force Captain from Louisiana named Jim "Viper" Mullins was trying to avoid the ground fire that was punching holes in the thin skin of the plane's wings. Mullins was chewing gum and grunting as he struggled to raise the plane's altitude, while rolling the wings up and down to make the slow plane less of a sitting duck. The Cessna was a high-wing plane with fixed landing gear and a top speed of 115 miles per hour. While it would be a great plane for a leisurely Sunday trip up the Pacific Coast in California, it is a very poor choice when people are shooting at you. O'Shea was about to get air sick when Mullins managed to duck into some low-ceiling clouds, making them invisible from the ground.

"Damn, Colonel, somebody down there is pretty pissed off," said Mullins, wiping the sweat from his face with a hand towel he kept at his knees. "That was close. We were about to be Swiss cheese."

No shit, O'Shea thought to himself. He had hitched a ride on the O-1 to see how the ARVN was performing in one of their first big battles since Diem had been overthrown. Outside the village of Long Dinh, almost 3,000 heavily armed ARVN fighters had surrounded some 600 members of the 514th Battalion of the Viet Cong. It was a prime opportunity for the ARVN to inflict real damage on the enemy. Instead of attacking with their ground forces, the ARVN commanders on the scene hunkered in, calling in U.S. airstrikes and artillery, leaving gaps in the lines through which a majority of the Viet Cong escaped. It was a fiasco.

Mullins banked the O-1 to the north and headed back toward Bien Hoa Air Base. Mullins was an Air Force fighter pilot currently assigned to the 19th Tactical Air Support Squadron. Normally, he worked as a forward air controller calling in airstrikes in support of the ARVN.

"This isn't much like flying an F-104, is it Captain?" O'Shea managed to joke, his stomach now back where it belonged.

"Not even close, sir. In fact, this plane feels slower than my car back in Louisiana. I've got a '57 Chevy with a Super Turbo Fire four barrel carb that puts out damn near 240 horses."

O'Shea knew these fighter jocks loved their fast toys. "So, how long have you been here in country?"

"About four months now, sir."

"What do you think of the South Vietnamese troops?"

"Not much. The ARVN is undisciplined, and left to its own devices, its soldiers tend to sit and wait for the VC to leave rather than engage. The only time we've had success is when our guys are pulling them along by their ears, or following them up with the pointy end of a bayonet."

O'Shea nodded. "Hard to see how we are going to be able to train them up to fight on their own, without actually getting drawn into the fighting ourselves."

"Hell, that's already happening. Most of our guys are in the thick of it, even taking point on patrols. It's the only way to get anything done around here."

O'Shea wasn't surprised by that. Most of the advisors were Green Berets, hard chargers who joined the military for just this kind of experience. But it wasn't scalable and wouldn't work unless in the end it left the ARVN able to fight on its own.

O'Shea breathed a sigh of relief when the O-1 touched down at Bien Hoa. As the O-1 pulled into its parking spot in front of a set of connected hangars, a ground crewman approached the plane, pointed up to the shredded wings and shook his head. Only then did O'Shea notice a clear fluid running from some of the holes in the left wing, creating a growing pool on the tarmac. O'Shea wondered just how much longer the plane would have lasted in the air. Mullins, sitting in the pilot's seat in front of O'Shea, got out first, helped by a Staff Sergeant who whispered something in his ear. Mullins let out a howl of laughter at whatever the sergeant had said. He didn't seem at all concerned about the holes in the wing.

O'Shea had been in country for a little more than a month. During that time he had kept a low profile, avoiding the tea and canapés at the Embassy in favor of time spent with the various advisor groups supporting the ARVN. He'd been asking a lot of questions and observing. And waiting for the president's courier to show up. It was only a matter of time, of course, before O'Shea's presence would create questions that would have to be answered, and he sensed that this time was now approaching.

As if on cue, just as he prepared to leave Bien Hoa he was handed a message.

9May64

To: Colonel Patrick O'Shea, USA c/o Bien Hoa Air Base

From: MACV Headquarters, Saigon

Message: Please report to General Harkins no later than 1400 hours 03June64.

Signed: Major General Price, Adjutant.

Office of the Secretary of Defense
The Pentagon
Washington, D.C.
10:20 a.m., May 9, 1964

Secretary of Defense Robert Strange McNamara, in shirtsleeves and a red striped tie, had just taken a phone call from General Paul D. Harkins from Saigon. McNamara was used to dealing with the vagaries of trans-Pacific phone calls, with the echo, the static and the delay that forced him to be patient and time his responses carefully, lest he talk over the other person on the line. It was a skill that the aggressive, energetic McNamara had willed himself to learn, though this moment was truly testing him. The Secretary of Defense was highly agitated by what he was hearing from Harkins.

"Mr. Secretary, Colonel O'Shea has been in Vietnam now for almost a month and I have yet to lay eyes on him. He's been in the field with Special Forces and CIA elements in the Central Highlands, moving from base to base in a plain uniform without insignia. He's damn near been a spy. If it were up to me I'd put him in irons and send him home on the slowest boat I could find. What is he doing here? And why was I the last to know about it?"

Doesn't that tell you something, General, thought McNamara.

McNamara paused before responding, momentarily enjoying

Harkins' fit of pique. McNamara was also irritated with O'Shea's trip to Vietnam, since it was outside of the Department of Defense channels and was thus something that couldn't be controlled—or closely monitored. But McNamara, who originally was attracted to Harkins' spit-and-polish demeanor and reputation for efficiency, had soured on the General as it became clear that he couldn't trust what he was hearing from the MACV command about the conditions on the ground. During McNamara's trips to Vietnam in 1962, and later with General Maxwell Taylor in late 1963, Harkins had made a coordinated effort to shield McNamara from bad news, going so far as to stage manage his visits into the field, making sure that only the most enthusiastic ARVN troops were present when the Secretary of Defense had the opportunity to ask questions. Harkins obviously wanted to impress McNamara, but the divergence between the rosy pictures painted by MACV and the reality of the increasingly dire situation was ultimately too much for even Harkins to hide.

By late 1963, McNamara had decided that after a suitable period of transition, Harkins would be relieved of command and put out to pasture in one of the Pentagon's many desk jobs until retirement. This made what McNamara was about to say to Harkins even more delicious.

"You do know that Colonel O'Shea is the president's personal representative to the military community, and is in Vietnam at his direction?"

"Yes, Mr. Secretary, I realize that. But—"

"But nothing, General. In any event, I'm sure that what he will find on the ground will be entirely consistent with the reports that I've been getting from you—that conditions are stable and that progress is being made."

Harkins was dead silent on the other end of the line.

"General, can you hear me?"

"Loud and clear now, Mr. Secretary. Is there anything else that I can do for you?"

McNamara smiled, enjoying the strategic retreat he was witnessing.

Harkins at least knew when to change the subject. You had to give him that. He was a consummate politician in uniform.

"That's all, General. Thank you for calling."

Click.

McNamara put the receiver down and punched the intercom on his desk.

"Jean, can you please call the White House and get me on the president's schedule? I'd like to go over the latest from Vietnam and discuss a few other matters with him."

"Right away, Mr. Secretary. Are you and Mrs. McNamara planning on attending the reception for the French president this evening?"

De Gaulle? Crap, that's all I need!

Charles De Gaulle was in town that week to pay his respects to the president, and a formal reception had been set up for him at the White House. McNamara disliked De Gaulle immensely, though he begrudgingly respected the Frenchman's unbridled national pride. But McNamara found De Gaulle to be imperious, contemptuous and flat-out arrogant. In particular, the Secretary of Defense knew that a lecture about Vietnam was going to be part of the evening; De Gaulle never let the embarrassing failure of the French in Vietnam cloud his opinion that he knew more about Ho Chi Minh and the Vietnamese communists than anyone else.

In general, McNamara was unmoved by De Gaulle's arguments, primarily because he was convinced that the French failure in Vietnam was a problem of execution, and not of strategy. The French were a second-tier military power that had fallen to Hitler in a month and a half during World War II. In McNamara's mind, France had great food and great culture, but their military prowess left a lot to be desired.

"Ah, Christ, Jean—I forgot that was tonight. If I don't go I'll never hear the end of it from Secretary Rusk. Can you have a car pick up Mrs. McNamara from home and I will meet her at the White House?" McNamara looked at his Omega Constellation chronometer, the watch his wife had bought him when he became president of the Ford Motor Company. "Around 6:30 should be fine."

McNamara turned his attention to the lengthy memo before him, addressed directly to himself and the president. The Joint Chiefs—the Chiefs of Staff of the Air Force, Navy and Army—were making a bold request to radically expand the war in Vietnam, banking that Kennedy, in a weakened state after Dallas, would finally cave to their pressure to take the gloves off and take the fight into North Vietnam. To the Chiefs, all problems could be solved by the application of more force: the challenges in South Vietnam, the crumbling of ARVN, and the failings of the advisory program—all could be fixed by the U.S. going on offense.

The Chiefs were pushing Kennedy to define Vietnam as America's war, and to enable the Pentagon to fully take charge of the battle, and McNamara realized he'd have to press the president hard to do so.

McNamara swung a very big hammer. And Vietnam was his nail.

Headquarters, Military Assistance Command, Vietnam (MACV)
137 Pasteur Street
Saigon, Republic of South Vietnam
3:45 p.m., May 11, 1964

MACV Headquarters inhabited a large pink building in the center of Saigon. It was four stories tall and had a guard shack at the front entrance, next to which stood one of the tallest trees in the area.

General Paul Harkins' office was on the building's top floor with a peekaboo view of the Saigon River, which meandered through the city on its way to the East Sea, some 20 miles northeast of the Mekong Delta. The office's walls were lined with pictures of Harkins posing with various dignitaries, including a large picture, displayed prominently behind his desk, of him next to General George Patton, taken when Harkins served on the staff of the Third Army in Europe during World

War II. Harkins enjoyed the cache that his work for Patton provided him within the Army, and wanted to make sure that everyone knew about it.

None of this was on O'Shea's mind as he cooled his heels in Harkins' outer office. He had been there for about an hour as staff officers came and went with officious purpose, curtly nodding to him as they passed by. He had presented himself first to Harkins' deputy, a pompous major general named Price, who had kept him standing at attention for a full minute as he pored over papers on his desk. After finally telling O'Shea to stand at ease without looking up, he neglected to offer him a seat, leaving O'Shea to stand with his feet shoulder-width apart and his hands interlocked at the small of his back, staring four inches above the general's head. Then, after another few minutes of silence, and still without looking up, he told O'Shea with dripping sarcasm that "the general" was extremely pleased that he had found the time in his very busy schedule to stop by and pay his respects to the senior U.S. military officer in Vietnam. While O'Shea was expecting an icy reception, this was even colder than he imagined. After five minutes or so, Price dismissed O'Shea and instructed him to wait in "the general's" outer office until he was called.

After about 40 minutes, Harkins' secretary came out to get him. "Colonel O'Shea, the general will see you now."

O'Shea rose, smoothed the blouse of his summer-weight khaki uniform, and walked into Harkins' inner office. He stepped forward toward Harkins' desk and saluted. "Colonel O'Shea reporting as requested, sir."

General Harkins sat behind his large oak desk and casually returned the salute. He then stood up and offered his hand to O'Shea. "Welcome to Saigon, colonel. I had hoped to have met you sooner." Harkins had a slight smile on his face as he said this, but his handshake was firm and his demeanor inviting. O'Shea was immediately put off balance, having expected more of what he'd gotten from the General's deputy. He wondered if they were playing a game of "good cop/bad cop" with him. He was about to find out.

"General, thank you. It's been a busy couple of weeks since arriving in country."

"More like a month, Colonel. Please sit," Harkins said, gesturing to one of the chairs facing his desk. "My people have been keeping tabs on you. I understand you've been visiting old friends in the field," referring to O'Shea's contact with Special Forces units in the countryside.

"A few. Yes, sir," O'Shea said.

Harkins sat staring at O'Shea, and the more he looked, the less he liked. O'Shea wasn't West Point and therefore wasn't a professional soldier, notwithstanding his distinguished combat record. He was a glorified amateur in Harkins' discerning eyes, a man who somehow had managed to skip over dozens of men more senior to him to take an unprecedented role in the Kennedy Administration. Yet here O'Shea sat, in *his* office in *his* building, in the country in which *he* was the supreme authority, and he was powerless over him. Harkins knew that O'Shea was there on behalf of the president of the United States and was therefore untouchable. And while Harkins could certainly make it difficult on O'Shea—putting up roadblocks to those under Harkins' command and making travel around Vietnam more challenging—in the end Harkins knew that he was up against a superior force, where discretion was the better part of valor. Discretion in this case came in the form of being "helpful."

"Colonel, I'd certainly like to help you get a solid picture of the progress we are making in our advisory efforts. Would you like me to set up a tour for you?"

O'Shea had been warned about the general's "tours." Harkins was well known for stage-managing the VIP tours of McNamara, Bundy, Rusk and others coming through Saigon. That was certainly not on O'Shea's agenda.

"I appreciate the offer, sir. But I must decline. At some point in the next few weeks I plan on heading out to the 7th Special Forces Group."

Harkins nodded. "The 7th has been very busy with CIDG and MIKE forces up around Nam Dong." The Civilian Irregular Defense Group was formed to organize and train "irregular" military units made up of local populations, forming Mobile Strike Force Command groups—or MIKEs. MIKEs were used as quick reaction forces to support ARVN troops in the field when they got into trouble, which was an all-too-common occurrence. Nam Dong, a province about 15 miles South of the Laotian border, was the sight of frequent incursions by North Vietnamese forces as they made their way into South Vietnam.

"I've heard the Nung have earned a reputation as tough fighters, sir," said O'Shea, referring to the ethnic Chinese peoples who fled China for Vietnam in the 11th Century, and who maintained a very distinct cultural and tribal identity. U.S. Special Forces teams had created a number of battalions made up of Nung fighters that had performed quite well in combat. They were natural warriors.

Harkins replied, "The Nung are solid soldiers when properly trained and equipped. We've seen very good results with the MIKE teams, but they aren't big enough to fight off regular North Vietnamese Army units. We need to have the ARVN fighting those battles, and that's where our efforts are concentrated now. I believe we are making good progress in many areas. But there is obviously more work to be done."

O'Shea smiled and nodded but offered no comment. He wanted to get through the meeting without alienating Harkins and hoped that the conversation would wrap up quickly.

Harkins, sensing that his charm offensive wasn't working, decided to abruptly switch tactics and send O'Shea a message he couldn't ignore or misinterpret.

"Colonel, I'll make this simple. I know why you are here and I don't like it. I can't stop you from making your rounds and taking notes on what you see and hear. But you are on your own. You don't work for me and I can't help you if you get into trouble. I've made it clear to my staff that if you find yourself in the bush, surrounded by VC, we aren't going to risk American lives to save you. You are, for all intents and purposes, an army of one."

Harkins paused, waiting for a reaction. When he got none, he went on. "Having said that, I expect you to check in with my office on a weekly basis, and to let my staff know where you are. I don't want to be completely in the dark if you go MIA and the president wants to know what's happened to you. Do we understand each other?"

O'Shea understood perfectly. While O'Shea took comfort that the soldiers in the 7th Special Forces Group and other Army units would certainly rush to the sound of gunfire if he were in trouble, he also knew that if he went missing or found himself in a position where U.S. Search and Rescue needed to be mobilized, he'd not get much—if any—assistance. He was a man without a country.

CHAPTER 9

122 Rue Gatons
Marseille, France
1:30 p.m., June 3, 1964

The Boulevard Rue Gatons runs from the center of Marseille directly to the waterfront, where a huge port services transport ships from all over the world. Marseille had long been the hub of France's industrial economy and for centuries served as the gateway to the French empire. It was also a linchpin in American efforts in Western Europe after World War II, serving as a vital access point for imports that fueled the rebuilding of Europe. The American government considered Marseille a strategic asset essential to winning the Cold War.

The offices of Antoine and Barthelemy Guerini were on the top floor of a squat stone building that faced the Mediterranean Sea. The façade of the building was a dirty shade of white, stained by the endless supply of coal dust and diesel that drifted up from the port and fouled the air. On the ground floor of the building sat the Bar de la Méditerranée, a sidewalk cafe where Antoine habitually took his morning coffee and read the *Le Monde* newspaper. Every half hour or so a visitor would sit down at his table and make small talk, making sure to slip an envelope of French Francs under Antoine's newspaper before leaving. Antoine and Barthelemy—nicknamed "Meme"—ran an extensive racketeering and loan-sharking enterprise in addition to transporting drugs, and Antoine's morning ritual was the fruit of that labor.

In reality, Antoine Guerini and the Union Corse, the secretive Franco-Coriscan mob of which he was a part, had long since bought off the Marseille police, and so Antoine's ritual with the envelopes was hardly necessary. The Guerini brothers and their associates had a long history of cooperation with police, military and intelligence agencies dating back to the Second World War, when the Union Corse had allied itself with the French Resistance, becoming effective saboteurs and spies against the Germans and later the communist party in Marseille.

Antoine Guerini was something of a legend within the Union Corse. His wartime activities as head of the mob laid the groundwork for the Union Corse's vast and profitable criminal activity of the 1950s and early 1960s. Guerini's personal relationship with Lucien Conein and the CIA was cemented in the political unrest of this period, when the U.S. focused on ensuring that communism did not gain a foothold in Western Europe. Any enemy of communism was a friend of the United States, and millions upon millions of American dollars flowed into the Union Corse coffers during this time, largely aimed at preventing Marseille from falling under communist control.

Among other activities the Guerini brothers parlayed their CIA ties and vast financial support into a global heroin empire that spanned what became known as the "Golden Triangle": Laos, Burma and Thailand. Raw opium was harvested in these areas and shipped via air to Saigon; from Saigon they were bundled into containers and put on ships bound for Marseille, where the docks controlled by the Union Corse were set up to receive them. A small cadre of Corsican chemists just outside the port would turn the raw opium into fine grade heroin—more than 100 kilograms a month by 1964—which would then be packed and returned to different ships bound for America. It was a highly efficient operation that lined the Guerini brother's pockets with millions of American dollars.

Earlier that morning, Antoine Guerini had arranged a meeting for the brothers with their chief lieutenant, Marcel Cordioni, to discuss the status of shipments from Saigon. The last few shipments of opium had been delayed and were smaller than expected, and Antoine was concerned that the chaotic conditions in Vietnam since Diem's coup were adversely affecting their business, despite Conein's assurances to the contrary. The Guerini brothers had paid dearly to buy stability in the Laos-to-Saigon pipeline, and the fact that it wasn't working made them livid.

"Marcel, please sit. *Café?*"

"*Oui, merci.* I've just been to the docks. It seems that this latest shipment was light more than 300 kilograms. This is the third time in the past month." Marcel Cordioni paused, knowing that he was treading on very sensitive ground. Lighting a cigarette he said, "It's very… problematic."

Antoine signaled his assistant to get Marcel a café, while his brother sat consulting his ledger. "Problematic? *Oui*, it's very problematic. I think it's time to send a message to Francisci and his CIA friend," Antoine said.

Meme Guerini grunted his agreement. "What I want is for Conein to know that we can make life very rough for him and the CIA here in Marseille. Perhaps there will be a strike at the dock next month. Perhaps we turn to Turkey for our supply of opium. We can quickly cut out Francisci from this whole enterprise and let the monkeys in Laos swing from vines in the jungle."

"If only it were that easy to get out of Laos," Cordioni said without thinking. The last thing he wanted was to dig a deeper hole for himself. He quickly added, "Francisci will do whatever is necessary to fix this, of that I am sure."

"He better not fuck it up," Antoine said. "I want you to send one of your men to Saigon to ensure we get results. I don't care how you do it, but make sure that Francisci and Conein—and anybody else who are getting in the way—know we will not tolerate any further disruptions."

Meme then slammed shut his ledger. "This all rolls downhill, Marcel. If Francisci's shipments are light when they reach us and then ours are light to Chicago." Then, looking at his brother, he said, "We don't have to tell you what happens when Chicago gets angry, do I, Marcel?" Salvatore Giancana of the Chicago Outfit was notoriously unforgiving of error.

Cordioni knew all-too-well what happened when Giancana last had an interruption in the supply of heroin feeding the American market. The Union Corse's man in Chicago had been beaten to an inch of his life and spent two months in traction, holed up in a cold-water flat on the South Side of Chicago. Word had eventually come back that the beating was personally carried out by one of Giancana's captains, Frank Nitti, who had opened up the heroin trade in Montreal and whose career was being made on the vast profits fueled by Guerini's shipments.

Marcel looked directly at Antoine Guerini. "*Non*. I know what happens."

The Salvatore "Sam" Giancana Residence
1147 S. Wenonah Avenue
Oak Park, Illinois
10:30 am., June 4, 1964

The home that Chicago mob boss Sam Giancana occupied in historic Oak Park was a nondescript red brick bungalow with three bedrooms and two baths. Its outward appearance belied the well-designed interior that the Chicago mob—formally called the "Outfit"—had retrofitted to be as secure as possible. Precautions included bullet-proof glass windows that faced the street, double-walled interior panels designed to block even the FBI's most sophisticated listening devices, and a variety of other measures that included a Doberman Pinscher innocuously named "Bella," which had been trained as an attack dog by German security forces in the Bavarian Alps.

At that moment Giancana sat in his den sipping an espresso. He was wearing gray slacks and a black cardigan sweater over a white golf shirt. With the exception of the gold pinkie ring on his right hand, he looked more like an accountant than the head of one of the largest organized crime syndicates in the world.

Giancana had summoned his captains to a meeting to address the dramatic decline in revenue from the drug trade that was putting intense pressure on their finances. Frank Nitti, Paul Ricca and Underboss Tony Accardo sat tensely across from him. Rarely was it good news to be called into Giancana's den in the middle of the day.

"What are we hearing from Marseille?" asked Giancana.

"They are trying to put pressure on Saigon, but aren't having a lot of luck," said Nitti. "Those fucking Nips can't seem to stay in power for more than a few weeks."

Ricca laughed. "Nips are Japs, Frank. These are Vietnamese."

"Nips, Japs, Gooks. What's the difference? They're all slant eyes."

Giancana shot a dirty look at Nitti. He didn't like the banter—not because it was racist, but because he was angry. The problems in Vietnam were costing him money and it was no time for jokes. "And what about our so-called friends in the CIA?"

"Francisci is supposed to be meeting this week with Conein," Nitti said.

Giancana was exasperated. "After all we've done for those fucking Kennedys and the CIA, I should hope they'd get this fixed. They wanted Castro dead and three times we tried to kill him. Three times! They needed help in the '60 election and we made sure that dead people all over Illinois voted for Kennedy. And we didn't take a fucking dime! All I asked was that they give us room to breathe and allow our trade to continue. Francis was supposed to fix that for us."

Accardo shook his head. "Fat chance. Sinatra's got no juice with Bobby Kennedy."

"No shit," said Nitti, "and we put a shit ton of pressure on Frank. I even threatened that we'd have Ross put a kilo of coke in his car and then arrange to have the FBI bust him." Rick Ross was an FBI agent assigned to the organized crime task force. He had the misfortune of being a drug abuser and degenerate gambler and had gotten deeply in debt to Giancana. He was now paid huge sums to be a fixer and killer for the Outfit.

"We've got Ross working on another job for us right now," said Accardo. "He's a ruthless son of a bitch and damn good at what he does."

"It didn't work with Sinatra because he's a worthless piece of shit," growled Giancana. "Francis talked a good game. But in the end, the president's baby brother was too smart for him."

Frank Sinatra and his "Rat Pack" made much of their living in Las Vegas, and in doing so, became friendly with the mob, which essentially ran Vegas as an extension of their racketeering business. Sinatra was also very friendly with John and Bobby Kennedy, who had been frequent guests at Sinatra's star-studded parties.

In fact, it was at one of those parties that John Kennedy had ended up in bed with a woman named Judith Campbell. Campbell, a beautiful brunette with almond shaped eyes, also happened to be Sam Giancana's girlfriend, a potentially explosive connection that Giancana assumed he could use to get favorable treatment from the Kennedy administration. Unfortunately, it had backfired. When Bobby Kennedy found out about Campbell's link to Giancana, he doubled down on his pursuit of the Chicago mob, ordering the Justice Department to step up the pace of prosecutions. He also moved quickly to exile Sinatra from the Kennedy clan, telling his brother that he'd have to "find another pond of starlets to fish in."

"So what do we do?" asked Accardo.

"It's not what we do. It's what we don't do," said Giancana.

Accardo, Nitti and Ricco looked at each other and then back at Giancana, clearly confused.

Giancana sighed. "The election! Kennedy only won last time because of us. Without organized labor he'd have lost to Nixon. So what if we stay home this time? And what if we put pressure on the New York families to help in Connecticut, Pennsylvania and New Jersey? If the election is as close as it was in 1960, that will be a lot of leverage."

Nitti smiled. This was the kind of strategy session he enjoyed. He had earned the nickname of "The Enforcer" by fixing problems that required head bashing. "So we get the Teamsters and the Auto boys engaged in organizing and intimidating voters, working on election officials and organizing in favor of Nixon. Piece of cake."

Giancana held up his hand. "Take it easy. Let's prepare ourselves, but no action yet. I plan to use this to threaten the Kennedys to get our pipeline restarted. If that doesn't work, we'll move on it and take our chances with whomever the Republicans put up."

Nitti sighed. "Yes, Boss."

"So how do we get the message to Kennedy?" asked Accardo.

Giancana took a final sip of his espresso and said, "Call Francis and tell him to call Bobby Kennedy. Tell him that his brother dodged a bullet once. He shouldn't press his luck."

The O'Shea Residence
2234 Scranton Place
Alexandria, Virginia
3:15 p.m. June 5, 1964

Sixteen-year-old Elizabeth O'Shea blew through the back door of the O'Shea house, dropped her book bag on the kitchen counter, and bounded up the stairs to her bedroom. On her bed lay the Beatles hit album, *Meet The Beatles*. Elizabeth had played it non-stop for the past three weeks. She loved every song, but her favorite was "I Want to Hold Your Hand." Her mother was now officially sick of hearing it, which was made even worse by the fact that it came on every five minutes on the car radio as well. The Beatles had taken the country by storm, and Elizabeth O'Shea was living proof.

Her father had been gone just a month—a nanosecond in the time frame of a military family. Elizabeth was used to long absences from her dad, and she and her mom had come to an understanding; when Patrick was away, Elizabeth and Maddie would spend lots of girl time together, going shopping and getting their hair and nails done. It was fun, and even at 16, Elizabeth liked spending time with her mom.

She was in middle of the chorus to "I Saw Her Standing There" when she sensed her mom standing in the doorway of her room. Maddie had just gotten home from the store, and held an Air Mail envelope in her hand. She mouthed the words "from your dad" and gestured Elizabeth to come downstairs.

The letter had been postmarked from Saigon on May 20—two weeks was about the time it usually took to get mail from Vietnam, and Maddie had learned to deal with the vast time delay between letters.

Dear Mads, Kevin, and Elizabeth,

Hello from Saigon! Since my last letter from the bush,
I've been in relative comfort of the Caravelle. Weather
has been cool but summer is definitely coming. Vietnam
remains a startling place of contradictions: People are
friendly and there are pockets of wealth, and you can feel
the French influence everywhere. Saigon seems like a slice
of Paris in some ways. But much of the country is poor and
subsisting on just a few dollars a day.

I did get to have dinner with Joe Jordan the other night.
Mads, you remember Joe? We were at Schweinfurt together
in '55. He's now with MACV Command here.

I plan on spending the next month up in the Central
Highlands area, so may not get another letter to you for a
bit, but don't worry about me. The troops are taking very
good care of me and I'm staying out of the line of fire.

If you need anything please contact me via the White
House. They know where I am and can get me a message within
a day or two.

Looking forward to coming home. Right now expect that
will be sometime in July.

Love,

Patrick

"July? Dad is going to miss my birthday! He was supposed to be here
this year!"

Maddie was, of course, used to this problem. "Honey, you know he'd
be there if he could. And who knows? He may be back in time. It's only
early June. Let's give it a few weeks to see how things go."

Elizabeth got up from the kitchen table and heard "That Boy" start up on her stereo upstairs. She had already forgotten about her birthday.

The Palmer House Hotel
Chicago, Illinois
11:10 p.m., June 5, 1964

FBI Agent Rick Ross knocked on the door of room 652. "Room service," he called out. Ross stepped to the right of the peephole so that if the room's occupant looked through the peephole they would only see the food cart. He pulled his gun and waited for the door to open.

"We didn't order any room service—" said a blonde woman in a negligee as she cracked open the door.

In the background a man yelled, "Don't open the fucking door!"

It was too late. Ross kicked open the door and stepped into the woman. Before she could scream, Ross punched her hard in the face, knocking her backward into the room. He strode forward into the room with his gun raised as a half-naked man reached for the phone on the nightstand.

"Don't move a fucking muscle or you are a dead man." The man abruptly stopped, one hand on the bed and the other in mid-air. "Lay facedown on the bed with your hands out in front of you."

The man complied, flopping himself down on his big belly. Ross kicked shut the hotel room door. He stepped over the woman on the floor. Blood was coming out of her mouth, and he rolled her over onto her stomach so she wouldn't choke to death. As he did he admired her ample breasts under the shear material of her negligee and nodded approvingly.

"Do you know who the fuck I am?" growled the man on the bed. "You are a dead man!"

Ross laughed. "I know exactly who you are, Mr. Sikes," Ross said with sarcastic formality. "You are the president of the Greater Chicago

Trade Unions." He calmly sat down in the armchair across from the bed.

"What the fuck do you want?"

"It's not what I want, Mr. Sikes. It's what Sam Giancana wants."

Sikes swallowed hard and started to visibly shake. Just the mention of Giancana's name sent fear coursing down his spine. "Wha...what can I do for Sam?"

Ross sat back and lit a cigarette. He always enjoyed this part, where grown men began to grovel and whimper in front of him. Giancana had tried all manner of physical intimidation on Sikes in the past, and it hadn't worked. It was now up to Ross to bring down the heavy hammer.

Taking out his FBI badge, Ross held it up for Sikes to see. He then pulled out a bag of heroin from his jacket pocket. "Well, what do we have here? Looks like smack. That's really unfortunate, Mr. Sikes. This is probably enough to get you rung up on dealing charges. And that poor girl on the floor? It would be a shame for her to overdose. That would probably add murder to the charges. Involuntary manslaughter if you're lucky. But I'm not sure you'll be very lucky."

Sikes started to panic. Physical intimidation was one thing, but what Ross brought was something much worse The power of the FBI and the threat of imprisonment was more than even the toughest men could withstand. Not that Ross was above the rough stuff; this job required the occasional use of blunt force to get his way. But usually the threat of spending the rest of your life in a federal penitentiary was persuasion enough.

"What can I do for Sam?" Sikes asked again, this time with more urgency.

"You can get your unions in line on the McCormick Place expansion. Mr. Giancana is very disappointed in your fees. They are exorbitant."

"Exorbitant? Are you fucking kidding me? I'm making maybe 10% after I pay points to every fucker in line—the aldermen, the ward bosses, the cement guys, the Outfit. Everyone's got a fucking handout!"

As Sikes was saying this, Ross pulled out a syringe, a lighter and a spoon and started to cook a dose of heroin. He heated it up, drew it into the vial, and stood up, walking toward the blonde on the floor.

"What the fuck are you doing? Don't touch her!" Sikes yelled.

Ross calmly picked up her left foot and spread her toes apart. He looked over at Sikes and said, "Pity she overdosed in your hotel room. And you are a married man! I have to give you credit, though—she's a fine piece of ass." As he pushed the needle into the space next to her big toe, Sikes broke.

"Ok, ok, ok! I'll do it. I'll take my cut down to 8%."

Ross again pushed the needle in further.

"No! Don't do that! Ok! 5%."

Ross just looked at Sikes. "You'll do it for zero percent. Nada. Nothing."

"I can't do it for nothing! The members will never go for that! I'll be out on my ass in no time!"

Ross shrugged. It didn't matter to him. He began to push the plunger down when Sikes screamed, "Ok, fuck! I'll do it for nothing! As a gift to Sam."

Pulling the syringe out, Ross spread her legs apart and took a gratuitous peek at her red panties. She had long beautiful legs. She was way too good for a fat slob like Sikes.

Ross stood up, unloaded the syringe onto the carpet and placed the needle back in its case. He put the bag of heroin back into his coat pocket and said to Sikes, "We have a deal. Don't make me come back here. Next time you will be the one that overdoses."

CHAPTER 10

Normandy American Cemetery
Colleville-Sur-Mer, France
10:00 a.m., June 6, 1964

President John F. Kennedy, with his back to the English Channel, stood at a podium and looked out over a field of white crosses gleaming in the morning sun—some 9,000 of them stretched out before him, as far as the eye could see. He was there to commemorate the 20th anniversary of the D-Day invasion of France.

On the dais behind him sat both General Dwight D. Eisenhower and French President Charles De Gaulle. Eisenhower had been Supreme Commander of Allied forces and had been the architect of the invasion—the hero of World War II, he was treated like royalty in France. De Gaulle had led the French government in exile during the war, and had done much to buoy the French resistance that fought the Nazi occupation. Kennedy had a good relationship with both men.

After giving a speech, Kennedy strolled with Eisenhower and De

Gaulle among the headstones. The Secret Service and the French police lined the perimeter, ensuring that the three men had privacy. Eisenhower was particularly emotional, standing before so many young men who had given their lives for an invasion he had personally ordered.

"My son John graduated from West Point on D-Day," said Eisenhower, choking up. "While he was throwing his hat in the air, these boys were storming these beaches. Not for conquest, nor for financial gain. But for freedom."

De Gaulle put his hand on Eisenhower's shoulder and squeezed. "My country will forever be indebted to you and these men."

A moment of silence passed.

Kennedy then said, "Gentlemen, while I have you here I want to discuss another war we've all been involved in."

De Gaulle looked at Kennedy and said simply, "*Indochine.*"

"Yes, Indochina. Vietnam. The situation there is very bad now. You've both had experience there, and I could use your counsel."

De Gaulle dove right in. "*Monsieur le Président*, I sympathize greatly with your situation. It would, of course, be nice if Vietnam could be made into something worthwhile, but it is a hopeless place. I feel that I am obliged to say that I do not believe the United States can win, and that the more you put in militarily, the more the population—both in Vietnam and in America—will turn against it. You will not be able to force your position there by power. The only path is to negotiate, as we did in Geneva." The French negotiated a settlement signed in Geneva in 1954 that split Vietnam into North and South.

Eisenhower nodded his agreement. "As you know, we resisted sending troops into Vietnam during my presidency. That was not by accident. We learned from Korea—a far more hospitable place to fight than the jungles of Vietnam—that a land war in Asia was a very bad idea."

Kennedy thought for a moment. "My advisors tell me that if we approve a ceasefire, Ho Chi Minh would exploit it, and ultimately overtake the South. If that happens, I'm told, all the dominoes will fall."

"*Oui, oui.* I know of this domino theory. It's *une ordure.* Rubbish. Yes, South Vietnam will fall to the communists. But it will be a messy kind of communism. I know about Vietnam. It's a filthy place, full of corruption. This will not start a domino falling. It will take many, many years for Vietnam to become a working nation."

"What would you do if you were me?" asked Kennedy.

"*Monsieur le Président,* my advice would be to find an event that you can point to which proves to the American people that Vietnam is not worth saving. My experience in France is that people are willing to send their sons to die if it is a cause worth fighting for. You must show your people that Vietnam is not."

De Gaulle was nothing if not confident in his opinions. Looking at Eisenhower, Kennedy said, "General?"

"The risks are real either way, Mr. President," Eisenhower replied. "But as I look around this cemetery, it's clear that no American boys should die because you are concerned about how it will play politically. Of course, that's easy for me to say now, since I'm retired. But I'd think very carefully about getting into a shooting war in Vietnam. Once you get in it will be tough to get out."

Just then, White House Press Secretary Pierre Salinger walked up, signaling to Kennedy that it was time to go.

"Thank you both for your time today," Kennedy said. "*Merci beaucoup.*"

"You are most welcome," said De Gaulle. "I pray for you and your people and that you make the right decision. And we stand by ready to help should you decide to negotiate. *Au revoir,* Monsieur President."

A tanned Frank Sinatra stood at the floor-to-ceiling wall of glass that separated the den from the large pool in his sprawling mid-century modern home. Craggy brown mountains loomed in the distance, framed by palm trees that swayed slowly in the hot, dry desert wind. Two attractive bikini-clad women sunned themselves on chaise lounges and sipped iced tea from highball glasses. But Sinatra barely registered them: Sam Giancana was on the phone.

"You want me to call Bobby Kennedy? Christ, Sam, I've been excommunicated. Like a Jew at the Pope's birthday party."

"Yes, Francis. You've made that very clear."

"So?"

"So I don't give a fuck. You promised me that you had influence with the Kennedys and could get them to back off our business interests. Not only have they not backed off, they've doubled down. I can't fucking breathe."

"I did everything in my power to help you. I told Bobby to lay off you as a personal favor to me. It didn't work. I can't help the fact that Bobby is on a moral crusade against you."

"Yes, the attorney general is a 'do as I say, not as I do' kind of moralist. I could write a book on the ethical failings of that corrupt family. You know how many women Bobby Kennedy has screwed outside his marriage? It would make even you blush, Francis."

Sinatra laughed. "I doubt that."

"In any event, you never delivered on what you promised. You owe me. And I'm going to collect on that debt one way or another."

Sinatra was familiar enough with how the mob worked, and he

knew a veiled threat when he heard it.

"Ok, Sam. I give. What do you want me to tell Bobby this time?"

"I need you to listen very carefully, Francis. For the past five years the CIA has been assisting our partners in France, the Union Corse, in moving opium out of Laos to Marseille through Saigon. That opium is the lifeblood of our heroin business."

"No shit? Why would the CIA do that?"

"Because they want the Union Corse's cooperation in fighting communists in France, and because they are using the funds to try and influence the government in South Vietnam."

Sinatra couldn't care less about communists in France. "So?"

"So we have a problem. The CIA has lost control of Saigon's government and shipments aren't getting through. Even worse, they are threatening to shut down the Laotian operation altogether, meaning that our supply could permanently dry up. This can't happen, Francis."

Sinatra thought for a moment. This was serious. "What do you think Bobby Kennedy can do about this?"

"A lot, if he's suitably motivated."

Sinatra knew that this could mean many things, and none of them good. He wanted to be very careful not to get himself sucked into something that could come back to bite him. He stayed silent waiting for Giancana to continue.

"I want you to tell Kennedy that if they don't straighten out the opium problem in Saigon, he's going to lose the election in November."

"You can really do that?"

"You bet your ass I can. We control the unions across Illinois, New Jersey, New York and Michigan. If the election is close, I can ensure he loses. Period."

Sinatra sighed. "Bobby doesn't like to be threatened. He's already gunning for you. You sure you want to pour gas on that fire?"

"I have no choice. We're being strangled by the supply issue. I need to make sure that the heroin flows or I'm going to have my own problems.

Sinatra knew that Giancana, like any mob boss, lived in a perpetual fear of being overthrown. His security was in keeping his men fat and happy, and enforcing order with brutal efficiency.

"Do we understand each other?" asked Giancana.

"Yeah, we do."

"So you'll make the call, Francis?"

"I'll make the goddamn call, Sam."

The Robert F. Kennedy Residence
Hickory Hill, Virginia
2:20 p.m., June 9, 1964

The Kennedy family was enjoying a quiet Saturday afternoon when the kitchen phone rang. 10-year-old Robert, Jr. answered the phone in the kitchen on the third ring.

"Kennedy residence, may I help you?"

"Is your father at home?"

"Yes, sir. He is. May I tell him who's calling?"

"Tell him it's Frank Sinatra."

At that moment, Ethel Kennedy came into the kitchen. "Robert, who is on the phone?"

"Some guy who says he's Frank Sinatra."

Ethel's face darkened. "Let me have the phone, Robert. You go see if you can find your father."

Ethel waited until her son had left the room. Then she spoke into the phone. "This is Ethel Kennedy. What do you want with my husband, Frank?"

Ethel's hostile tone surprised Sinatra. She had originally reveled in her husband's friendliness with the Rat Pack and the celebrities they attracted. But that had changed when she began hearing rumors of the starlets hovering around her husband at the various parties he and Jack had attended. She had confronted Bobby at one point over the rumors and been left underwhelmed by his denials. She had been immensely relieved when Sinatra was exiled from the Kennedy family in 1961.

"Hi Ethel. I need to talk with your husband. It's business."

Ethel smirked. "Business, huh?"

"Really, Ethel. I swear it."

At that moment Bobby came into the kitchen and took the receiver from his wife. "Hello Frank."

"Thank you for taking my call."

"What can I do for you?" asked Bobby curtly.

"Actually, I'm calling to give you a message from a mutual acquaintance in Chicago." Sinatra didn't need to spell it out more than that—they both knew whom he was talking about.

Kennedy was silent for a moment. "What does that scumbag want?"

Sinatra proceeded to recite Giancana's story about the CIA's role in the opium trade in Laos and what it was doing to the mob's business. He then plainly outlined the threat about the election and what Giancana wanted in return. When he was done, he waited for Bobby to react.

After 30 seconds of silence, Sinatra said, "Bobby? Are you there?"

Bobby Kennedy cleared his throat. "Thank you for calling, Frank." He hung up the phone.

"Fuck!" Bobby Kennedy said, louder than he intended. His wife ran into the kitchen.

"What's the matter?"

"Oh, nothing, honey. It's election stuff. Nothing we can't handle."

Ethel was unconvinced, but didn't press it. She knew sometimes it was better to be in the dark.

Kennedy went into his home office. His mind was reeling. He had no knowledge about what the CIA had been doing in Laos and Vietnam. He knew the lengths the CIA would go to promote U.S. interests abroad, but even he was surprised that they were helping to bring the scourge of heroin into America's inner cities.

He grabbed his keys and headed for the car. It was time to see his brother.

Bobby Kennedy found his brother sitting in the solarium on the third floor of the White House. The president was wearing deck shoes with no socks, tan khaki pants and a tattered sweatshirt with "Harvard" emblazoned across the front. A stack of papers was scattered about in front of him.

"Where are the kids?" Bobby asked as he entered the room.

"They're with the nanny. I needed a few hours to myself today."

Bobby took a seat in the sofa across from his brother.

"What's up?" the president asked Bobby. "It sounded urgent."

"Guess who called me today?"

The president sighed. "I'm not really interested in playing twenty questions. Why don't you just tell me?"

"Frank Sinatra."

"Now Bobby, I know what you are thinking. And I haven't seen Sinatra since Jackie's funeral. And only for a few minutes."

Bobby was amused that his big brother, the president of the United States, was worried he'd be in trouble if it came out that he'd been cavorting with Sinatra. Bobby had done a good job of putting the fear of God—or at minimum J. Edgar Hoover—into his brother.

"I wish that's all it was, Jack. Frank called to give us a message from Sam Giancana."

The president's eyes narrowed. "Oh?"

"It seems that the Chicago mob is upset because their heroin business is being interrupted by opium supply problems in Laos and Saigon."

Bobby waited for his brother to react. When the president said nothing, he went on. "Apparently, the CIA has been facilitating this supply chain, ensuring safe passage of the opium to ships bound for Marseille. From there it ends up in Chicago, New York and other cities."

The president said nothing.

"You don't seem surprised by this, Jack."

The president shrugged his shoulders and again said nothing.

"Seriously, Jack?" Bobby knew his brother and understood the silence to mean that Kennedy knew much more than he was divulging. "Did you know about the CIA's opium operations?"

The president paused. "Yes," he said.

"Jesus Christ! You can't be fucking serious! How could you keep this kind of information from me?"

"It got started as a part of the covert operations the CIA has been conducting in Laos when Eisenhower was president. I just let it continue. I didn't think it was that extensive."

"Oh, it's pretty fucking extensive all right. As a matter of fact, it extends all the way to the Oval Office!"

The president looked confused. "I don't follow."

"That's why Frank called. Giancana is threatening to rally organized labor against us in the election. He's claiming he can take Illinois, New Jersey, West Virginia and Michigan from us."

"Can he really do that?"

"You bet your ass he can, Jack. We only beat Nixon last time because of the work that Giancana did with Daley in Chicago."

"What does he want?

"He wants you to get the CIA to restore the supply of opium so he can get his drugs on the street."

"How the fuck do I do that? Saigon is out of control and Khanh's gone rogue. We have no control over what's going on there now."

"Tell that to Giancana. He thinks you can fix this."

"I'll talk to Frank and tell him to explain it to Giancana."

"You want that conversation ending up on a Hoover wiretap? You think we're in trouble now? Hoover will blackmail us for the next twenty years. That's suicide."

"Jesus Christ."

Bobby got up and started pacing the room. "We have two choices here. Either we play ball and see what the CIA can do about increasing the opium supply in and out of Saigon, or we can tell Giancana to fuck off and take our chances that the election won't be that close."

Kennedy shook his head. "Nixon is running strong again. I think we'll be lucky to win by a couple of points. We may very well need Illinois and those other states."

"So can we give Giancana what he wants? At least until November?"

"I think so," said the president. "I'm sure the CIA can get some shipments through without Khanh knowing it, even if we have to use American planes to do it."

Bobby shook his head in disgust. "This is great. So we give that crook Giancana what he wants and at the same time we contribute to the supply of heroin that is poisoning our youth. What a deal!"

The president knew that politics made strange bedfellows. "This is temporary. After November we'll move to destroy the Laotian opium business. And we'll crush Sam Giancana as well. Ok?"

Bobby Kennedy looked crestfallen. He hated Sam Giancana with a passion. But he loved power more, and knew that if his brother weren't reelected, the fate that his brother dodged in Dallas would amount to little. His brother lived and Jackie died. Unless he beat Nixon, that supreme sacrifice would be for naught.

"Yeah, okay," he conceded.

CHAPTER 11

Café La Parnasse
110 Ham Nghi Boulevard
Cholon District, Saigon
11:30 a.m., June 20, 1964

Lucien Conein sat at an inside table in the crowded Café La Parnasse. The restaurant was just down the street from the Vinh Loi Bachelor Officer's Quarters (BOQ), where many Americans serving MACV were housed. The proximity of the café to the BOQ was a plus in Conein's mind: security was tight on the street, but the café's prices were so high that Americans rarely dined there.

Conein had gone through a very tough month. The instability that wracked Saigon since the Diem coup had continued unabated. General Khanh was far more interested in purging the ranks of those he deemed disloyal than he was in consolidating power and ensuring that the economic engine that was fueling the South Vietnamese regime continued. This included the opium trade which, when properly managed, was an unlimited source of cash. Unfortunately, Khanh was proving to be rash and unpredictable in a business where predictability was essential. The opium trade operated on trust and timing; when either was broken, shipments missed their connections and people invariably ended up dead.

All of which was creating problems for Rock Francisci, the Union Corse's point man in Saigon, who was under increasing pressure from Marseille to fix the opium supply problem. Francisci had personally gone to Laos, flying one of his planes into dirt airstrips carved out of the jungle, to meet with his suppliers, but it quickly became apparent that the supply of raw opium was not the issue. Shipments were leaving Laos intact. The problem was at the Ton Sun Nhut airport, where Francisci's Air Laos Commerciale had its hangar operation. Francisci learned that various South Vietnamese government officials were skimming off the top, removing raw product and diverting it to factories in the Mekong Delta, where the opium turned into heroin found its way into Saigon's black market. Francisci paid the CIA very well to ensure that this kind of thing wouldn't happen, and he was about to make it clear to Conein the stakes involved if it didn't get fixed.

Francisci pulled up a chair just as Conein's Vietnamese coffee arrived. He wore a white coat over blue linen pants and a straw hat in the shape of a fedora.

"*Bonjour*, Rock," said Conein, lighting a cigarette. "Smoke?"

"*Oui, Lucien. Merci.*" Francisci took out an ivory cigarette holder, placed the cigarette firmly in the tip, and accepted the light proffered by Conein. He took a long drag and exhaled, adding to the haze of smoke that filled the café's ceiling—like a chimney without a flue.

"So, Rock, I gathered from your message that this is not a social call."

"I got a message from Marseille last night. It was in the form of a brick thrown through the front window of my flat. Tied around it was a note. You know what it said?"

Conein had a good idea, but didn't want to say. He gave a slight shake of his head.

"It said, get your bricks in order or the next time this will be a bomb." Francisci stopped for effect, watching Conein's eyes. He didn't seem to be surprised.

"Rock, I know that we have a problem, and I know where the problem is."

Francisci laughed. "Tell me something I don't know. I went to Laos and spent a week getting bit by mosquitos. I know where the problem is and it's right here under our noses. The question is why is it happening and what are we going to do about it?"

Conein shrugged. "It's happening because Khanh is an amateur and doesn't have control of his people. He's not watching the store. In the meantime, his people are robbing us blind."

"*Non*. Not us. Me."

Lucien looked at Francisci and said, "You think that I don't have a lot riding on this? This is hurting me as much as it is hurting you. All my credibility is wrapped up in being able to influence Saigon and right now I'm not able to do that."

Francisci didn't say what he was thinking, which is that losing your career in the CIA is hardly the same as losing your life. Instead, he pressed Conein further: "Why, with all the influence of the CIA and all the money you pay General Khanh, do his people think they can get away with robbing us blind?"

"Because Khanh has signaled to his men that he doesn't give a shit about it. They are under the impression that the U.S. government is going to crack down on the opium trade and that in the end it's all going to go away. So Khanh's men are taking advantage of the opportunity while they still can."

Francisci took another long drag on his cigarette before replying. He was trying to make sense of what he was hearing, and it wasn't adding up.

"What in the world gives them the impression that the CIA is going to crack down on this source of funding and influence?"

"I didn't say the CIA. I said the U.S. government. There are many, many questions being asked by the U.S. military and MACV on the impact of the opium trade on our efforts to influence the ARVN to fight. While Harkins seems willing to turn a blind eye for now, there are others who are clearly not."

"Others? Such as?"

"Word is that the American Ambassador Lodge is soon going to be replaced by Maxwell Taylor."

"Taylor? Isn't he in the Army?"

"He is Chairman of our Joint Chiefs of Staff—the top officer in the military."

"You stupid Americans. You put a general in a political job?"

"Yes, well, Taylor has the trust of the president. But more importantly, if Taylor comes he likely brings a new commander with him, which means Harkins goes, too."

Francisci sipped his coffee. "And do you think that this new Ambassador Taylor will move against us?"

"It's very possible. Yes."

Francisci lit another cigarette. "I will have to report back to Marseille on this. The Guerini brothers will not be happy, and neither will our friends in Chicago."

"You do what you need to do, Rock. In the meantime we have a more immediate problem here in Saigon. There already have been enough mixed signals to give some of Khanh's men the idea that they can move against us, take our shipments, and not pay a price."

Francisci looked hard at Conein and said, "But they will pay a price. Right Lucien?"

Conein paused a minute before replying. He knew this was where Francisci would be looking for action. "Yes."

Francisci looked at Conein and waited. He was prepared to wait all day if necessary, but he was going to force Conein to make the first move. After about a minute, he lit another cigarette and ordered another coffee.

Conein finished his own coffee and put out his cigarette in the ashtray. He stood up and reached into his inside coat pocket, pulling out a list of names on lined yellow paper.

"Fortunately, my sources inside the Interior Ministry are still good. I think you will find what you are looking for here," Conein said as he laid the paper down in front of Francisci. "I trust you will use this information with discretion." With that, Conein walked out of the Café Lu Parnasse.

Francisci picked up the paper and unfolded it. On it were the names of two South Vietnamese army officers, two officials in the Ministry of Trade, and one senior government official in the Ministry of Transportation. He folded it back up and slid it into the left breast pocket of his coat. He was very pleased at how the meeting with Conein had gone.

The Special Warfare Center and School - Headquarters
Fort Bragg, North Carolina
2:45 p.m., June 23, 1964

Sergeant Major Richard Ambrose, sitting outside the office of Colonel Ed Summers, picked up the telephone on the third ring.

"Ambrose" he barked into the receiver.

A man's voice said, "The president is calling for Colonel Summers."

Funny guy, Ambrose thought. His nemesis on base, the sergeant major of the 82nd Airborne Division, was obviously pulling a fast one on him.

"I'm sorry, the colonel is currently indisposed. He's on the can reading the Sunday funnies. Can I take a message?"

There was silence on the other end of the phone. "Ah, excuse me. Is this the office of Colonel Edward Summers, Commandant of the Special Warfare Center?"

Ambrose's stomach sank as he immediately realized that this was no prank. "Yes, sir. It is. How may I help you?"

"The president of the United States is calling for Colonel Summers."

"Yes, sir. Please hold."

Ambrose jumped up and ran over to Summers' open door. "Sir, the president of the United States is on the horn."

Summers looked up, ready to laugh at what he thought was a joke. When he saw that Ambrose was dead serious, he said, "No shit?"

When Ambrose nodded, Summers picked up the receiver and punched the line.

"Colonel Summers speaking."

"Please hold for the president."

"Colonel, I understand you are close friends with Colonel Patrick O'Shea," Kennedy said without preliminaries.

"Ah, yes, sir."

"I also understand that you fought together in Korea."

"We did, sir."

"And that you saved O'Shea's life at the Chosin Reservoir."

Summers let out an embarrassed laugh. "That's O'Shea's version, Mr. President."

The president was quiet for a moment. "Colonel, here's why I'm calling. I need you to come to Washington, D.C. and pick up a sealed message. I want you to personally deliver it to O'Shea in Saigon."

Summers was now thoroughly confused. "Sir?"

"I know this is a strange request. I have a critical message to get to O'Shea, and I don't trust the telephone and can't use the diplomatic pouch. I can't tell you what is in the message you are carrying, but it's of the utmost importance that O'Shea gets this message, and it must come from someone he trusts completely."

"Yes, sir."

"I will have travel authorized for you. You will leave for Washington tonight. Tomorrow morning you will fly to Saigon, meet with O'Shea and then return to Bragg. As far as your staff and anyone else are concerned, your mother in Idaho has become ill and you must go home to tend to her. Is that understood?"

"Yes, Mr. President."

Office of the Under Secretary
The Department of State
Washington, D.C.
10:45 a.m., June 25, 1964

They buried it, thought Under Secretary of State George Ball.

He held in his hands a copy of a memo he had written in April to his boss, Secretary of State Dean Rusk, on Vietnam. It cogently outlined his argument against escalation. When he had written it he had assumed that the memo would ultimately reach the president, but it was clear from the notes in the margin that Rusk had reviewed it, then filed it away. He felt a twinge of betrayal from his boss, and now knew that Rusk was fully in the grips of McNamara and the Pentagon who wanted to bury any dissenting views that might be presented to the president. Ball would now have to figure out a new path to getting his ideas in front of Kennedy.

Vietnam had become something of an obsession to Ball—so convinced was he that the United States was heading down a perilous and foolish path. He had begun to voice these concerns to Rusk as early as mid-1963. The Secretary of State was always willing to listen to Ball and never tried to silence him. But neither was Rusk willing to let Ball's well-reasoned concerns shake his faith in McNamara or the military's ability to succeed in Vietnam. Ball came to see his boss as a true believer in the scientific certitude that McNamara brought to the Kennedy Administration. And true believers like to be around other true believers. So, as Ball watched, Rusk moved to gradually silence many of the Vietnam pessimists at State.

First came Paul Kattenberg, who had spent most of the 1950s in Saigon and knew more about Vietnam than almost anyone. Kattenberg was moved out after voicing his views that Vietnam was "nothing less than poison" and would lead to disaster for America. Then there was Bill Trueheart, who had spent most of 1962 and 1963 as a primary political officer at the Saigon Embassy, only to be moved out to a peripheral job at State focused on "Southeast Asia" but specifically excluding anything to do with Vietnam. Trueheart's crime was modifying some of the military's estimates of progress in Vietnam to be more realistic—for that, Harkins and McNamara wanted Trueheart's head. In the spring of 1964, they finally got it.

Ball's own opposition to American policy in Vietnam was largely pragmatic: he simply didn't see how the U.S. could win. He was convinced that the U.S. military was ill-suited for an air or land war on the Asian mainland. Ball had been a member of the Strategic Survey team that studied the effects of Allied bombing on Germany during World War II. The study had come to two conclusions: First, the massive and sustained bombing that had pummeled Germany day and night had, in the end, been largely ineffective in destroying the Third Reich's industrial capability; and second, that instead of punishing the Germans into capitulation, it had actually served to strengthen the morale of the German people to carry on the fight. This experience on the survey team lead Ball to immediately reject the military's view that the U.S. could bomb "North Vietnam back to the stone age," noting that Vietnam had surprisingly little industrial infrastructure to hit, and that massive bombing would likely steel the North Vietnamese people into fighting to the bitter end.

Perhaps most importantly, however, was that Ball didn't see this effort as worth a fight, no matter the odds of success. He saw the government of South Vietnam as hopelessly corrupt and without legitimacy, the product of an artificial agreement struck in Geneva in 1954 that divided Vietnam into two halves at an arbitrary line on the map. He had supported the coup against Diem because he saw the Diem-Nhu regime as an abomination. But it was clear now that what had taken Diem's place was just as corrupt and unworthy of American support. Ball believed that principles still mattered in how the United States should conduct its foreign policy, and he had convinced himself that President Kennedy, when faced with all the facts, would choose to not throw good money after bad.

So, Ball was marshaling his forces to make an end run around McNamara and the Pentagon to get to Kennedy to advocate for his position directly, and to convince him to get out while he still could.

The American Bar
Hotel Caravelle, Saigon
5:20 p.m., June 26, 1964

The bar was packed tight with a mix of American reporters and Vietnamese women in flowery dresses and high heels. Some were the "girlfriends" of journalists assigned to cover Saigon, and others were high-class escorts that quietly served the Caravelle's clientele without attracting undue attention.

Patrick O'Shea sat on a stool at the far end of the bar, nursing a scotch on the rocks while reading the *International Herald Tribune*. For the past two weeks he had been in and around Saigon meeting with various Embassy and MACV personnel, including members of the Special Forces command. O'Shea had also made several forays into the bush, including a rather harrowing trip down the Mekong River into the southern delta area. While he hadn't been under fire, he did have an unpleasant experience with a poisonous puff-faced snake that had nearly bitten him when he was washing his socks in the river. He'd decided from that point on he would wear his socks dirty, thank you very much.

He felt the presence of someone behind him, looking over his shoulder, and figured it to be one of the Vietnamese women looking for a "date." When he turned to say something, he found himself looking into the eyes of Ed Summers.

If O'Shea was surprised to see Summers he didn't show it. "You're cute but not really my type."

"Really? And I got my hair cut just for you."

O'Shea laughed since Summers had worn the same crew cut for the past 20 years.

"What brings you to beautiful Saigon?" O'Shea asked, knowing full well why he was there.

Summers smiled, looking into O'Shea's eyes. He knew he didn't have to answer. "Let's go to your room. And don't get frisky. I'm armed and dangerous."

*   *   *

O'Shea poured bourbon into two water glasses and handed one to Summers, who sat in an armchair by the open window in O'Shea's simple, yet elegant room. The window was open, and a warm breeze drifted in; the Saigon summer was just heating up, and both men were in shirtsleeves.

"Your boss says hello," Summers offered.

"I take it you went to Washington before coming here?"

"I did. Kennedy had me come to the residence, and asked me to wear civvies. I had never been to that part of the White House before."

"What did he say?"

"It was pretty surreal. He invited me in and handed me an envelope," Summers said. He reached over to his coat that was draped over the back of his chair, and took out a white envelope. Handing it to O'Shea, he said, "He told me that it was a personal note to you, and that I was to keep this on my person at all times. Must be pretty damn important."

O'Shea nodded slightly.

"Do you know what's in it?" Summers asked.

"I have an idea. It's instructions for the delivery of a letter."

"A letter to who?"

"Honestly, I don't know."

Summers paused for a moment when it became clear that O'Shea really didn't know. "Jesus, Patrick, sounds pretty cloak and dagger. Hard to understand why he couldn't have just put it in a diplomatic pouch."

"I guess Kennedy feels like he can't trust anyone on this. He's very worried about getting railroaded by the Pentagon in Vietnam. So whatever I'm delivering, he didn't want anyone at MACV or the Embassy to know about it."

Summers' curiosity was killing him. "Aren't you tempted to open it?"

O'Shea looked at his oldest, closest friend and said, "Of course. But…"

"Ah, crap. I know you can't open the damn thing. I'm just dying here. Maybe it's to the hot wife of an Embassy staffer."

They both laughed. Finally, O'Shea said, "When do you go back?"

"Tomorrow morning," Summers said. He looked at his watch. "How about dinner? I'm starved."

* * *

Later that evening, after Summers retired to his own room at the Caravelle, O'Shea sat on the edge of his bed, holding the letter bearing his instructions. It was an expensive envelope, made of heavy linen paper, worthy of something personally sent by the president of the United States.

O'Shea carefully opened the envelope and pulled out a single sheet of paper. On it was a typed note:

John P Kennedy

O'Shea pulled a map of Vietnam out of his valise and unfolded it on
the bed. He quickly found the coordinates that Kennedy provided,
which corresponded to a point on the map just inside the Laotian
border. Tracing his finger along the map into Vietnam, he put his finger
on Nam Dong, where he knew the U.S. 7th Special Forces Group was
located. He figured from there he would be able to get into Laos to
make the connection with this man named Nguyen Tai.

CHAPTER 12

7th Special Forces Base at Nam Dong
Republic of South Vietnam
7:25 a.m., July 2, 1964

Sitting inside the Command Post—CP—of Special Forces team A-726, Communications Sgt. Keith Daniels listened to chatter over the airwaves. Most days, when not on patrol, he sat with one ear listening to the din of transmissions from various units in the field, and one ear tuned to his radiophone where direct instructions from headquarters would come in. Across from him sat base commander, Captain Roger Donlon. Tall, lean with a square jaw and crew cut, Donlon at that moment fingered a well-worn copy of Louis Lamour's *Dark Canyon*, trying to find the last page he had read before finally falling asleep at 3 a.m. Donlon wasn't previously a fan of westerns, but in the bush you read whatever was handy, and Donlon had taken a liking to Lamour's classic novels where the good guys and the bad guys were easy to tell apart—it certainly wasn't that way in Vietnam.

Donlon had been a Green Beret only a short time, and he'd had an unusual career even by the standards of the Special Forces, where many men came in with backgrounds that could charitably be called "unconventional." He had joined the Air Force in 1953 at the end of the Korean War and eventually decided he wanted to make the Army a career. He applied and was admitted to West Point in 1955, only to leave after a year. It turned out that the structure of the U.S. Military Academy was just too strict for Donlon, who preferred a more dynamic and free-flowing environment—traits that would come to make him an outstanding Special Forces officer. He rejoined the Army in 1958, went to Officer Candidate School and finally found his true calling in the Green Berets.

Staff Sergeant Rick Evers poked his head in the CP. "Choppers are in-bound."

Donlon put his book down carefully next to his rack and stood. He grabbed his beret, put it expertly on his head at precisely the right angle, picked up his M16 and exited the CP, making a hard right turn toward the clearing where the choppers set down. ARVN and Nung forces were stationed at regular intervals all along the perimeter and were instructed to be ready to lay down suppressing fire anytime a chopper came in, knowing that the slow moving birds were fat targets for the Viet Cong, especially during take off and landing. As Donlon caught up to Sgt. Evers, he said, "This should be the colonel who is visiting us for the next few days."

"Sir, that's all we need. More REMF brass hanging around looking for ways to ding us," Evers said. MACV was notorious for ordering senior officers out from behind their desks in Saigon to "observe" field operations, ostensibly to provide direct feedback to command on progress being made. In reality it almost invariably turned into an opportunity for some major or colonel to show up for a few hours, take a few pictures and write a report about how things could be improved. Since shit always rolled downhill in the army, these reports tended to become the basis for a bunch of unnecessary, often dangerous "improvements" to how they conducted their work. Donlon's team had been no exception, and visiting brass were uniformly referred to as "REMF"—Rear Echelon Mother Fuckers.

They reached the clearing just as a pair of Bell H-1 Hueys came into view. Just as the skids of the helicopter touched the grass, out jumped a lone passenger. He wore green fatigues and jump boots, and had a bag slung over his shoulder. In his right hand he held an M16 rifle, and in his left he held his jungle hat. Three long strides later Patrick O'Shea was shaking hands with Captain Roger Donlon.

* * *

"So where do you call home, Captain?"

Donlon and O'Shea sat in the CP eating a lunch of spaghetti and canned peaches. "I'm from New York originally, sir. Ended up going to Officer Candidate School after a detour through West Point." Donlon smiled, not offering more details.

O'Shea thought he understood what Donlon was saying. He knew that officers that thrived in Special Forces were independent, unconventional and often a poor fit for the spit and polish of the Military Academy.

"So you decided to become a snake eater instead, huh?" Green Berets were often derisively called "snake eaters" by the regular army, given their unique training regimen and their propensity to go native in the bush, including eating snakes, when necessary, to survive.

Donlon laughed. "It just fits me, I guess."

"What is it that you like so much about it? I'm genuinely curious."

"I love the challenge of it. I love the idea of training a country to defend itself. Obviously, we can't solve every problem ourselves, no matter how much hardware we throw at it. Especially here, where it's hard to tell friend from foe. No way any white man can tell a good gook from a bad gook. It's just not possible."

O'Shea nodded. "Which leaves us with our ARVN friends. And the Nung."

"Exactly."

"Since you arrived in May, can you tell me about your experience? How it's going with the ARVN, and what you see as the biggest problems we face?"

"Sir, may I speak frankly?"

O'Shea nodded. "Of course you can, Captain."

"I'm happy to give you my full and unvarnished opinion. But we have all heard the tales of officers who have dared to speak the truth to the powers that be in the Pentagon and who ended up cashiered. I love my job, Colonel. It took me a long time get this far. And I don't want to end up in charge of latrines in Alaska."

O'Shea smiled broadly. "No, I wouldn't guess that latrine duty would suit you. Look, I'm not here on behalf of MACV or the Pentagon. I'm actually here to get the straight scoop on the war effort, unfiltered and raw. I'm not here to report to Harkins or McNamara or anyone else in the chain of command." O'Shea didn't mention the letter or the mission from the president. He wanted to feel Donlon out first.

Donlon liked this colonel and really wanted to believe him. "So you aren't just another REMF? My team here thinks you're here to screw with us."

O'Shea laughed. "I've never thought of myself as a rear echelon guy, but I will admit that there are more than a few who probably think I'm a motherfucker."

Donlon smiled. "So who do you work for? The CIA?"

O'Shea had until that moment, been exceedingly careful about divulging who his patron was. But he knew at that moment that he had one chance of gaining Donlon's trust, and to do so, he'd have to be totally honest with him. He saw a lot of himself in Donlon, and his gut was telling him to take the young captain into his confidence.

"I work for the president of the United States," O'Shea said simply.

Yeah, right.

Donlon waited a moment for O'Shea to give up the joke, but the expression on his face was deadly serious.

"You work for President Kennedy?"

"I do."

"You mean, you work in the White House for someone on his staff?"

"No. I actually work directly for the president. Personally."

With that, O'Shea reached into the side pocket of this jungle fatigues and pulled out his wallet. He handed Donlon the laminated card that President Kennedy had given him in the Oval Office. It was the first time that he had actually shown it to anyone.

Donlon looked at the card closely, shook his head, and handed it back to O'Shea. "So, if I share my views with you they will actually get to the president?"

"Just the views worth sharing," O'Shea said, cracking a smile.

Donlon felt satisfied that this colonel, who had shown up at his base with little notice, was not going to ruin his career if he heard something that he didn't like. In any event, if this was a chance for Donlon to help educate the president on what was happening out here in the bush, he was going to take it. His life—and the lives of his men—might depend on it someday.

* * *

Later that night, O'Shea "knocked" on the canvas of Donlon's tent, who was sitting on his cot reading a letter from his wife.

"There's something I need to discuss with you in private, Captain. Can we take a walk?"

"Yes, sir."

Donlon and O'Shea walked to a clearing in the middle of the camp. In a low voice he said, "I didn't tell you the full story of my visit earlier."

"Sir?"

"I am here to carry out a mission on behalf of the president—to deliver a letter to a representative of the Vietnamese government. I've been given coordinates to a location near here." O'Shea pulled out a three-by-five card and handed it to Donlon. On it were the map coordinates

Kennedy had given him.

Donlon could just make out the numbers in the moon's ambient light. Without a map, they meant little to him. "And where is this exactly?"

"It's just inside the Laotian border at the site of an ancient Buddhist temple."

Donlon looked at O'Shea with wide eyes. "Inside Laos?"

O'Shea nodded. "I'm supposed to meet a man named Nguyen Tai there tomorrow night. He will be at the meeting site for only two hours, and it's essential that I be there to meet him. I need your help in getting there."

Donlon's mind was racing. This was not good. "Sir, I've been specifically ordered not to go into Laos. If we do cross the border and get into hot water, it will be my ass in a sling. The only way I'll do it is to run it up to Special Forces HQ and get permission."

O'Shea blanched. "Negative, Captain" he said, with real ice in his voice. "This mission is top secret and I'm taking a risk even telling you about it. I understand your position and I'm prepared to go it alone if I have to. But under no circumstances are you to report what we are discussing to your superiors. Is that clear?"

Donlon shook his head, momentarily forgetting he was talking to a superior. No way was he going to let this colonel wander into Laos alone. "Not a goddamn chance."

O'Shea was startled by Donlon's response. He stared through the dark trying to take his measure. After their earlier meeting, O'Shea had felt confident that Donlon would cooperate or, at the very least, not prevent him from going. Now he wasn't so sure. Would Donlon stand in the way of him delivering the letter?

And then, as if reading O'Shea's mind, Donlon said, "Sir, here's what we'll do. I'll have a small SF team escort you to the border, and I'll assign three of my best Nung fighters to go with you into Laos. They can provide you some security, and they know that area pretty well, which will lessen the chance that you'll end up wandering in the jungle for the next year."

O'Shea smiled. He hadn't misjudged Captain Donlon after all.

CHAPTER 13

Near the Vietnam Border
Kingdom of Laos
4:30 p.m., July 4, 1964

Nguyen Tai sat with his back against a tree at the edge of a clearing. He could just make out the jagged outlines of the ancient Buddhist temple, now little more than a mound of rocks. Tai and four North Vietnamese agents of the Public Security Ministry had been flown into Laos the previous day, and then hiked more than four hours to get to the rendezvous point. Tai's shirt was stained in sweat and his boots were caked in thick red clay. He wore a camel colored pit helmet and he cradled an AK-47 in his lap.

Tai was a veteran of "the Revolution," having joined the Vietnamese independence movement in 1944 as a teenager. He made a name for himself as a resistance leader, first against the Japanese and later the French—operating in the shadows, he was ruthlessly effective. By the time the French left Vietnam in 1954, Tai had become a leader in North

Vietnam's internal security directorate. Now, ten years later, he was fighting the Americans and their puppet regime in the South. It mattered little to him who the enemy was; he would unify his nation or he would die trying. He doubted the Americans understood the commitment he and millions of others like him made to their independence, and the lengths they would go to ensure that all of Vietnam was united and free. The Americans would find out at their peril.

Tai had been told little about why he was there. He knew that he was to meet an American to pick up a letter, and he knew that the letter was to be delivered personally to Ho Chi Minh. That was quite an honor, and one he had been thrilled to receive. But he hadn't liked anything else about this mission, which was to be done with no communication or coordination with the American. Meeting the enemy in the jungle at dusk was a recipe for disaster—the jungle was an eerie place that made men nervous. And nervous men tended to have itchy trigger fingers.

The four Public Security Ministry agents were fanned out around the perimeter of the temple. One climbed a tree and set up a WWII-era sniper rifle. The others were in positions where their fields of fire would overlap, making it virtually impossible for the American to approach their position without being in the crosshairs. Tai wasn't expecting trouble, but neither was he willing to take any chances.

At precisely 5:15 p.m. the agent in the tree made a clicking sound with his tongue, the alert they had set up to signal that movement had been detected. Tai stood up quietly and peered round the tree, straining to see through the gloom. He could just make out the outline of five men spread out over about 20 yards, moving slowly and methodically through the bush. One of the shapes appeared to be significantly larger than the others—that would be the American, Tai guessed. While Tai hadn't expected the American to come alone, for some reason the presence of the others made him angry. He promptly put his AK-47 to his shoulder and drew a bead on one of the figures, now no more than 50 yards away.

As he did so, Patrick O'Shea stopped in his tracks, a shudder of fear suddenly washing over him like a wave. It was a sixth sense that one only had if they'd been in combat before; he knew that someone at that moment was aiming a gun at him. He dropped down prone on the wet jungle floor and flipped off the safety of his M16 and tried to see what was ahead of him.

There had been no instructions on how to make the exchange of the letter with Tai. So far, O'Shea had to play the whole thing by ear. Just then one of the Nung fighters accompanying O'Shea took the matter into his own hands and started yelling in Vietnamese. "We and the American are here to deliver the package. We are here to deliver the package! Do you hear me?"

O'Shea waited for a response. When there was none, O'Shea yelled in English. "I am an American officer here to peacefully deliver a letter!"

Moments passed with no response. As O'Shea contemplated his next move, shots rang out from Tai's AK, shredding the foliage around the Nung closest to O'Shea. Tai purposely missed the man, but the noise from the gun filled the tight space around them with devastating effect. O'Shea instinctively yelled out to his men, "Hold fire, hold fire!" not wanting the Nung to return fire until it was clear that they were going to have to fight their way out.

As the deafening noise finally subsided, Tai yelled out, first in Vietnamese and then in English, "Put down your weapons and stand up. You will not be hurt."

The Nung nearest O'Shea looked for a signal. After a few seconds, O'Shea decided that his best bet was to comply. Nodding to the Nung, he stood up, dropping his rifle to the ground. "We are complying!" O'Shea yelled in English. "Don't shoot!" One-by-one the Nung followed suit, until all five men were standing with their arms out to their sides. Though O'Shea knew Vietnamese, he preferred to keep that fact a secret. He wanted to be able to eavesdrop on Tai's conversation with his men.

Now in English Tai said, "I have a sniper in the trees and will fire if you make a move for your weapons. Stay where you are."

At that moment, Tai and the three agents on the ground rose up from their spots and approached O'Shea and his men, who were now soaked in sweat and caked in mud from the jungle floor.

Tai walked directly up to O'Shea and examined him. O'Shea wore a plain camouflage uniform without obvious rank or unit. In English, Tai asked, "You are an American army officer?"

O'Shea swallowed hard, not knowing whether saying yes would help or hurt his chances of getting out of this alive. He decided to tell the truth. "Yes. I am a colonel in the United States Army."

Tai looked momentarily surprised. In the North Vietnamese hierarchy, a colonel was a high rank that tended to sit behind a desk. He looked at O'Shea and decided that this letter must be pretty damn important for a colonel to personally make the delivery.

"And who are you?" asked O'Shea.

"I am Nguyen Tai of the Public Security Ministry."

O'Shea nodded. "I have a letter for you."

It was now almost dark, and O'Shea moved to turn on the flashlight he'd been carrying. As he did, Tai raised his AK-47 and pointed it at O'Shea's chest. "Easy there, I'm just getting my flashlight to show you the letter," said O'Shea. Tai nodded but didn't lower the muzzle.

O'Shea flicked on the flashlight and illuminated himself and Tai. He could see now that Tai was of a wiry build with very dark, dead eyes. Not taking any chances, O'Shea said, "Ok, I'm going to reach into my pack and take out the letter now. It's wrapped in a plastic bag."

After Tai nodded his assent, O'Shea slowly pulled out the white envelope. He shone the light on it so Tai could clearly see what it was, turning it over in his hands. O'Shea then said, "This letter is of great importance to the president of the United States. Before I hand it over, do I have your assurance it will be delivered to its intended recipient?"

"Tai laughed, "Colonel, you are in no position to make demands of me. But I can assure you after all this trouble, this letter will reach its destination."

Satisfied, O'Shea handed over the letter.

Tai promptly put the envelope inside his tunic. He looked at O'Shea a final time, smiled slightly and again raised the barrel of his AK. Sweat dripped down O'Shea's face, and he stared into Tai's eyes. O'Shea's gun was still on the ground at his feet, and there'd be no chance he'd be able to get to it. O'Shea was now praying that Tai was not a cold-blooded killer.

Suddenly Tai raised a finger, signaling to his men to back away. Within seconds Nguyen Tai had disappeared into the black night and was gone.

O'Shea stared after him for a few moments. He was suddenly very tired and incredibly thirsty.

"Let's get the hell out of here."

7th Special Forces Base at Nam Dong
Republic of South Vietnam
4:25 a.m., July 5, 1964

After an hour of tossing and turning, Patrick finally gave up trying to sleep. His encounter with Nguyen Tai had left him physically and mentally exhausted. It was a feeling he hadn't had since Korea, and it quickly took over his thoughts.

It was an unbearable cold that burned like fire on O'Shea's toes and fingers. He was 22 years old and in charge of a platoon of men who were hungry, tired and scared. It was hard to see how they would survive. The Chinese had poured over the North Korean border in endless suicidal waves. The first wave would get mowed down and then another wave would follow.

They would surely run out of ammo before killing them all.

After two days of fighting, O'Shea and his platoon hunkered in a ditch east of the Chosin Reservoir awaiting orders to retreat—it was impossible to do anything else. Some of his men were wounded while others were shaking so badly—from cold and from fear—that they couldn't shoot their weapons.

He hated what had transpired, the careless way that his superiors used his men as fodder, ignoring the obvious signs that the Chinese were coming, unwilling to listen to what was really happening on the ground, and unwilling to hear the truth.

O'Shea finally dozed off, and after several hours of fitful sleep he awoke with a start to the sound of automatic gunfire. As his head cleared he realized he was no longer dreaming, he rolled out of his cot, grabbed his weapon and went out to see what was happening.

He quickly found Roger Donlon, weapon in hand, moving around the back of his tent. He then heard another short burst of fire, and identified it as coming from the mess tent. Within seconds he heard more shooting, an M16 on full auto and the staccato boom of a .45 semi-automatic. When the shooting stopped he could hear the shouts of one of Donlon's men yelling, "Clear!" accompanied by lots of yelling in Vietnamese.

When Donlon and O'Shea arrived at the mess tent they found the dead body of one of the ARVN soldiers under his command. He'd been shot multiple times in the chest and at least once in the head, a growing pool of blood now flowing onto the earth beneath him.

"What the hell happened?" Donlon asked.

Lt. Van Tho, one of the ARVN officers, pointed at the body and said, "He turned his rifle on Captain Tran. Shot him through the head and then sprayed a few of the tents. Two of my men are wounded. Captain Tran is dead."

"Goddamn it!" Donlon said. "Is he VC?"

Lt. Van Tho spent several minutes speaking to two of his platoon sergeants. They went back and forth trying to agree on what had happened. Finally Van Tho said, "We believe he is a VC infiltrator. He joined the unit just two months ago and was always asking many questions about our plans. Last week one of my sergeants found him talking to a local villager in a whispered voice, and it appeared like he was giving the villager information. When my sergeant approached he immediately struck the villager and claimed he was trying to bribe him. It seemed suspicious at the time. Now we know why."

Donlon nodded. This was not good. Turning to Sgt. Evers he said, "Have Sgt. Jones get on the horn and get a medevac chopper up here for the wounded, and ask the Doc to do what he can for them." The Doc was the Team medic, Sgt. Alonzo Towers.

"Yes, sir."

"Let's get this body into a bag and get the ground cleaned up."

When they returned to the CP, Donlon reported the incident to headquarters. When that was done, he found Colonel O'Shea back at his tent.

"Has that kind of thing happened before?" O'Shea asked.

"Not here, sir. But I've heard it happening with other A-teams. It's damn hard to tell the good guys from the bad. I wonder how many more there are."

7th Special Forces Base, Nam Dong
Republic of South Vietnam
11:20 p.m., July 5, 1964

Donlon sat on his cot, and in the glow of his lamp, wrote a letter to his wife Anne. All that day he'd had this feeling in his gut that something was not quite right. He told his team sergeant to get everyone buttoned up tight. He felt sure they were going to get attacked that night. His letter to his wife was unusually raw, as if Donlon sensed that it might be his last chance to tell her he loved her. He hoped that if he got killed someone would find the letter and make sure it reached her, so he placed it in an envelope and wrote her name on the front in big block letters and laid it on his pillow. He knew he wouldn't be sleeping tonight.

He was particularly concerned about the presence of O'Shea in the camp, who was due to leave early the next morning. He didn't want a dead colonel—particularly one working for the president—on his record or his conscience. But that was out of his control now. If they were hit, O'Shea would have to be a grunt again and fight it out like the rest of them. Earlier he had stopped by O'Shea's tent and told him to expect trouble, to be ready to move and to sleep with his boots on. Donlon knew that O'Shea was a soldier, a combat veteran, who would keep his head when shit hit the fan. He had nonetheless assigned two of his best Nung fighters to positions just outside O'Shea's tent, and had instructed them to go wherever O'Shea went. It wasn't much, but at least Donlon had done what he could to ensure O'Shea would survive the night.

Just before 1 a.m., as Donlon entered the mess tent to check the guard roster, he heard the shrill whistle of an incoming mortar round. Before he could react, the round exploded. The concussion blew Donlon back out the tent door and flat onto his back. For a few moments he lay there, his eyes open to the night sky, seeing nothing but tracers crisscrossing above him. As his head began to clear, he could hear a cacophony of explosions and screams. All hell was breaking loose around him as he struggled to get back on his feet. As he looked around him he could see the CP on fire and hear machine guns opening up around the perimeter.

Donlon, finally on his feet, stumbled forward and ran headlong into his lead sergeant, Gabriel "Pop" Alamo. Alamo was called "Pop" because he had served in World War II with the 82nd Airborne and in Korea. At 45 years of age, he was the oldest member of the A-team.

Alamo looked at Donlon and yelled over the din of gunfire, "The CP's on fire—I'll clear out the weapons and make sure we have enough to fight this out!"

Donlon nodded and quickly moved toward the other supply tent that was now also burning. Battling the flames and heat, he managed to pull out a number of M16s, along with a 57mm recoilless rifle, while salvaging several crates of ammo. As he did, Sgt. Evers ran by carrying an M16, and stooped to grab a sling with 10 fully loaded magazines. He looked at Donlon and their eyes met—no words were required. They were under attack and it was time to get moving. Evers gave Donlon a slight nod and disappeared into the darkness.

When he got to the CP tent, Alamo found his radio operator attempting to stomp out the fire that had ignited the walls of the tent. His left leg and arm had been peppered by hot shrapnel and half his uniform was shredded.

"Pull your gear out of the tent and call HQ," Alamo yelled. "Tell them we're under attack and we need reinforcement."

"Roger that. Anything else?"

"Yeah, tell them to hurry the fuck up!" Alamo grabbed whatever weapons he could find, and promptly ran back toward where he had last seen Donlon.

Meanwhile, O'Shea, who had been in a dead sleep when the first mortar came in, rolled out of his rack and managed to quickly grab his M16 before being almost smothered by his Nung chaperones, who pushed him toward the bunker area adjacent to the mess tent. The bunker had a reinforced roof with sand bags at the entrance, and Donlon had told the Nung's to take O'Shea there in the event of an attack. When O'Shea realized where the Nung's were taking him, he stopped in his tracks.

"I'm not going to sit in this goddamn bunker while the base is under attack," he told them. "Take me to where I can help provide perimeter defense."

The Nungs didn't argue, quickly moving off toward one of the south-facing perimeter positions.

Donlon was attempting to get over to the forward mortar pit when he saw an enemy sapper team trying to blow a hole in the front gate. Using his M16, Donlon quickly killed the three sappers, leaving their bodies piled in a heap at the mouth of the gate. Then, reaching the 60mm mortar, Donlon jumped in the pit and was trying to set-up the mortar for firing when an incoming round came down nearly on top of him. The concussion from the blast blew him up and out of the pit. Again lying on his back in a daze, Donlon heard the youngest member of his A-Team, Sgt. John Houston, yelling into the night.

"Houston!" yelled Donlon.

Through the explosions he could just make out Houston's response. "They're coming though the line over by the ammo bunker!"

Donlon started running on wobbly legs towards Houston's voice and in the general direction of the ammo bunker.

Then another mortar round came in.

This round's aim was true, killing Sgt. Houston in his tracks and blowing Donlon back onto his back. Shrapnel from the mortar had ripped into Donlon's arms and stomach, and he began to bleed from his wounds. Crawling around in the dirt and momentarily blinded by the dust and smoke, he came upon Houston's lifeless body, his young face impossibly serene in a moment of shocking violence. It was an image that would stay with Donlon for the rest of his life, for Houston had confided in him just the day before that his young wife was pregnant with their first child. Now this child would forever be without a father.

Closing Houston's eyes with his hand, Donlon managed to crawl a few yards to one of the abandoned mortar pits. Catching his breath, he peered over the rim of the pit and could see enemy soldiers through the haze, just twenty yards away.

By this time at the other side of the camp, O'Shea had made it to a perimeter position and had jumped into a fighting hole, with the Nung fighters right behind him. As soon as they jumped in, one of the soldiers already in the hole turned his rifle on O'Shea. Before O'Shea could react, he pulled the trigger.

Fortunately for O'Shea, the jam-prone M16 failed to fire. The Nung nearest O'Shea immediately opened up on the soldier, killing him instantly. When O'Shea moved closer he could see that the solider had shed his uniform and was wearing the black pajama-like uniform of the enemy. Beside him was another ARVN soldier slumped against the mud, with lifeless eyes staring straight ahead, his throat slit. O'Shea guessed that the man who tried to kill him was another infiltrator. After his heart stopped pounding and he could talk, O'Shea said to the Nungs, "Keep your eyes open for infiltrators—there will probably be more." O'Shea wondered just how many traitors were in their midst.

Across the camp, Alamo had made it back to the 60mm mortar from which Donlon had been blown. The mortar was still operational, and Alamo worked to set it up for firing. As he did he could see more sappers attempting to breach the main gate of the base, which he feared would allow the enemy to pour into the camp. Scrambling out of the pit, Alamo grabbed the 57mm recoilless rifle and several grenades, and ran toward the main gate in a hail of gunfire. Crouching low, he began to hit the enemy with 57mm shells, killing a half dozen more and adding to a growing pile of bodies at the gate entrance. Gradually he was able to push the enemy back, forcing them to fall back into the jungle.

While Alamo had bought some time, he knew that they had to get their mortar into action if they were going to have any chance of deflecting the attack. Moving back to the pit, he began to direct mortar fire outside of the perimeter, alternating with shots from the rifle. By this time, Donlon had made his way back toward Alamo's position, and was about to join him when he saw a grenade fly through the air, bounce once and roll into Alamo's pit.

"Grenade!" screamed Donlon.

The grenade exploded in a plume of smoke and dirt. Donlon crawled over to the lip of the hole and could see that "Pop" Alamo, a veteran of three wars and the heart and soul of A-Team 726, was dead.

Acting instinctively, Donlon pulled Alamo's broken body out of the pit and dragged him toward the center of the camp where he knew Doc Towers was working on the wounded. Donlon knew it was too late, but he wasn't going to leave Alamo alone in that pit where the enemy might mutilate his body. Seeing Donlon dragging a body toward him, Towers ran over.

"What have you got?" asked Towers.

"It's Pop. He's dead," Donlon said so quietly that Towers could barely make it out. He refused to put Alamo down.

"It's ok, Captain. I'll take care of him." Slowly, Donlon lowered Pop back onto the ground. He took a step back and realized he had to keep moving. There'd be a time for mourning, but that time was not now.

For the next several hours, Donlon was a blur of action, dragging himself from position to position, carrying ammo and supplies where needed and coordinating the defense of the camp. Donlon had not seen O'Shea for several hours, and had no idea if he was dead or alive. When Donlon finally ran into him after stumbling into O'Shea's fighting position, he was not surprised to see O'Shea firing his M16 with deliberate care, saving his ammo and being sure to hit whatever he was firing at. O'Shea, however was shocked to see Donlon's condition; barefoot and bloody, wearing a tattered uniform, O'Shea couldn't believe that Donlon was still alive. He looked at the man and saw the true embodiment of a warrior – resolute in the face of the enemy, worried about his men, and determined to ensure that his team had what it needed to get the job done.

"Any word on reinforcements?" O'Shea asked Donlon.

"No." Donlon looked at his watch. It was almost 4:30 am. "We called almost four hours ago."

O'Shea didn't say what he was thinking. Could this be Harkins' way of teaching him a lesson? Harkins had made it pretty clear that he was on his own. Would he really do such a despicable thing?

Probably, thought O'Shea.

"Just keep doing what you're doing," Donlon said, slipping out of O'Shea's hole and heading toward the East perimeter.

By daybreak, Donlon had sustained three more wounds from shrapnel, and his body was riddled with holes. That he survived was a miracle—none of the shrapnel had hit vital organs, and though he lost a lot of blood during the night, his adrenaline had kept him moving. In the process, he had saved the lives of several Nung fighters when finding them wounded, he used one of his socks as a tourniquet and tore what was left of his uniform blouse into bandages. He encouraged them to continue to fight, leaving them propped against a berm with their weapons in their hands.

As the sun rose the morning of July 6, an eerie quiet settled over the camp, broken only by the moans of the wounded and the dying. By this time it was clear that the VC had broken off the attack, and O'Shea found Donlon lying prone against the edge of a mortar pit. He was unable to walk, covered with dirt and blood. Doc Towers was hunched over him trying to bandage his left arm while Donlon smoked a cigarette. Donlon already knew that Gabriel "Pop" Alamo and John Houston were dead, but all of Donlon's other A-Team members had survived the night. 55 ARVN and Nung soldiers were also dead, at least 10 killed by infiltrators, their throats slit or their necks broken just as the battle had begun.

"Donlon, it is sure good to see you," said O'Shea, his smile appearing even whiter due to the mud and dirt caked on his face.

"Well, at least I won't get cashiered for losing my VIP," Donlon replied. "Good thing you remembered how to shoot, Colonel."

O'Shea laughed. "It appears that I can still shoot straight. But all this diving into foxholes is a bit much. I'm getting too old for this crap."

"Don't make me laugh. It hurts too much."

Just then, the distinctive sound of incoming helicopters could be heard. Help had finally arrived.

About damn time, thought O'Shea.

CHAPTER 14

Ly Tru Trong Boulevard
Saigon, Republic of South Vietnam
6:00 a.m., July 8, 1964

Rock Francisci sat slumped in the front seat of his car facing a luxury apartment building two blocks from the Transportation Ministry offices. For the past week he had been periodically conducting surveillance on the men from Lucien Conein's list. He quickly honed in on one person in particular, Deputy Minister of Transportation Pham Li Hung. If Francisci had harbored any doubts that Hung was an active participant in Khanh's efforts to steal his opium, they were quickly dispelled by the Deputy Minister's opulent lifestyle. Hung was always impeccably dressed in fine Italian suits that cost more than a month's pay on his government salary, and he often frequented two of the most expensive restaurants in Saigon. He was married with two grown children, and his wife lived outside of Saigon in what he called his "country house." During the week Hung stayed in this luxury Saigon apartment where he frequently entertained various beautiful young women. Hung was obviously living large on the fruits of Francisci's labors.

That would change this morning. Hung had the misfortune of being a creature of habit. Like clockwork, he left his apartment every morning at 6:05 a.m. for the ten-minute walk to his office. He followed a route that, for a half block, cut down an alley between two large buildings. It was the perfect place for Francisci to send a very direct message to Khanh and his minions: Back off or go to war with the Union Corse.

Francisci looked at his watch and waited. At precisely five after the hour, Hung exited the front door wearing a tan suit and brown fedora, and carrying a black leather briefcase. He made a quick right turn and headed down Ly Tru Trong Boulevard toward the Ministry offices. Francisci watched him move purposefully down the street until he disappeared into the alleyway. Satisfied that the prey had arrived at the trap, Francisci started his car and drove off in the opposite direction.

Hung entered the darkened alley with his head down, taking care not to scuff his fine Italian shoes on the cobblestones. He didn't notice the two men who had quietly moved in behind him until it was too late. Without a sound, they quickly looped a garrote around Hung's neck, pulling so tight that the wire cut through flesh and bone, almost severing his head. He was dead before he hit the ground. The larger of the men efficiently placed a tarp on the ground, rolling Hung's body up like an oversized bloody burrito. Hoisting Hung easily over his shoulder, he walked to a panel van. In a span of two minutes it was over.

As Francisci had instructed, the van was driven over to Khanh's office and Hung's body was dumped conspicuously in the gutter. To Khanh the message would be unmistakable. The highest ranking name on the list Conein had given Francisci was now dead, murdered the way the mob murders people—with brutal efficiency and copious amounts of blood.

O'Shea, sitting in seat 3A of the first class section of the Boeing 707 as it winged its way toward Honolulu, cradled a glass of whiskey on his knee as he poured over his notes. He was on the first leg of his trip back to Washington, D.C., after spending the better part of three months in Vietnam. He was going to use the long flight to work on the report he'd be presenting to the president upon his return.

On this flight, O'Shea sat next to a very attractive woman in her mid-20s, who kept stealing glances at him. She wore a patterned floral dress with black heels and a string of pearls around her neck.

He wasn't sure what she was looking at, but it was making him uncomfortable. Looking over at her, he said, "Do you live in Saigon?"

"Oh, Goodness, no! I live in Los Angeles."

O'Shea nodded. Now curious about what she was doing in Saigon, he asked, "In Saigon on business?"

She gave him a dazzling smile. "I'm an actress and a singer, and I've been on a USO tour with Bob Hope."

O'Shea looked at her face more closely. He didn't know many actresses and didn't see many movies. But she certainly was beautiful enough to be an actress, and she did look vaguely familiar.

She looked at O'Shea's uniform and studied his ribbons. "You sure have a lot of those ribbon-things on your chest. You must be a hero of some kind."

O'Shea laughed and tried to deflect. "Not really. If you are around long enough they give you these just for breathing."

"I doubt that," she said, flashing him another winning smile.

O'Shea attempted to get back to work, but he could feel her eyes still on him. He looked over again at her.

"I'm sorry. I don't mean to bother you. I just don't like to read on airplanes and I'm a very nervous flier."

O'Shea knew that 99.5% of men in the world would be eating up this beautiful young woman's attention with a spoon. But O'Shea wasn't really interested in flirting and didn't want to waste the quiet time of this long flight to chitchat with an actress. But he also wanted to be polite. Maybe, he thought, if he chatted her up for a bit she might get tired and go to sleep.

After some small talk about her career, the USO, Bob Hope and Hollywood, the discussion turned to O'Shea's job. He was circumspect but told her that he worked in the White House. That really got her interest.

"Oh my! Do you work near the president? Do you actually see him?"

O'Shea smiled. "Sometimes."

"I met President Kennedy last year. I sang for him at his birthday at the Waldorf Astoria."

"Really?"

"Yes. It was such a great moment! Jackie was there. She was so elegant, so beautiful. That poor man! Losing his wife like that. It's just tragic!"

O'Shea wasn't sure how to respond. "It was very tragic."

She suddenly looked sad. "It's terrible losing your spouse like that. My Aunt Doris lost her husband suddenly in a car accident. She was never the same." Tears began to form in her eyes. She looked at O'Shea with total sincerity and said, "I'm going to give you my phone number, colonel. I want you to give it to the president. And I want you to tell him that if he ever needs comforting, to call me and I'll come. Wherever he is in the world." She took out a slip of paper and wrote:

Ann-Margret
Richmond 9-4175
Call anytime!

After some more small talk, Ann-Margret finally got tired and fell soundly asleep, her head resting on O'Shea's shoulder—he could smell her perfume, and it made him think of Maddie. He closed his eyes and thought of the last few weeks. He realized that he should be dead and that he had come closer to dying than at any time in his life—including in Korea, and that was saying something.

He didn't know why the VC infiltrator's gun had jammed, anymore than he knew why he had survived at Chosin when so many of his men had not. But he took both instances as a sign that God wasn't finished with him yet. In this sense what happened in Nam Dong had given O'Shea a much deeper appreciation for what the president must be experiencing after Dallas. How do you process surviving what should have been certain death? Do you chalk it up to chance? Or do you see it as a sign that there is a bigger purpose for your life?

After the fight in Nam Dong, O'Shea had accompanied Captain Donlon back to the U.S. Naval Station Hospital in Saigon. Donlon had undergone surgery to repair the wounds he had received during the course of the battle. Two other soldiers from Donlon's A-Team had also ended up in the hospital. Fortunately, all would recover fully from their wounds.

Though he wasn't technically required to do so, O'Shea had written a detailed after-action report of the battle, and sent it both to Harkins at MACV and through a separate channel inside the Special Forces community. He wanted to make sure the full account of the battle, including the infiltrators among the ARVN and the long delay in receiving reinforcements, was heard up the chain of command. Given what was in his report, he ventured to guess that MACV would do what it could to whitewash it. He couldn't let that happen.

Privately O'Shea still wondered whether the failure of MACV command to come to their aid that night had been Harkins making good on his threat that O'Shea was "on his own" if he got into trouble. Was it possible that Harkins would carry out that threat to the point where he'd put an entire A-Team in danger of being annihilated? Did Harkins see this as his best chance of getting O'Shea out of his hair? By having him killed by the VC? A year ago, before Dallas, O'Shea would have laughed at such a possibility.

Now he couldn't be so sure.

Somewhere over the Midwest
Aboard Air Force One
1:00 p.m., July 16, 1964

The Chief Steward aboard the president's plane made his way back from the communication room that sat just behind the cockpit of the converted Boeing 707. He passed the president's stateroom, where Kennedy was resting after having delivered a pair of campaign speeches in Los Angeles, and headed toward the small conference room in the center of the airplane. There he found Bobby Kennedy sitting with political aide Kenny O'Donnell pouring over a district-level map of the United States. The reelection campaign for the president had begun. Bobby, as the sitting attorney general, could not officially serve as his brother's campaign manager as he had done in 1960, though he'd certainly be pulling many of the strings behind the scenes. They fully expected New York governor and moderate Republican Nelson Rockefeller to secure the GOP nomination, and had placed pins on the states that they thought were still "in play."

"Excuse me, Mr. Kennedy. This message just came in for you," the steward said, holding up a folded piece of paper.

Kennedy took the paper without a word and unfolded it.

RICHARD NIXON SECURES NOMINATION OF GOP ON FIRST BALLOT. GOLDWATER VP.

"Goddamn!" exclaimed Kennedy.

Bobby knew that all their campaign plans had just been upended; Nixon was an experienced campaigner who wasn't afraid to mix it up. He also had a deep reservoir of connections throughout the country, and had a visceral dislike for the Kennedys. Nixon had risen from poverty to become a Congressman and Vice President of the United States for two terms under President Dwight Eisenhower. Having gone to Whittier College, a small school in California, Nixon was insecure about his lack of an Ivy League education, a trait that made him both paranoid and ruthless with those who he saw as "Harvard types." He had come within a whisper of beating Kennedy in 1960, and would have won had it not been for the help provided by Sam Giancana in Chicago. This was a rematch that would likely go down to the wire, and meant that the Kennedy camp could take nothing for granted.

"Jesus, this is going to change our strategy," said O'Donnell. "Now it seems to me that the race is going to shape up a lot like 1960. Nixon will take California and the West, most of the Midwest, Florida, Iowa, Michigan, Maine. It's going to come down again to Texas and Illinois. As they go, so goes the election. Am I missing something?"

"That's if we hold what we won four years ago," Bobby replied. "My biggest concern is that if we don't get out in front on foreign policy we could be in trouble in some of these other states. Before Dallas, Jack had a real problem with the press, which painted him as a neophyte and as someone that the Russians could push around. Cuba changed much of that," said Bobby, referring to the Cuban Missile Crisis, where Kennedy had stared down Soviet Premier Nikita Khrushchev. "But I still think Vietnam is a weakness for us. There's been a steady stream of bad news coming out of Saigon, and I fear that Nixon is going to wrap it around Jack's neck."

O'Donnell nodded his agreement, even though was not an area on which he had any influence. O'Donnell and the rest of the staff were only political operatives. Their job was to get the vote out and to make sure the local political parties played ball, and they were very good at it. "You know what my biggest worry is? That Johnson can't hold Texas and we don't get the same kind of 'help' from Mayor Daley in Chicago this time around. We need to make sure we get the union vote out big in Illinois."

Bobby nodded. Then considering the sympathy effect of Dallas, asked, "Do you think that Jackie's death in Dallas will give us a boost in Texas?"

"It might. But you know, there could be a dark side to that. There may be a backlash against the Democrats in Texas after the rest of the country has spent the past year bashing it as a place where Republican red necks shoot guns and drink beer."

Bobby grunted. "That's pretty ironic since Oswald was a Marxist who tried to become a Soviet citizen."

O'Donnell shrugged. Public perception had little to do with reality. "We need to get our operation in Texas up and running. I'll work on getting the Vice President down there on a campaign swing just after Labor Day."

"And I'll work on the president to make sure we hold the line in Vietnam until November," Bobby responded. "We don't want the war to become the story. If that happens, the president may find himself on the defensive. That could make all our organizing for naught."

Patrick O'Shea had been home for ten days and he wasn't sleeping well. The battle of Nam Dong was in his dreams—the noise and the smell of cordite in the air, so real that he'd often wake up and not realize where he was. The dreams always ended the same way: with VC inside the wire and the Nung guarding him dead. Donlon screaming in the distance. The "click" of a trigger being pulled. Then he invariably wakes up with a start, breathing heavily, waking Maddie in the process. She'd never seen her husband so bothered, and she was worried. It didn't help her that he had declined to give her many details about what had happened while he was in Vietnam. She knew he had been in a camp that had been attacked, because he did tell her about Roger Donlon. But she had no idea about his detour into Laos to deliver Kennedy's letter, or just how close she'd come to losing her husband.

Lying in bed O'Shea stared at the ceiling and listened to his wife's steady breathing. He thought about how his mother became a widow at the age of 38, suddenly alone with two kids to feed.

The year after his father died his mother met a man at church. He was a teacher at the local college, an educated man. He was thus the opposite of Patrick's father, who had a high school diploma and had earned lots of credits from the school of hard knocks. The man's name was John but his mother called him "professor." He was 12 years her senior, and possessed a preternatural calm that was a stark contrast to his father's intensity. For the first time in 20 years his mother felt like she mattered. Her face brightened.

Watching his mother heal her wounds taught Patrick a lot about the power of the human spirit. It was a different kind of resilience than his father taught him, which was more about grit and determination. His mother showed him that life went on even in the face of loss. And sometimes it even got better.

Finally, at 6 a.m, O'Shea got up, made a pot of coffee and went into his study. On his desk was an IBM Selectric typewriter and the final chapter of his report to the president. It had taken him the better part of the past week to put it all together, and he intended to have it on the president's desk as soon as he finished his conclusion. He knew the president liked to be briefed verbally, and usually would ask so many questions that O'Shea was bound to cover all the points in their meeting. But he also knew that Kennedy liked detail, and would want to have it in written form to be able to refer to it when needed. Kennedy would be having dozens of meetings on Vietnam over the next several months, and his goal was to arm the president with a first-hand perspective.

Looking at the clock, O'Shea picked up the phone and placed a call to the one person he could talk to about what he had seen and done in Vietnam.

After three rings the phone was answered at Fort Bragg. "Summers," Colonel Ed Summers said in a loud whisper. O'Shea knew that he was still in bed and didn't want to wake his wife.

"So, you snake-eaters sleeping in now?"

Summers immediately recognized the voice. "Shit, Patrick, I got up this morning, shot a hog, made fresh bacon and eggs and am on my third pot of coffee."

"I'm sure. Listen, old man, get out of bed and call me back when you actually do have your first cup of coffee. I've got some things to talk over with you."

"Roger that" Summers gently hung up the phone and got out of bed. His wife stirred and rolled over to go back to sleep.

Fifteen minutes later, fresh coffee in hand, Summers called back.

"So I hear you ended up eating some dirt out there in the bush, Patrick. The tea and canapés in Saigon weren't enough for you?" Summers knew enough not to mention the instructions he had delivered on behalf of Kennedy. If O'Shea could divulge any details now that he was back in the States he would. Otherwise he wouldn't. But regardless, Summers wouldn't be bringing it up.

"Before I ran into your Captain Donlon, I had actually thought it was more dangerous being anywhere in the vicinity of Paul Harkins. But I was violently disabused of that notion."

"Based on that after-action report you filed, I guess Donlon and my guys did us snake-eaters proud." Summers was very possessive of the men that came through the Special Warfare Center. They were all "his guys."

"Ed, I have to say that I was never prouder to be a part of the army than I was that night. Donlon is a superb officer and his men all performed with skill and courage. You should be a proud papa."

Summers laughed. "I am. But losing Alamo and Houston was a tough blow. I'd known Pop almost as long as I've known you."

"I know, Ed." O'Shea lifted his mug and said into the phone, "To absent companions."

Summers, on the other end of the line, did the same.

"So to what do I owe this wake up call?"

O'Shea paused before replying. O'Shea was hesitant to tell him about his nightmares and his difficulty sleeping since getting back from Vietnam. Members of the martial profession don't like to show weakness, even among friends. "I've been having trouble sleeping. Jet lag, maybe. I don't know."

"Jet lag? Right. Ok, Thinker. What's really going on?"

O'Shea smiled. "Maybe I am living up to the nickname."

"Well, that would be understandable, given the pressure cooker you are in. Whatever you tell the president—wait, have you already given Kennedy your report?"

"Not yet. I'm actually just finishing it up as we speak."

"Shit, Patrick, whatever you tell Kennedy you are going to be pissing people off. And some of them sign your paycheck."

O'Shea sighed. "Yep, but that bed's made. I'm guessing that my career is going to be over one way or another. Kennedy himself told me that if he wins reelection he would protect me. That gives me until at least '68 in uniform. So, best case is I don't do 30 and I get out early. But if he loses to Nixon I'm toast. Even if I come out now strongly supporting an expansion of the war, my future is over inside the Army."

"We discussed this before Christmas last year. You knew the risks. So what's changed?"

"What's changed is that what I found in Vietnam was much, much worse than what I expected to find; when we last discussed this, I had no idea just how screwed up things were. When you actually see it yourself—and I did see it, firsthand and in living color—it takes on another meaning altogether."

Summers grunted. "So you know what a mess the ARVN is, then?"

"I wish that were the extent of it. That's only the tip of a very rotten iceberg," said O'Shea, uncharacteristically mixing metaphors. "The CIA is working with the French to smuggle opium out of Laos, and funneling the profits to Khanh and his henchmen. And guess who is at the center of it? Our old friend Lucien Conein."

"No shit? The CIA is smuggling opium?"

"Apparently they are facilitating it, in partnership with the Corsican mafia. And even worse, I think Harkins is allowing it to happen. It's utterly corrupt."

Summers let that sink in. Given how compromised Harkins and the MACV leadership had become it didn't surprise him. "Wow. Is that what you will be telling your friend the president?"

O'Shea paused for a moment, then said, "Yes."

Both men were silent for a moment. Summers then said, "Well, for what its worth, most of my men who have been on an advisor tour think that it's just not a war that the regular army is prepared to fight. And there aren't enough of us snake-eaters to make a real difference if this becomes a full-scale American war."

O'Shea knew that this line of argument would resonate with Kennedy, who had created the Green Berets for just the kind of challenge that Vietnam represented—small regional wars of national liberation. Only Vietnam wasn't so small, and there weren't enough Green Berets to handle something on this scale. He'd definitely be making this argument to the president.

"Well, thanks for listening, Ed. By the way, how is Donlon doing?"

"He's on the mend. He'll be in the hospital for another month or so. He's definitely on the fast track for the Medal," he was referring to the Medal of Honor.

"Well, if he doesn't get it then nobody should. Let's hope politics don't get in the way."

"You helped with that, sending your report up the back-channel through Bragg. MACV didn't get a chance to bury it, or leave out the fact that 30% of the ARVN infantry at Nam Dong were infiltrators. Can you imagine how pissed Harkins was when it became clear that he couldn't keep you from reporting that embarrassing fact?"

"I can. And to be honest, it gives me great pleasure."

CHAPTER 15

The Oval Office
The White House
Washington, D.C.
9:50 a.m., July 27, 1964

Colonel Patrick O'Shea carried his report, officially entitled "Findings from Presidential Mission to Vietnam," under his arm as he entered the Oval Office. He had made one extra copy of the report. Uncertain if Kennedy would want a copy floating around, he decided to bring both, along with his source notes. He was prepared to give it all to the president if he so desired.

O'Shea was shocked to see his smiling wife Maddie and their two children, Kevin and Elizabeth, standing with the president. "Colonel O'Shea, I hope you don't mind me asking your lovely wife and children in for a visit. I can see by your face that you don't know anything about this," said the president.

A genuinely surprised O'Shea said, "Sir, my wife is apparently very good at keeping a secret."

"Jackie was like that, too. She was great at surprise parties…" The president's voice trailed off, as if he was momentarily lost in a vision of his late wife. Snapping out of it, he said, "Well, this is a happy occasion and I wanted to make sure your family was present."

"Sir?"

The president reached into his pocket and pulled out a pair of silver stars. Stepping forward he said, "With the advice and consent of the United States Senate, I am pleased to pin these stars on you, Brigadier General Patrick O'Shea, United States Army."

Maddie, Kevin and Elizabeth O'Shea clapped and a photographer appeared to memorialize the event. The president unpinned O'Shea's silver eagles and replaced them with a single star on each epaulet of his uniform. Stepping back, he shook O'Shea's hand and said "Congratulations, General."

"Thank you, sir."

"Now, let's get a few more pictures." The family crowded around the president, and the photographer took a half dozen photos. "Mrs. O'Shea, we'll make sure to get you copies of these as soon as we can. I'm sure you'll want to frame a few," the president said, smiling.

After the photos, the O'Shea family left and the president pushed the intercom button on his phone. "Mrs. Lincoln, in five minutes please ask Mr. Hilsman to join us."

Kennedy walked over to where O'Shea was standing. He raised his eyebrows and cocked his head slightly.

O'Shea knew what the president was referring to. "Mission accomplished."

The president nodded. "How did it go?"

"It was…intense."

The president looked into O'Shea's eyes. Instinctively, he knew that O'Shea was soft-pedaling, but he decided to let it go.

He stuck out his hand. "Well, thank you for what you did. Sometime soon we'll talk about what was in the letter you delivered."

O'Shea wasn't sure how to respond. So he simply said, "Yes, sir."

Just then Roger Hilsman appeared. He congratulated General O'Shea on his promotion, and sat down next to the president. "I've asked Roger to be here, since he's the schemer that helped me commission your trip. Roger may be the second least popular person as far as the Pentagon is concerned." The president paused and gave O'Shea a slight smile. "I guess you know who least popular is, Colonel—Excuse me! I meant to say General."

O'Shea nodded. "I won't be expecting many Christmas cards this year, Mr. President."

The three of them shared a little laugh at that understatement. The president then nodded toward the binder O'Shea carried. "Is that the sum of your efforts, General?"

"It is, Mr. President," O'Shea said, pushing the copies of his report across the coffee table. "How would you like to proceed, sir? I can give you an oral overview now and leave it with you for further study. Or you can read the executive summary and we can discuss the points in depth. I'm at your disposal, sir."

"Let's take 15 minutes and read through the exec summary. If we have questions we can take it from there."

* * *

Findings from Presidential Mission to Vietnam
Colonel Patrick O'Shea, USA
July 21, 1964

EXECUTIVE SUMMARY

The purpose of the presidential mission to Vietnam was to assess the conditions on the ground with respect to U.S. policy, and to provide unfiltered analysis to the president of the United States.

Summary of Findings:

1. The U.S. mission in Vietnam–defined as creating an independent, quasi-Democratic South Vietnam that can protect its own borders with its own forces, is failing.

2. The Government of South Vietnam is corrupt and lacks any legitimacy of the people. U.S. policy is propping up a dictatorship in the guise of a democracy.

3. The ARVN is ineffective, unable to fight independently and is riven with corruption and political infighting. It is my estimate that more than 30% of ARVN troops are VC sympathizers and/or infiltrators.

4. While U.S. Special Forces are performing exceptionally well, their numbers are too small to make a material difference, and the indigenous troops they assist are incapable of taking on the fight (see point #3 above).

5. The MACV command is providing inaccurate and misleading reports to the Pentagon. This is, in my view, an intentional effort to deceive the civilian decision-makers in Washington.

6. The enemy is determined, well organized, well trained and well equipped, and will not be dissuaded from unifying the country by force.

7. The enemy is highly effective at fighting in the jungle and operates with a very small footprint. Bombing and other forms of interdiction are unlikely to be successful.

8. There is no plausible way to achieve success in Vietnam as we have defined it; the U.S. Army is doctrinally ill-suited to fight a land war in Vietnam.

9. It is my considered opinion that the continuation of our involvement in Vietnam will ultimately lead to failure.

* * *

When the president finished reading, he thumbed through the 85 pages of the report, noting the detail and then looking at several of the maps. When he finally looked up he glanced over at Hilsman, who was busily jotting down notes in the margins.

The president said after a moment, "General, my faith in you has been vindicated by this report. Not your conclusions, mind you—those we can debate. The fact that you gave it to me straight is commendable."

"Thank you, sir. My father always used the expression, 'in for a penny, in for a pound.' I guess it stuck."

"So it seems from your report that the advisory effort is not working," asked the president. "Is that correct?"

"It's not that it isn't working. In many cases it is working very well. There are some basic issues that could be fixed, of course. The language barrier is a huge problem—many of our advisors don't speak Vietnamese, and it creates confusion and hampers effectiveness. The ARVN doesn't promote or reward its officers and men based on merit, so there is little incentive to excel. The supply system is corrupt and poorly designed, and leads to a lack of combat support when and where it is needed most. But in the end, the real problem is more fundamental: our advisors need a partner to advise who is capable of taking the fight to the enemy. Those conditions are not present in Vietnam, in my opinion."

"And what makes you think that there are so many infiltrators among ARVN troops?"

"Mr. President, almost getting shot by an infiltrator is something that makes an impression on you. Are you familiar with what happened to me at Nam Dong?" O'Shea asked. Both Hilsman and Kennedy nodded.

"Secretary McNamara filled me in on it and told me the Pentagon is reviewing a potential Medal of Honor award."

"The ARVN unit embedded with the A-Team was infiltrated by dozens of VC sympathizers. When the attack came, they stripped off their uniforms and killed the ARVN soldiers next to them."

Hilsman then asked, "What do you make of such a high percentage of infiltrators?"

"I think it signifies a couple of very serious problems."

"Such as?"

"The Viet Cong have created a vast and sophisticated infrastructure in South Vietnam—a shadow government, in effect. This government provides recruits, money and intelligence to the military units fighting us. They levee taxes, encourage the rural population to join military units, and gather information from farmers and others in the countryside about both ARVN operations and police units, and the identity of government informers."

"In other words, they are winning the 'hearts and minds' of the people."

"Yes, sir," O'Shea said, nodding emphatically. "The VC have convinced the people that the South Vietnamese government is out to tax them, repress them and conscript them into the army. So they've been able to turn many against the ARVN, and part of that is getting young men to join up and infiltrate. They essentially lie in wait for a time to strike, often during an attack like at Nam Dong. It's very difficult to defend."

"Difficult or impossible? That's the question, really," Kennedy said. "Will we ever be in a better position than the communists to influence the people at the village level—either by the carrot or the stick? What percentage of the South Vietnamese people live in the countryside? 85%? If we can't get them to follow us—meaning the government of South Vietnam *and* the ARVN—how can we possibly be successful?"

Hilsman tapped his pen on his pad. "Mr. President, I agree. We are fighting a war that is simultaneously both a military and a political battle—the two cannot be decoupled. If we can't win both, we can't win either."

"Does that sum up your view as well, General?" asked Kennedy.

"Very succinctly, Sir. But there's something else we need to discuss."

"Go on."

O'Shea proceeded to tell Kennedy about what he learned from Tucker Gouglemann. When he finished, the room was silent.

Kennedy looked at Hilsman before responding to O'Shea. "General, I'm already aware of this issue, and am taking steps to deal with it."

"Yes, sir. In my view this really calls into question whether the government of South Vietnam—"

"General," the president interrupted O'Shea. "Thank you for your report. Are there other copies of this document?"

O'Shea got the message: the president had heard enough. "I've brought the only two copies in existence, and also my source notes in case you want to keep it under your personal control."

"Do you have a safe at home?"

"I do."

"I think I'll keep this here," gesturing to the report in front of him. "I'd like for you to keep Roger's copy and the source notes in your safe. I want to make sure we have a back up in case my copy grows legs and disappears. As always, this discussion is to remain in confidence."

O'Shea was taken aback by this last statement. Everything that happened in his job was confidential. "Of course, sir."

Kennedy then smiled, turning on his well-honed charm. "Welcome home and congratulations again, General. I'll be setting up some meetings on our path forward on Vietnam and I'll want you there. My staff will be in touch on timing."

O'Shea stood. "Thank you, Mr. President."

<hr/>

The George Ball Residence
1221 N Street
Washington, D.C.
2:45 p.m., July 25, 1964

Under Secretary of State George Ball desperately wanted to take a vacation. He'd lived in the nation's capital long enough to remember when it virtually shut down during the summer months. That was before World War II and the vast expansion of the federal government under Roosevelt. Who in their right mind spends the summer in a veritable swamp surrounding the Potomac? 95 degrees and 95 percent humidity were enough to make you sweat sitting in place. Ball hated D.C. in the summer.

Today he sat comfortably in his air-conditioned living room sipping an iced tea. He was preparing yet another memo for Kennedy on Vietnam when the phone rang.

"George, sorry to bother you at home." Ball immediately recognized the voice of his long-time friend Clark Clifford.

"Clark, don't be silly—it's always good to hear from you."

"I had a long talk last week with McGeorge Bundy after a PFIAB meeting and wanted to visit with you a bit about it." Clifford, now Chair of the Presidential Foreign Intelligence Advisory Board that provided Kennedy with analysis on intelligence matters, was also an old friend of Ball's. They had spent many hours discussing Vietnam.

"What's Mac asking for now? To drop nukes on Hanoi?"

Clifford laughed. "Not exactly. But he is again pressing his case for bombing North Vietnam as way to get their attention."

"My God, Clark. We already have their attention. We've really been quite busy in the North. We have navy ships routinely patrolling the Gulf of Tonkin just daring the North to attack. And we've been blowing bridges, attacking naval installations and sabotaging power lines. The French Resistance would have been envious."

"I know. But Mac thinks it's not enough."

"For my money it's already far too much. It's provocation with little chance of success. Worse than that, it's likely to lead to an event that we will have a hard time backing away from. What if one of our covert teams gets detected? What happens if one of our ships gets attacked?"

"I tend to agree. But I'm sensing that there is the beginning of a consensus between McNamara and Bundy and the Joint Chiefs to escalate the war with bombing strategic targets inside North Vietnam."

"This doesn't have something to with General Taylor leaving for Saigon to become the Ambassador, does it?"

"I think it might. Taylor has been playing defense with the Joint Chiefs and has been working to shield President Kennedy from their views. With him gone the Pentagon sees an opening to push Kennedy to escalate."

"Who's taking over for Taylor?"

"Earle Wheeler," said Clifford. Wheeler had been the Army chief of staff.

"Do you know him?"

"Not personally. What I have heard is that Wheeler is in a different mold from Taylor and the other chiefs in that he's not a combat commander. He's been a staff officer his whole career—a very good one. I hear he's smooth, well-educated and intellectual."

"In other words, he's a Kennedy general."

"Precisely. But unlike Taylor, he's on record as being a proponent of using maximum force to get results."

"Oh, boy. Here we go. Why is it always the armchair generals who want to go in with guns blazing?"

Clifford laughed. "I don't know. But I do know that pressure on the president to escalate is going to increase," said Clifford.

"It sure will. Thank God it's an election year. At least we have that going for us."

Clifford, the old political hand, knew that Ball was right. It would take a massive provocation to get Kennedy to make any decisive move to escalate in Vietnam during a presidential election. "Lets just hope that nothing blows up in Vietnam between now and November," Clifford said.

"You can hope, Clark. But I'm going to do whatever's necessary to get in front of Kennedy before it's too late."

CHAPTER 16

Aboard the USS *Maddox*
The Gulf of Tonkin, North Vietnam
3:30 p.m., August 2, 1964

The USS *Maddox*, a 376-foot Sumner-class destroyer with a complement of 336 officers and men, knifed its way up the coast of Vietnam at a speed of 20 knots. It had arrived in Southeast Asia just a few weeks prior, having sailed from Long Beach, California to join the fast carrier force of the 7th Fleet patrolling the waters off Vietnam. The *Maddox* had a distinguished combat record in the Pacific during the Second World War, having survived a kamikaze attack off Formosa, while later supporting U.S. troops at the invasion of Okinawa. This day its mission was to gather signals intelligence off the coast of North Vietnam.

Aboard the *Maddox* was the commander of the 7th Fleet's Destroyer Division, Captain John Herrick. A tall, austere officer with a booming voice, Herrick was known for decisive action and a quick temper. As division commander he was responsible for all the destroyers in the 7th

Fleet, including the *Maddox*'s sister ship, the USS *Turner Joy*, presently en route to the area from the South. Also on board the *Maddox* was the ship's captain, Commander Herb Ogier. Ogier was Herrick's opposite: soft-spoken, cerebral and with a fine wit.

At that moment the *Maddox* was some 28 miles off the coast of North Vietnam, steaming perpendicular to the coastline, with its radar tracking a number of small bogies some 15,000 yards out and closing fast.

"Battle stations," Herrick said to Commander Ogier.

"Yes, captain." Ogier hit the horn, and battle stations blared from the PA across the ship.

"Radar, please report range and direction," Ogier said into his microphone.

"14,000 yards and closing at 40 knots, sir." They were fast boats moving directly towards them.

"Can you identify target type?" asked Herrick.

"Motor-torpedo PT-type boats, approximately 50 feet in length, Captain."

Herrick keyed his mike again. "Signals, anything from the net?" referring to the radio traffic.

"Captain, chatter indicates enemy assumes we are part of the earlier actions taken against the Hon Me and Hon Nieu islands." That action, taken earlier that same day, was part of extensive covert operations against North Vietnam.

Here we go, thought Herrick, who knew they were about to get attacked.

Having been provoked by the earlier action, the North Vietnamese Navy now saw the *Maddox* as an offensive threat, and not simply an intel-gathering cruise in international waters. Turning to Ogier he said, "Commander, when these targets get within 10,000 yards, fire three warning shots."

"Aye, Aye, sir."

Ogier relayed the command to his gunnery officer and waited as the seconds ticked off. At the precise moment the three boats came inside the 10,000-yard mark, the *Maddox* fired its 5-inch gun three times in quick succession. As the smoke cleared the bridge, it was apparent to both Herrick and Ogier that the boats were not breaking off their attack.

Herrick issued another order to Ogier. "Begin evasive action and commence firing on targets when they get within 5,000 yards."

"Yes, sir."

"And contact the *Ticonderoga* and let her know we are under attack," Herrick said to Ogier. "See if they can get some birds in the air."

Aboard the USS *Ticonderoga*
Gulf of Tonkin
4:05 p.m., August 2, 1964

Commander James Stockdale rushed to the ready room aboard the USS *Ticonderoga,* an Essex-class Fast Carrier with a full complement of F-8E Crusader attack aircraft armed with Zuni air-to-ground missiles. Word had just come in that the USS *Maddox* was under attack, and was requesting air support.

"What's the situation?" asked Stockdale, the wing commander of navy attack squadron VF-51. A graduate of the Naval Academy and Stanford University, Stockdale was an aggressive former test pilot who was excited to get into the fight.

"*Maddox* reports multiple fast boats heading toward them at high speed. Have fired warning shots to no effect," replied the *Ticonderoga's* intel officer.

"Weather?"

"Visibility good, winds out of the south at 15 knots."

Stockdale grabbed the weather print out, turned to his wingman and two other pilots and said, "Let's go."

Together, the four pilots ran out of the Ready Room and onto the deck of the carrier. Stockdale's heart was racing. He loved flying low over the ocean, and fed off the danger that it presented. It was the kind of stress that made lesser men buckle. He reveled in it.

Stockdale was first to his plane. Buckling in, he lit the huge single engine of the supersonic fighter and began his checklist. The Crusader was a devastatingly effective attack aircraft, but was known to be a difficult plane to control and required above average skill to master.

Within five minutes, all four Crusaders were launched by catapult into the sky over the Gulf of Tonkin.

* * *

On the *Maddox*, Captain Herrick was searching desperately for the incoming boats. Radar indicated that the three boats had split their attack, with two coming up from behind while one was attempting to flank the *Maddox*, going for a side shot with its torpedoes. Herrick knew the precise moment that the boats reached 5,000 yards, because the destroyer's six 5-inch guns opened up with a roar, sending 55 pound shells hurtling toward them at 2,600 feet per second.

Once the 5-inch guns opened up, all hell broke loose. The two boats approaching from the stern fired their torpedoes.

"We've got three torpedoes in the water bearing 22 degrees at 65 knots!" yelled the radar operator.

"Hard left, full speed ahead!" Ogier shouted into his microphone.

The *Maddox* heeled quickly to the left and Herrick was suddenly off balance. Grabbing the rail, he managed to look down as the three torpedoes passed harmlessly off the starboard side of the ship. Looking through his glasses, he could see the telltale muzzle flashes that told him all three boats were now firing on the *Maddox* with their 14.5mm deck guns. They were small guns by naval gunfire standards, but could still do some damage to the destroyer with a lucky shot into the bridge.

At that moment, the two F-8E Crusaders flown by Stockdale and his wingman screamed overhead at 300 feet off the deck, immediately launching Zuni air-to-ground missiles at the boats, while strafing with their 20mm canon. As Herrick watched, one boat was set on fire and the other two began racing for shore at top speed. Not a minute later, the other Crusaders chased the other two boats toward shore, firing their guns until they were clearly within North Vietnamese waters. They then formed up and returned to the *Ticonderoga*.

Herrick surveyed the ship for damage: several shells had hit the *Maddox* leaving a few superficial scars. No crewmen were injured. One of the Crusaders had a chunk of its wing taken out by a 14.5mm shell, but landed safely. Additionally, one of the PT boats had been destroyed and the two others damaged.

The Situation Room
The White House
8:35 a.m., August 3, 1964

When Patrick O'Shea received the flash message on the incident in the Tonkin Gulf, two things were immediately clear. First, the attack was a natural response by the North to the regular covert incursions being made against coastal installations, and second, this was a potential powder keg if not handled with care. Attacks against U.S. naval forces on the high seas rarely went un-responded to, and in an election year, it was anybody's guess how this might escalate. O'Shea wanted to make sure that cool heads prevailed.

O'Shea ripped the Teletype from the machine and put it in his briefcase for the three minute trip to the Oval Office. As he exited the elevator from the basement, O'Shea saw a group of senior military officers standing in the hallway outside the Oval. He immediately recognized the new chairman of the Joint Chiefs, Earle Wheeler, as well as the chief of Naval Operations, Admiral David McDonald. Standing off to the side was Air Force General Curtis LeMay, an unlit cigar between his teeth and an aide carrying his attaché. As he walked by, O'Shea nodded at General Wheeler, who was watching him carefully. As he passed by O'Shea could feel the venom in the air.

As O'Shea approached the Oval Office, Mrs. Lincoln gestured to him. "The president wants to see you alone first. Secretary McNamara, Secretary Rusk and Mr. Bundy are on their way." Lincoln looked at her watch. "The meeting will start right at 9 a.m. sharp. So you have about 10 minutes."

Inside, O'Shea found Kennedy sitting in his rocking chair facing the fireplace, in between two couches that faced each other.

"Sir, I've brought the latest intelligence from CINCPAC, including the after action report from Admiral Sharp. It's there on the top," O'Shea said, pointing to the Teletype.

The president took the papers from O'Shea and scanned them briefly. Looking up, he said, "Can you summarize it for me?"

"The reports suggest that the *Maddox* was attacked by PT boats roughly 28 miles off the coast of Vietnam—"

"So, the *Maddox* was in international waters?"

"Technically, yes, sir. However, the intel also shows that the North Vietnamese clearly saw the *Maddox* patrol as a continuation of two days of covert attacks on naval installations in North Vietnam. In that sense, the North believed it was defending itself against our offensive operations."

"And that's clear from what? The radio intercepts?"

"Precisely, sir. The *Maddox* is a souped-up destroyer filled with sophisticated radio intercept equipment. They were able to clearly identify the chatter from the attacking boats. There was no doubt that the North believed it was under attack. And the *Maddox's* commander," O'Shea paused, referring to his notes, "Captain Herrick, made clear in his report to MACV and the Pacific Fleet that this was the case."

Kennedy nodded. "Ok, thank you." The president reached over to the intercom on the table next to him. "Mrs. Lincoln, please show everyone in."

O'Shea stood and took his place outside the circle, standing at attention at the back of the room. It was customary for O'Shea to stay for these meetings as an observer but not to participate in any way. His role was to prepare the president beforehand and then be there to decipher the meetings after they were over.

Once everyone was settled, Secretary McNamara began the meeting by retracing the facts of the attack, which generally mirrored what O'Shea had told the president. On the issue of whether the North saw the *Maddox* as an offensive threat, McNamara was more guarded. "There is some intel that suggests this to be the case, but to my mind it's not definitive," concluded McNamara.

Kennedy interjected. "Not definitive? My understanding is that the *Maddox*'s Captain believed there was conclusive evidence to this effect."

"I'm sure he does," said McNamara.

"But you don't believe him?"

"It's not that I don't believe him, Mr. President. It's just that my experience with men under stress is that their recollections are often clouded in the heat of battle. I'm just saying that in my mind, it's not conclusive."

Kennedy stared at McNamara. There was no doubt that he was one of the smartest men Kennedy had ever known. But it was becoming increasingly clear to the president that his Secretary of Defense had a confidence in his own judgment that bordered on narcissism. When everyone is telling you how smart you are all the time, you start to believe it.

The president turned to the Joint Chiefs and asked them to weigh in. They were unanimous in their view that, irrespective of whether the attack by the North was offensive or defensive in nature, the military saw this as an act of war.

"Mr. President, this attack cannot go un-responded to," said General Wheeler. "It invites further aggression against our ships and puts our forces in further danger. We strongly recommend a proportional response, and have put together a list of targets, including fuel supply depots and naval shipyards."

The president took the list and reviewed it carefully. He was doing this purely for show, as he had no intention at that moment of escalating the war by bombing the North. "Where is the *Maddox* now?"

Admiral McDonald answered. "Sir, we've told the *Maddox* and its sister ship, the *Turner Joy*, to stay on station. We want to send the signal that we aren't going to be intimidated by these attacks."

Kennedy thought for a moment. Given his approval of the covert actions against North Vietnam that provoked all this, Kennedy felt he owed it to the U.S. military to support them when they were in harm's way. He also wanted to let the North know that the United States wouldn't be bullied from international waters.

"General," the president said at last, addressing Wheeler, "I approve of you keeping the *Maddox* and *Turner Joy* on patrol. But I want you to take precautionary measures, providing air cover during daylight hours and avoiding close approaches to the coastline when covert activities are underway. Let's not throw sand in their face."

General Curtis LeMay couldn't constrain himself any longer. "Mr. President, I say we use our B-52s to send them a real message—one that they won't soon forget. We're sitting here like a debating society while our men are being shot at. It's bullshit, sir."

Kennedy didn't particularly like LeMay. He was an old-school pilot who flew B-29s against Japan in World War II and pioneered strategic bombing. He was gruff and full of spit and vinegar—not the kind of erudite military leader Kennedy generally preferred.

"Thank you, General. I know that when we need to flatten someone, you'll be there to do the job. I'm not sure this is the time and place for that."

Just as LeMay was about to respond, Kennedy decided that he had heard enough. "Thank you gentlemen, I'll consider all this and will communicate my decision to Secretary McNamara." Kennedy rose slowly, signaling to the group that the meeting was over. He caught O'Shea's eye and raised his finger ever so slightly, indicating that he wanted O'Shea to stay behind.

When the room had cleared, Kennedy said to O'Shea, "Well, that was about what I expected. They massaged the facts to suit their views, hoping I'd pull my six-gun and start firing. It's clear to me that this was not an unprovoked attack, and that it doesn't merit a response. We gave them a black eye, correct? Sunk one of their boats?

"Yes, sir. That's what the report says."

"That's enough. For now."

Office of the U.S. Ambassador
U.S. Embassy, Saigon
8:00 a.m., August 4, 1964

The United States Embassy in Saigon resembled a mini version of the Flatiron Building in New York City. It took up the entire corner of Ham Nghi Street and was rounded in front and flat along both sides. The face of the building had small symmetrical windows that faced the street; it looked more like a fortress than the welcoming diplomatic headquarters of the world's greatest democracy.

Ambassador Maxwell Taylor had been in his new job for only a few weeks, but already he was sensing trouble. Earlier that morning he had fired off a cable to the State Department recommending that the president announce the U.S. would attack North Vietnamese patrol boats "wherever they were found" in international waters, lay mines in the approaches to the patrol boats' harbors, and "enhance the capability of the South Vietnamese Navy to hit targets in the North." He called Secretary of State Dean Rusk.

"If we don't do something definitive to respond to this attack it will leave our ally here in the South with the impression that America flinches from direct confrontation with the North. We're asking the ARVN to stand and fight, and we won't do it ourselves? We need to send a signal that we aren't going to be intimidated."

"I understand your position, Max. But the president is balancing a variety of interests here. He's worried that a retaliatory attack will force us to reveal our covert activities, and will otherwise inflame public opinion."

"Look, I understand the political implications. But my view of everything has changed now that my boots are on the ground here. I'm more concerned that we not undermine our position with Khanh and the ARVN. It will reduce our leverage here if they don't think we are willing to respond when our own ships are attacked."

"Understood. I'll pass on your views to the president personally."

Taylor paused. He sat staring out the window, suddenly feeling very alone. "It's worse here than I expected. Khanh's government is a cesspool, full of corruption. Khanh himself seems unstable, neurotic, paranoid, disliked by his officer corps. My first meeting with him was a disaster. We could be the best army and political corps in the world and still not make this work. It keeps me up at night."

Rusk just listened, waiting for Taylor to continue. After a moment, he did. "I've been reading the after-action reports, reviewing the counterinsurgency results. It's not pretty. We've got a tremendous infiltrator problem in the ARVN and we are losing at the village level. The number of VC in the South is at its highest levels since we started keeping track. I'm concerned that if we don't bring the fight to the North we're going to lose."

There. I said it, thought Taylor.

Maxwell Taylor was no defeatist. He'd been a winner all his life and was now proconsul of the greatest power in the world in one of the poorest, most corrupt nations on earth. But, now more than ever he was unsure if he could succeed.

"Are you arguing that we should bomb the North?"

"Yes. We must show the North that we are willing to do what it takes to force them to sue for peace. If we hit their industrial base maybe they'll call off their war in the South."

Rusk took a deep breath. 30 days in Saigon had done a number on Taylor, he thought. He didn't like the air of desperation in Taylor's voice. "I'll make sure that the president sees your cable, and I'll convey your views, Max. Hang in there. It's not over by a long shot."

"I hope you are right, Dean. We need to be aggressive if we are going to hold the line here. Words aren't enough."

Rusk, who as a diplomat made his living with words, thanked Taylor and hung up.

Aboard the USS *Maddox*
The Gulf of Tonkin, North Vietnam
11:20 a.m. August 4, 1964

In 30-knot winds and a howling rain, the *Maddox* and the USS *Turner Joy* were some 100 miles off the Vietnamese coast, heading north. Commander Ogier was at the helm, while Captain Herrick sat off to the side on the bridge, clutching a coffee and trying not to spill it. In 20 years at sea, Herrick had always been amazed by how the ocean could take a destroyer displacing 5,000 tons and make it feel like a tin can.

Herrick was in a mood as foul as the weather. He had urged his bosses in the Pacific Fleet to resist the temptation to return to the scene of the attack on August 2. It was clear to him that the North saw his ships as an offensive threat, and in Herrick's mind, it made little sense to poke the bear. Unfortunately, the Pentagon had seen it differently.

At 2:45 p.m. the skipper of the *Turner Joy* radioed that his radar operators were picking up targets that indicated an impending attack. Herrick immediately went down inside the combat information center one level below the bridge. Three sonar operators were hunched over their screens, marking a series of objects that were moving toward the *Maddox*.

"What have you got?" asked Herrick.

"Sir, we are seeing target signatures at 12, 10 and 9 miles out. They are moving toward us at more than 20 knots."

"How sure are you that these are enemy targets and not noise signals from the storm?"

"These don't appear like storm signals, Captain. They read like boats at speed."

Herrick thanked them and returned to the bridge. He pulled Ogier aside and told him what he'd seen. Ogier indicated that he'd been in radio contact with the *Turner Joy* and they were requesting permission to fire on the targets.

"Permission to engage, Captain?" Ogier asked.

Herrick was uncertain, but decided that being aggressive in this case was the prudent choice.

For the next three hours, both the *Maddox* and the *Turner Joy* moved aggressively to avoid the enemy boats while firing their 5-inch guns, targeting radar signals that appeared and disappeared in the stormy sea. The *Maddox* crew, perhaps spooked by the attack of August 2, was particularly active, reporting that they had been repeatedly fired upon by boats that were coming from all angles and identified sightings of torpedo wakes, enemy cockpit lights and numerous radar and surface contacts. By the time the destroyers broke off their "counterattack," they had fired 249 5-inch shells, 123 3-inch shells, and dropped five depth charges.

Early that evening, Herrick began to have his doubts about the attack. He suspected that his sonar operators were overeager and prone to what he termed "situational paranoia." After speaking with the captain of the *Turner Joy*, he learned that only the *Maddox* had detected any torpedoes in the water. After some discussion with his signals team, Herrick determined that the *Maddox*'s operators were probably hearing the ships propellers reflecting off her rudder during the sharp turns made during evasive maneuvers. They had fired all those rounds at ghosts.

By 9 p.m. on August 4th, Herrick sent a flash—highest priority—message to Washington declaring his doubts:

Review of action makes many reported contacts and torpedoes fired appear doubtful. Freak weather effects on radar and overeager sonar men may have accounted for many reports. No actual visual sightings by MADDOX. Suggest complete evaluation before any further action taken.

Herrick spent the next hour reviewing more signals intelligence and then started to second-guess his previous flash message. Maybe an attack had occurred? Such was the fog of war. Herrick decided that he knew enough to know that he didn't conclusively know anything, and the smart thing to do would be to send all the signals intelligence he could to the Pentagon and let them figure it out.

National Military Command Center
The Pentagon
7:25 a.m., August 5, 1964

It was early the next morning in Washington when word of this new "attack" reached the Secretary of Defense in his office in the Pentagon, he immediately convened an emergency meeting in the "Tank," the Joint Chief's secure conference room on the Pentagon's "E" ring.

When McNamara entered the Tank, Deputy Secretary of State Cyrus Vance and National Security Advisor McGeorge Bundy accompanied him. Without preliminaries McNamara said, "I want to discuss specific options for retaliating against North Vietnam for what I consider to be an unprovoked attack against the United States."

McNamara found a willing audience for this discussion. He asked the Chiefs for the relative advantages and disadvantages of either retaliating with a "sharp limited blow" or mining the North Vietnamese coast to hobble their navy.

LeMay spoke first. "Mining the coast won't get their attention like airstrikes, Mr. Secretary. We can have B-52s in the air in," LeMay paused to look at his watch "90 minutes from the time you give the word." I recommend we hit them hard where it hurts. Let's grab them by the balls and squeeze."

Thank you for the visual, thought McNamara.

General Wheeler agreed. "Why are we talking in terms of 'limited' reprisals? Seems to me that if we are going to bomb them, we should make it really sting. Maybe they will think twice about challenging us again. We've already given the president a list of targets to hit, including fuel depots and naval yards in the heart of North Vietnam."

McNamara thought carefully about what he was about to say. He wanted the Chiefs to provide recommendations that were proportional to the attacks in the Tonkin Gulf, knowing that Kennedy would have little appetite for a substantial bombing of the North.

"General," McNamara said, addressing Wheeler, "your list is too broad and too aggressive—at least for now. The president has approved a limited strategy of 'graduated pressure' against the North. While this second attack may change his calculus, I'm proceeding as if he will want to have a proportional, targeted response. That means a sharp but limited strike, or something that hits right at their ability to launch their PT boats."

With the exception of LeMay, the Chiefs seemed mollified by McNamara's answer. They proceeded to discuss options, and together came up with a list:

```
Sharp limited strikes against such targets as PT boats, PT
bases, oil depots, etc.
Continued pressure by laying mines off the coast of Vietnam.
A combination of both 1 and 2.
```

The Chiefs then provided detail on the location of targets to be hit, and a plan for additional actions 24, 38 and 60 hours after the first attack.

Satisfied they had what they needed, Robert McNamara and McGeorge Bundy left for the White House.

CHAPTER 17

2234 Scranton Place
Alexandria, Virginia
8:20 a.m., August 5, 1964

"I got it!"

The O'Shea family was just finishing a quick breakfast of cereal and eggs when the phone rang. Elizabeth and her brother Kevin simultaneously jumped up and raced each other into the kitchen to grab the phone. Kevin was about to go off to college at William and Mary in the fall, and his summer was full of social activities fitting of a young man about to leave the nest.

Elizabeth, who had been closest to the kitchen when the phone rang, won the race and grabbed the receiver off the wall.

Giggling she answered, "O'Shea residence, Elizabeth speaking."

"This is the White House operator. Is General O'Shea available?"

Rolling her eyes as if getting a call from the White House was routine—which of course it was—Elizabeth said, "Dad, it's for you. Again."

Patrick got up from the table and went to the phone. "O'Shea here." He listened for a few seconds and hung up without another word.

Maddie O'Shea knew what was coming. She asked simply, "How much time do you have?"

Looking at his watch, O'Shea said "I need to be at the White House in 45 minutes. So, not much."

O'Shea sat back down and managed to finish enough of his breakfast that he wouldn't be starved; he had no idea when he'd be home or when he'd be able to eat again. It was an occupational hazard of his always-on-call work life.

The Residence
The White House
11:10 a.m., August 5, 1964

As O'Shea exited the elevator on the third floor of the White House, he bumped into a woman who was just leaving the residence.

"Well, I was hoping I'd run into you again!" said Ann-Margret, kissing O'Shea on the cheek.

"How have you been?" he finally asked, not knowing what else to say.

"Oh, I've been wonderful. I'm in town for the premier of my movie with Elvis called *Viva Las Vegas*." She reached into her purse and pulled out a pair of tickets. "Short notice, but come if you can. It's tonight."

O'Shea took the tickets. Maddie would probably enjoy going. "Thank you."

"Oh, no. I should be thanking you for passing my number to the president," she said with a wink.

"My pleasure." *Or more accurately, his pleasure*, thought O'Shea.

O'Shea and Ann-Margret stood there for another awkward moment before the Secret Service agent motioned toward the elevator and said, "This way, ma'am."

"Hope to see you at the premier!" Ann-Margret then gave O'Shea a dazzling smile and entered the elevator.

O'Shea watched the elevator close and stood there for a moment, marveling at what had just happened, before entering Kennedy's outer room in his bedroom suite. He found the president looking into a mirror as he tied a dark red tie. He looked refreshed, his face deeply tanned. On the outside, Kennedy appeared to be a vigorous healthy man, who had a visceral, physical appeal that he used—with both women and men—to great effect. Those who were close to Kennedy knew that this appearance of vitality hid a number of very serious health issues, the most significant of which was a chronic adrenal insufficiency malady called Addison's disease. The president wore a back brace, had special inserts in his shoes to assist with back pain and was otherwise generally in a state of discomfort.

It certainly didn't slow down his libido, O'Shea thought to himself.

Picking up a glass pitcher full of water, Kennedy motioned to O'Shea, silently asking him if he wanted some. When O'Shea declined, the president poured himself a tall glass and sat down in the chair opposite O'Shea.

"I've got McNamara, Rusk, Bundy and a few others coming to the White House to meet with me in 30 minutes. McNamara indicates that there has been another attack in the Gulf of Tonkin, and he has a revised list of retaliatory measures he wants me to review. That's all I know at the moment. Can you add some color to this?"

O'Shea nodded. "I stopped into the Situation Room before coming up and reviewed the messages from the *Maddox* and CINCPAC. There wasn't much that was definitive, but there were some discrepancies."

The president took a gulp of water and raised his eyebrow. "Such as?"

"Well, Captain Herrick seems confused about whether a second attack on the *Maddox* actually occurred; at first he said it definitely had not, and then later seemed to backtrack on that, saying it very definitely had. He sent a large number of the signals they received, and much of it is contradictory."

"So what's your sense of what happened?"

"Hard to say with certainty but my sense is that the *Maddox* crew, in the same waters where just two days before they were attacked, were jumpy. The possibility they picked up storm noise is pretty plausible."

"That's my guess, too. I know a few things about operating on the ocean in bad weather. It's scary and confusing." For a moment Kennedy was silent, lost in thought.

Finally, O'Shea said, "If there's nothing else, sir?"

"Actually, there is something else."

"Sir?"

"Do you mind when we are in private if I call you Patrick? It seems overly formal for me to be calling a fellow Irishman "General" when nobody else is around. Particularly now that you are helping me arrange my social calendar."

O'Shea was flattered. "I wouldn't mind at all, sir."

Kennedy laughed. "But you still have to call me 'Mr. President.'"

* * *

The meeting of the administration's foreign policy team was held in the Cabinet room inside the West Wing. The president sat at his designated chair, with his name engraved on the backrest, at the head of the long rosewood conference table. As was customary, immediately to his left sat Secretary of Defense Robert McNamara and to his right sat Secretary of State Dean Rusk. Also present around the table were Attorney General Bobby Kennedy, National Security Advisor McGeorge Bundy, CIA Director John McCone and Roger Hilsman. Rusk had purposely not invited his deputy, George Ball, preferring not to make this meeting on a Tonkin Gulf response into a debate on general Vietnam policy. O'Shea sat along the back wall, with McNamara's aide and an assistant to Secretary Rusk.

President Kennedy opened the meeting by asking McNamara to report on what had transpired in the Gulf of Tonkin. McNamara went over the details of the events in chronological order with his usual efficiency. He concluded by saying, "Mr. President, there has been some confusion as to whether this attack really took place, or whether it was due to bad weather and overanxious radar operators. Based on my discussions with Admiral Sharp and our analysis at the Pentagon, we believe the attack was real. It happened, for the record, well outside Vietnamese territorial waters and thus constitutes an attack on U.S. forces on the high seas."

The president said, "Are you saying that we have twice been attacked by the North without provocation?"

"Yes, sir. That's about right."

"Anyone here disagree with this conclusion?" Kennedy asked.

His brother Bobby and Roger Hilsman signaled that they did.

"Bobby."

"We don't have any real idea what happened out there, and given the covert activities we've been doing, you can hardly blame the North for defending themselves. I'm not sure that the second attack happened, but even if it did, it's pretty hard to see how this is not a clear-cut case of self-defense on their part. We've been playing in their backyard and they kicked us in the nuts. It isn't like we were walking down the sidewalk and they came over and coldcocked us for no reason."

As the Attorney General spoke, McNamara looked like he was going to come out of his skin. The president then turned to Hilsman, "Roger?"

"Mr. President, I have to say that striking North Vietnam on the basis of this evidence is dubious at best. It is one thing to make an affirmative decision to widen the war by striking North Vietnam as matter of policy; it is another thing altogether to do so like this, as retaliation for an attack that may or may not have taken place. This is a bullet that once shot, can't be put back in the barrel."

The president nodded. "So let's say for argument's sake that the second attack did happen, unprovoked in international waters." Looking right at McNamara, he asked, "What do we do about it?"

McNamara handed the president and others around the table a copy of the list of targets he had compiled with the Joint Chiefs, and explained to Kennedy that the Pentagon felt that these were in line with a limited 'graduated pressure' strategy: targeted strikes against specific targets related to the Tonkin Gulf attacks.

The president read the list and put it down before him. "Dean, what is likely to be the political fallout of striking the targets on this list?"

"Mr. President, I don't see any international fallout as long as we make clear that we are defending ourselves against an unprovoked attack in international waters. None of our allies are going to take issue with that."

"Mr. McCone, what impact would this have on our covert operations in the North and the activities of the CIA in Vietnam?"

"Sir, I think this will be a boon to the covert activities we are carrying out in the North," the CIA Director responded. "I can't say how this will impact the covert operations in the South, or whether this will encourage the VC to be more aggressive. Either way, I think we can handle it."

"Mac?" said the president to Bundy.

"I agree with Secretary McNamara. This list is proportional and well-designed. It will send a message without risking widening the war unduly, and I think will have a salutary effect on our South Vietnamese allies."

Kennedy listened but didn't say anything. He was having a sensation he'd felt more than once since surviving Dallas. It was like a form of déjà vu—an opportunity to see things again with a fresh perspective. He was again reminded of the gift of fate he'd been given, and how important it was for him to do what was right, and not just what was politically expedient.

After a few minutes the president ended the meeting.

Following the meeting, the president entered the Oval Office with O'Shea close behind, and walked immediately over to the bar on the credenza at the far side of the Oval Office. With his back turned he asked, "Gentlemen?"

Bobby looked at his watch and said, "It's a bit early for me." Looking at O'Shea, he raised an eyebrow.

"Nothing, Mr. President," said O'Shea.

"You guys are no fun," said the president, pouring himself a finger of scotch. "Bobby, General O'Shea has agreed that I can call him by his Christian name when we are alone. Since you're part of the family, I think that includes you. He's now officially 'Patrick.'"

How chummy, thought Bobby.

Bobby was unsure of what to make of O'Shea. He wanted to like him because he was Irish, but he was never truly comfortable with anyone who was close to his brother in a way that could undermine Bobby's influence.

They took their seats and the president sipped his scotch. O'Shea, still in uniform, sat ramrod straight and tried to look relaxed. It was hard for him to pull off. Bobby shed his coat and rolled up his sleeves and sat back deep into the cushions. "Christ, that McNamara sure wants to use his toys," Bobby blurted.

The president laughed and then looked at O'Shea. "Patrick, this is off the record, ok?"

O'Shea nodded, knowing that Kennedy wanted to speak freely, "Yes, sir."

"I'm clear about two things now," the president said. "First, the Pentagon really wants a fight. I think the Chiefs want to go much further than McNamara recommended. You heard what LeMay said after the first Tonkin attack—no question, he'd drop an H-bomb on Hanoi tomorrow if we let him. And second, I'm increasingly paranoid about the law of unintended consequences. I know that once we cross the threshold of sending jets into the North we won't be able to predict what happens next."

Bobby said, "The unintended consequence I'm really worried about is how Nixon is going to wrap this around your neck. When this gets out to the press—and it will get out—Nixon is going to skewer you with whatever decision you make. If we retaliate in a limited, controlled fashion, he's going to say it wasn't enough. And what if we do nothing at all? Well, he's going to brand you as soft on communism and you are going to be playing defense on this for the next three months."

The president knew his brother was right. Kennedy was really in a no-win position. The domestic political aspect of this was dangerous, which was why he needed to be very careful about how he played it.

Both Kennedys looked at O'Shea, expecting a comment. "Mr. President, you know my views already. I think that the Pentagon feels that since we are there we need to do what we can to support our forces and those of our ally. That's the mission they've been given. The real question is, I'm afraid, a political one."

"And what question is that?"

"Mr. President, I'm a military man. I don't even vote. Political questions are above my pay grade."

"Well, as the Commander in Chief, I'm ordering you to answer my question, General O'Shea."

O'Shea looked at the president and said, "The question really is should we be there at all?"

"Leave it to an Irishman to get to the heart of the matter," the president replied. Looking at Bobby he said, "Why couldn't you have come up with that?"

Bobby laughed. "Because he doesn't have to spend Christmas with you, Jack. That's the kind of question that can get you into a ton of trouble. Look, the reality is that we've spent the last three years talking about how vital South Vietnam is to our fight against global communism. We can't just say, 'Oops, never mind.' It doesn't work that way. We inherited a commitment from Eisenhower and we've continued and expanded that commitment. This is a mess we've helped make, and we aren't going to be able to just cut and run. At least not without paying a political price."

The president took a sip of scotch and said finally, "I know that."

The three sat in silence. Then the president said, "Patrick, if you don't mind, I'd like some time with my brother."

O'Shea stood up. "No problem, sir. You know where to reach me should you have any other questions."

"Thank you."

Once O'Shea had closed the door behind him, the president turned to his brother. "You remember how we handled Cuba? The Joint Chiefs—especially LeMay—wanted to commence bombing immediately and then invade. We resisted. We used the blockade and pressure to stare the Soviets down, and they blinked."

"They blinked because of the blockade and because there was a credible threat of force behind it."

"Exactly. That's my point. Military force isn't just a blunt instrument. It's also a tool of coercion. What I'm saying is that I don't trust the Pentagon to use it in that way. And maybe that's ok. That's not their job. But it means that I will never take the military's recommendations at face value."

"But you have O'Shea here inside our tent! He's part of the military. Aren't we taking a risk by having him as part of our internal deliberations?"

The president smiled. "Ah, little brother. That's where you are wrong. O'Shea is an intellectual as much as a soldier. He understands the stakes here, and I'm convinced that he doesn't want to waste the lives of his friends and brothers if it's a hopeless war. That's why I trust him. He knows that he has already put his military career in a vice and isn't likely to get it back."

Bobby nodded. "Well, I hope you're right."

"Me too, Bobby. Me too."

The Press Briefing Room
The White House
Washington, D.C.
8:30 p.m., August 7, 1964

Pierre Salinger, the White House Press Secretary, stood next to the president in an anteroom next to the briefing room. Kennedy was well schooled at dealing with the press; during his first term, he gave a nationally televised press conference on average every 16 days. Salinger was reviewing the briefing paper that had been put together on various subjects that might come up in the press conference, but Kennedy knew that the main topic that night was going to be Vietnam.

Since the meeting with his foreign policy team at the White House, the president had been busy laying the groundwork for this moment. He had met one-on-one with leaders in Congress on both sides of the aisle, and had put Vice President Johnson to work getting the Democrats in Congress on board. Kennedy found that there was very little appetite among Congressional leaders for getting deeper into Vietnam.

Just prior to going on television, Kennedy called Secretary McNamara and informed him of his decision: he was not going to authorize a retaliatory strike against North Vietnam at this time. But he offered the Pentagon a few consolation prizes, including an authorization to mine the PT bases if the aggression against DESOTO patrols continued. McNamara was disappointed but told Kennedy that he would inform the Joint Chiefs of the decision.

At 9 p.m., Pierre Salinger took the podium. "Ladies and Gentlemen, the president of the United States of America."

Kennedy strolled in and everyone in the room rose to their feet. Taking the podium, he said, "Please be seated." Hands immediately went up, but instead of calling on a reporter for a question, Kennedy said, "I have a short statement before taking questions. As many of you know, North Vietnamese PT Boats in the Gulf of Tonkin attacked the USS *Maddox* on August 2nd. Over the last 72 hours I have met with my National Security team and I have assured them that we will remain resolute in protecting our forces serving in Vietnam. However, the incident in the Tonkin Gulf does not change our stated policy in Vietnam, which is to support the South Vietnamese government against the communist forces inside of their borders. This is their fight and they need to wage it. We are there to assist them in every way possible short of engaging in offensive military operations against North Vietnam. That is a line I am not willing to cross, as it would signal a fundamental shift in our policy. This should not be done on the basis of retaliatory attacks, but after a careful consideration of our global strategic priorities and in full consultation with the Congress of the United States.

"That concludes my statement. Now I'm happy to take some questions…"

CHAPTER 18

431 An Duong Street
Cholon District, Saigon
9:10 a.m., August 19, 1964

Rock Francisci's .45 caliber automatic lay before him on the table in his dining room as he finished a breakfast of eggs, white rice, coffee, and orange juice. Francisci knew that he was now a marked man and didn't trust the lone doorman downstairs to stop a panhandler, let alone armed thugs doing the bidding of Nguyen Khanh.

Khanh's reaction to the Deputy Secretary of Transportation's murder the night of July 8 was swift, but it wasn't exactly the reaction that Francisci had hoped for. Rather than pull back, Khanh did the opposite, raiding the offices of Air Laos Commerciale twice over the past several weeks, wreaking havoc on Francisci's shipments and creating even more problems for him with the Guerini brothers. Using Conein as an intermediary, Francisci had tried to get a message to Khanh that he was willing to renegotiate the terms of their trading relationship. He was still waiting for a response. In the meantime, Francisci now knew that he was going to have to start looking for alternate routes to get his opium from Laos to Marseille. There were few good options given the security required and the need for a deep-water port that could handle freighter traffic.

Francisci could see that things were changing in Saigon, and not for the better.

Conein had been at MACV headquarters when word came down that Kennedy had sent his personal military advisor on a fact-finding mission to Vietnam, and that it was clear the president was reassessing everything the U.S. was doing. Harkins was apparently apoplectic about the visit, which he considered an intrusion upon his prerogatives as the head of the U.S. military effort in Vietnam. He even tried to get Conein to tail the colonel wherever he went. Though Conein refused that request, his network was deep enough that he was able to keep tabs on the colonel's activities. The colonel was asking a lot of questions that signaled that the status quo was not going to hold. Change was coming.

The one change that would be catastrophic for Francisci would be for the Americans to cut and run. The American presence in Vietnam was vital for the opium trade in Laos to continue. The Americans made Francisci's access to Laos possible, and any possibility that they could be pulling back was a direct threat to Francisci's business. That meant it was also a threat to the Guerini brothers and the Chicago Outfit as well.

The Playboy Club
116 East Walton Avenue
Chicago, Illinois
9:10 p.m., August 20, 1964

Hugh Hefner's members-only club had opened in 1960 and was an immediate smash hit among Chicago's movers and shakers. Drawn by the allure of exclusivity coupled with scantily clad waitresses dressed in bunny outfits, it was the place to see and be seen. It employed an elaborate system to alert Hefner when a particularly important VIP showed up. So when Sam Giancana showed up this night, the valet in front of the entrance immediately raised his hand with two fingers, making the sign of the "V." That told the bouncer just outside the door that a VIP was about to enter the club. The bouncer then pressed a hidden button; this button activated a buzzer inside the executive offices on the top floor of the five-story building, which in turn alerted the manager on duty. The manager then picked up the house phone that automatically rang the head of security, who knew where Hugh Hefner was at all times. The head of security then alerted Hefner and by the time the VIP reached the inside hostess desk, the owner and founder of Playboy Enterprises would be there to greet them.

"Sam, very nice to see you tonight," Hefner said as Giancana proffered—unnecessarily since everyone knew who he was—his Playboy Key, signifying his membership in the club.

Giancana nodded, handed Hefner his hat and said, "Who's playing tonight?" As a Chicagoan, Giancana was a blues lover, and the Club had a fine roster of talent that played there nightly.

"Luther Allison and Bo Diddley."

Giancana smiled. Once he got his business done he was going to very much enjoy the evening.

"Your guests are upstairs in your room." Hefner offered. Giancana had a regular table in the club's upper floor. He also had access to a private room where he attended to mob business, as well as the occasional tryst with one of the Bunnies who waited tables. As a rule, fraternization between the Bunnies and Playboy Club members was strictly prohibited; but then again, every rule was meant to be broken, and VIPs like Giancana broke them often.

When Giancana entered his private room his favorite Bunny waitress was just setting drinks down. The Bunnies were taught a specific backward lean called the "dip" which gracefully put drinks down while at the same time accentuating their bust line for the guests. It was extremely effective.

"Estelle, doll," Giancana said when he saw her. She was a tall, very buxom and very platinum blonde who had been Playboy magazine's "Miss October" of 1963. "I'll have the usual." Estelle gave him a dazzling smile and winked. Giancana felt a stirring in his loins; he'd definitely be seeing more of her later.

Around the table were the Chicago Outfit's capos—Frank Nitti, Tony Accardo, and Ross Prio.

Without so much as a hello, Giancana said, "Let's make this quick. I want to catch Luther's next set."

Nitti, Accardo and Prio all looked at each other. None of them wanted to be first to talk. The boss was not going to like what he heard. Finally, Accardo broke the silence. "Boss, we got potential problems with our opium supply in Laos."

"Laos? I thought we took care of that problem. Francis got Bobby to back off, and we've had good supply over the past few months."

Accardo nodded. "Yes, yes. The supply issue was taken care of. This is a different problem."

"Christ, what now?"

"Francisci is reporting that the CIA is saying that Kennedy may pull out of Vietnam altogether."

"So?" Giancana apparently didn't immediately grasp the consequences of what Francisci was reporting.

"So if Kennedy pulls out we lose all our influence with the South Vietnamese government, our access to the Laotian supply lines and our ability to get raw opium to Marseille."

"Fuck!" Giancana suddenly understood the problem. After a moment he asked, "How does Francisci know all this?"

"Apparently Kennedy sent his primary military aide to Vietnam earlier this year. According to the CIA, he was very pessimistic," Accardo replied.

"Who is this guy?" asked Giancana.

Just then Estelle returned with Giancana's drink. Standing next to the table, she dipped backward and placed the drink down. As she did, Giancana could smell her perfume. He again got aroused.

After Estelle left the room, Accardo said, "We don't know his name. But I'm sure Ross can find out."

"Ok. Let's do what we do. Get Ross to find out who this aide is and let's put the squeeze on him. I want him to be convinced he needs to recommend that America stay in Vietnam until the 21st century."

Nitti looked confused. "When is that?"

Giancana rolled his eyes. "The year 2000."

Nitti whistled. To him that seemed like forever.

The Old Ebbitt Grill
1427 F Street NW
Washington, D.C.
7:10 p.m., September 5, 1964

The Old Ebbitt Grill is the oldest saloon in Washington, dating from the mid 1850s. It was a favorite of D.C.'s lobbyists, where the "two martini lunch" was a staple and the dark booths offered plenty of cover for deals to be negotiated out of the public eye. It was also a place that Patrick and Maddie O'Shea had good memories, including a celebratory dinner the night that Patrick had been named as Kennedy's military advisor. Today was their 20th wedding anniversary and for the first time in a long time they were having a date night.

The waiter, dressed in a white shirt, black vest and black tie, came by to drop off a loaf of warm bread on a cutting board and take their drink order. "I'll have a Famous Grouse neat and the lady here will have a white wine," Patrick said. As the waiter retreated, Patrick looked at his wife and thought again how lucky he was. She was beautiful and had been a fantastic partner for the peripatetic life they'd lived over the past 20 years.

"What will happen now, Pat?" Maddie asked. Without specifying what "now" was, he knew what she meant.

"Honey, I don't know. I guess a lot of it depends on what happens to Kennedy in November. If he wins relection we'll be here for another four years. If we want, that is."

"Do you want?"

"I thought I did." Patrick reached for a piece of bread, slathering it with warm butter. "But the past several months have changed things. Changed me, actually."

She had an idea what he meant, but wanted to hear it from him. They hadn't talked much about his time in Vietnam since he'd returned. Patrick had been too busy, and too stressed putting the report to the president together. But over the past few weeks, things had begun to settle. She wanted to know what had happened in Vietnam. "Sweetheart, I need to know what's changed and why. Otherwise I can't help you. And whatever we do next, I want it to be our decision."

Patrick knew that she was right, and more than that, felt she deserved the truth. "It's hard to explain, Mads. I've always been a soldier. I take orders and then do my job to the best of my ability. That's the deal I made when I joined up. I always told myself that when that became impossible to do, I should get out." His voice trailed off. Maddie waited for him to continue. "I don't know anymore."

Maddie had never heard her husband talk like this and she needed to know why. "What's happened, Patrick?"

"When I was in Vietnam this last time, I watched good men die for something that I don't think is worth dying for." He stopped and looked at her. "I almost died for something that isn't worth dying for."

She suddenly felt a pit in the bottom of her stomach. She swallowed and asked, "How?"

He paused for a moment, considering how much detail to give her.

Finally he said, "We were in Nam Dong, up near the Laotian border. An infiltrator had gotten into our lines—in fact, there were many infiltrators that night—and he pointed his gun at me and pulled the trigger. Thankfully, the gun jammed."

Tears filled Maddie's eyes. She reached over and put her hand on his arm. "Oh my God," she said softly.

"You know, as bad as that was, it wasn't the worst of it. I've been shot at—hell, I've been shot before—and in combat you know that when your time is up, it's up. My time wasn't up. That makes sense to me. What doesn't make sense is the realization that we've been totally co-opted into an unholy alliance with people who don't deserve our support. And the CIA is even worse…" Patrick knew that he needed to stop talking. He looked around at the adjoining tables and lowered his voice. "It's a train wreck, Mads."

Maddie wasn't sure what to say. Luckily, the waiter returned with their drinks and she had a moment to compose herself. Patrick picked up his glass and raised it for a toast. "To us," he said.

She smiled. "To us."

After a moment, Maddie responded, "I've never seen you like this. You seem disillusioned. Are you?"

"Disillusioned isn't the right word. More disappointed. Not in the president. Not yet, anyhow. But by senior leadership in the Pentagon and at MACV in Saigon. I feel betrayed. I guess you go to war thinking that those who send you there are going to think carefully about why they are doing so. Of course politics are always a part of the equation. I know that. But in the end, you expect that you won't be sent on a march of folly."

"Is that what Vietnam is? A march of folly?"

"It is. It's absolute folly. Can't be won, shouldn't be fought and isn't worth a single American life."

Maddie nodded. "Wow," she said. "Where is Kennedy on this?"

"I'm not certain. He has a lot of pressure to maintain the status quo.

All I can do is try to influence him in the right direction. After that its truly up to him."

"What if he doesn't make the right decision? What then?"

Patrick had obviously given this question a lot of thought. He was torn between principle and pragmatism. "Honestly I'd be tempted to retire. But I'm not sure we can afford that. With your parent's medical bills and the kids going to college, I'm not sure how we would make ends meet."

Maddie didn't know how to respond to that. She knew he was right, and she'd been stressed about their finances herself lately. "I'd feel awful if you stayed in just for the money."

"You know my father worked his job long after he loved it. He was the oldest patrolman on the force. But he had two kids to feed and a wife to support. He'd never have quit in protest of anything. He'd have tried to fix whatever it was, but he wouldn't have quit."

Maddie never got to meet Patrick's father. But she knew what a deep, complex influence he had on her husband. And she knew that what Patrick was really saying was that quitting wasn't an option for him. He wasn't built that way. Kennedy might make the wrong choice, but Patrick was going to stay with Kennedy for the duration.

"To the future," Maddie said, raising her glass.

Office of the Under Secretary
The Department of State
Washington, D.C.
10:45 a.m., September 16, 1964

"Mr. Secretary, I have a Patrick O'Shea for you."

Punching the intercom he said, "Do you mean General O'Shea?"

"I'm not sure. Should I ask him?"

Ball sighed. "Yes, Mrs. Jenkins. Thank you."

After a moment she said, "Mr. Ball, yes, he says he's General Patrick O'Shea."

Interesting.

"Mrs. Jenkins, which phone line is he on?"

"He's not on a line, Mr. Ball. He's here. Standing in front of me."

"Please send him in."

Ball stood up and reached for his coat, which he put on, buttoning the top button. He knew O'Shea was the president's military advisor, and had met him on several occasions. He wondered if Kennedy had sent him here to get Ball to reconsider his views on Vietnam.

When Patrick O'Shea walked through the door he was not in uniform. He wore a tailored dark suit, white shirt and striped tie. If Ball didn't know O'Shea was in the military, he'd have mistaken him for a business executive. After shaking hands, Ball gestured for O'Shea to sit down at the conference table in his office.

"General, to what do I owe this impromptu visit?" asked Ball.

"Mr. Secretary, please forgive me for dropping in unannounced. I thought of calling, but…well, it didn't seem like the appropriate topic for the telephone."

"Oh? Really? And what topic might that be?"

Without missing a beat, O'Shea said "Vietnam."

I knew it. He's here to try and talk me into supporting escalation, thought Ball.

"General, I'm flattered that the president thinks my opinion is that important, and I appreciate you coming all the way over here. But I'm not interested in having you try and turn me into a supporter of any plan to bomb the North, or to otherwise escalate our involvement in that Godforsaken place."

"Actually Mr. Secretary, the president doesn't know I'm here. But I know he does value your opinion, which is why I wanted to meet with you. Only I want to join forces with you in making sure that we get out of Vietnam as soon as we can."

Ball sat with his mouth slightly agape, trying to make sense of what he just heard. "So you are against us escalating in Vietnam, General?"

"I am, but I wouldn't stop there. I'm for de-escalation. I'm for getting out. Full stop."

"Can I ask why?"

O'Shea spent the next 20 minutes talking about his trip to Vietnam and his findings, making it clear that above all else, he didn't believe that the South Vietnamese government was worth fighting for, and could never become a viable democratic government. He left out any discussion of the opium issue. "It's not a fight we can win, Mr. Ball."

By the time O'Shea finished, Ball believed that he was sincere. And the prospect of having an ally so close to the president was something Ball couldn't have planned, but would certainly prove beneficial. Ball had been looking for a way inside the Kennedy inner-circle. Now he had it.

"General, what plans do you have for the rest of the day?" When O'Shea indicated nothing, Ball looked at his watch, checked his calendar and punched the intercom. "Mrs. Jenkins, please clear my schedule until just after lunch. General O'Shea and I will be in a conference. Please hold my calls unless it's Secretary Rusk, the president himself, or Nikita Khrushchev."

Even after three years working for her boss, Mrs. Jenkins still didn't get his sense of humor.

"Sir?"

Ball sighed. "Just hold my calls, Mrs. Jenkins."

Ball took off his coat and hung it up next to the door. He then turned to O'Shea and said, "You might want to get comfortable General. We're going to be here awhile."

CHAPTER 19

Arlington National Cemetery
Arlington, Virginia.
2:20 p.m., September 19, 1964

Frank Nitti had been standing in Section 20 of the cemetery for more than thirty minutes. It was a lovely fall day but he was getting increasingly agitated that his contact in the FBI was late. Arlington's vast open space was a great place to meet someone in private without fear of someone eavesdropping. Ironically, Nitti, who'd put more than his fair share of people in graves, hated cemeteries—he was superstitious, and didn't like being among the dead.

By the time FBI Special Agent Rick Ross approached, Nitti was pissed. "Where the fuck have you been?"

"Take it easy, Frank. I'm risking my ass even being here. You should be thankful I came at all."

"You should be thankful I don't put a bullet in your head."

Ross hated the situation he was in—his weakness for gambling had put him in debt to the Giancana's crew when he'd been stationed in the Chicago field office. He'd been offered a choice: work for them, pay back the $100,000 he owed them with interest, or take a bullet to the back of the head. It was an easy decision. He'd been on the "payroll" ever since.

"So what'd you find out?" Nitti asked.

"My sources at the White House tell me that Kennedy has a military aide who is advising him on Vietnam, and is very close to the president. He lives in Virginia. He has a wife and two kids. We did a deep background check on him. He's pretty clean. Main thing is that he's having some financial challenges. His wife's parents are both ill and he has a kid in private college and another about to graduate high school."

"What's he do for Kennedy?"

"He's the president's point man on Vietnam. Went there earlier this year on behalf of Kennedy. Has unfettered access to the Oval Office. He's as close as you are going to get to Kennedy without getting to Bobby or his kids."

Nitti thought for a moment. "This is good. What's his name?"

Ross handed over an envelope. "It's all in there. Every Thursday after work he goes to a bar in Georgetown near the university to meet with fellow Citadel graduates. It's an informal alumni club. That's your best bet to get to him."

Nitti took the envelope and smiled. "Ok. We'll arrange a sting and you will be there to make it stick."

"Listen, this has got to stop. If this pans out for you, I want out."

Nitti grinned. "You'll get out when we tell you. Not a moment sooner. Got it?"

"Yeah, Frank. I got it."

Cooper's Bar and Grill
Georgetown, NW
6:30 p.m., September 20, 1964

The blonde woman wore a tight blouse and a pencil skirt, with black pumps. She was tastefully sexy in a way that would fit in with the college coeds and business people who frequented Cooper's. All eyes were on her as she made her way along the bar, eyeing an open seat next to a handsome gentleman in uniform.

"Excuse me, is this seat taken?" she asked the man.

Patrick O'Shea, nursing a scotch and soda, looked up at her and smiled. If someone was going to sit there, it might as well be her. She was undeniably beautiful. "Please" he said, pulling out the stool for her. He watched her shimmy onto the seat, and she pressed against him as she did so. He could feel her soft breast on his arm and caught a flash of her legs as she swiveled to the bar. He felt a flash of adrenaline—even as a married man, the power of a beautiful woman had a visceral effect on him.

O'Shea caught the attention of the bartender. "What are you drinking?" he asked her.

"Vodka tonic, please."

O'Shea ordered her a vodka tonic and another scotch and soda for himself. When the drinks came he turned to her and said, "Cheers." They clinked glasses.

After an hour or so of small talk and several more drinks, O'Shea realized that the woman was becoming increasingly tipsy—and increasingly handsy. She was testing every ounce of willpower he had. She'd inched closer to him and frequently placed her hand on his thigh as she talked, rubbing her breasts up against his arm and giving him winning smiles. She was very randy and made it clear she was available to him.

O'Shea was about to pay his check so he could avoid this danger zone when she knocked over the remnants of her drink onto O'Shea's lap and uniform tunic. She shrieked and started apologizing profusely, while grabbing a napkin she proceeded to pat the napkin all over O'Shea's crotch area. O'Shea abruptly stood up, embarrassed that her touch had begun to actually arouse him. He mumbled, "It's fine, it's fine," and turned to find the restroom.

As he did, the woman fell against him, putting her arm around his waist and whispering, "Don't go." At the same time she deftly dropped a small vial in the pocket of his jacket. He quickly disengaged himself from her and headed down the bar to the safety of the men's room.

When O'Shea returned to pay his check he found the woman had disappeared. With a mixture of relief and disappointment, he paid for the drinks. It was time to go home before he got himself into trouble.

* * *

As O'Shea crossed Holmes Run creek in Alexandria he noticed a patrol car pull in behind him. He thought about how much he'd had to drink and was pretty sure he wasn't drunk. He slowed down just in case, and made sure to come to a complete stop at Sanger Avenue before turning right.

The patrol car lights came on even before he'd finished the turn, followed by a single blast of the siren. O'Shea swore to himself and pulled over to the side of the street. He knew the drill from his father: stay calm, roll your window down and make sure you don't make any sudden movements.

"Is there a problem, officer?"

"Good evening sir. Can you please get out of the car?"

"What for? I wasn't speeding and I made a complete stop."

"Sir, have you been drinking?"

"I had a few drinks over the past three hours. I'm not drunk."

"Yes, sir. Please step out of the car."

O'Shea sighed and opened the door, stepping out on the street. He then noticed another patrol car had stopped, and two more police officers were standing by.

"Seems like overkill for a traffic stop," he said.

"Sir, please step onto the sidewalk."

O'Shea complied. He stood before the officer and was then asked to perform what is known in the trade as a field sobriety test. He was asked to walk in a straight line and touch his nose while standing on one foot. He performed it perfectly.

"Sir, it appears you are driving while under the influence. I am hereby placing you under arrest. Please turn around, face the patrol car, put your hands on the trunk and spread your legs."

"I am not drunk and I performed that test perfectly." O'Shea knew enough not to invoke his status as a senior army officer or tell them he worked in the White House for the president. That would likely only inflame the situation, and require them to call a supervisor. O'Shea didn't want any more attention on this.

"Sir, you can tell it to a judge. Please turn around and face the car."

O'Shea reluctantly complied. He would fight this tooth and nail. As he tried to remember his lawyer's phone number, the officer patted him down, emptying his pockets out on the car's trunk. When he reached into his jacket pocket and pulled out a vial, he whistled. "Well, well, what do we have here?" holding the vial up for O'Shea to see.

"What the hell is that?" O'Shea asked loudly.

The officer held the vial up to the light. "My guess is that it's cocaine, or maybe heroin. Hard to tell until we get it tested."

"What the hell?" O'Shea's mind was racing. He was confused. How had this happened?

Taking out his handcuffs, the cop cuffed O'Shea and read him his *Miranda* rights. He put O'Shea in the back of the patrol car, drove him to the station and placed him in a holding room. After 45 minutes a man in a dark suit came in.

"General, my name is Ross and I work for the FBI."

O'Shea was visibly surprised. "What does the FBI have to do with this?"

Ross pulled out the vial. "This appears to be cocaine," he said, not answering O'Shea's question.

"I've never seen that before," said O'Shea.

"Maybe the judge will buy that explanation. Maybe not. But I don't have to tell you what even being accused of felony drug possession will do to your career now, do I? There goes your pension and there goes your job in the White House. That would be a real shame."

Ross' mention of the White House set off alarm bells in O'Shea's head—he hadn't said anything about working there. There was something else going on here. Was he being set up? If so, why?

"How do you know I work in the White House?"

Ross smiled. "I've got my sources."

"Fuck you. What do you want?"

"I represent some powerful interests that want you to do whatever you can to convince the president to stay the course in Vietnam."

O'Shea was totally taken aback. Who would want that and why? He could think of a few obvious answers—the military, the defense industry—but he knew there were other ways that they could send this kind of message to an active duty officer. This was something else. "How do you know the president is evaluating Vietnam? What makes you think I can influence him?"

Ross sighed. "Look, let's cut the shit, ok? I know that you are the president's primary military advisor. I know that there are discussions going on right now on whether to expand the war. We want that to happen."

O'Shea sat in stony silence. His mind was reeling. Finally he asked, "This isn't the FBI who is asking this. So who wants it?"

Ross smiled. "It doesn't matter. What matters is that there are powerful forces very interested in the war continuing. All we are asking is that you do your best to ensure that happens."

"And if it doesn't happen?"

"Then this arrest report," Ross said, holding up a folder, "lands on the desk of the *Washington Post*."

O'Shea hated being squeezed like this. He had no idea who these "powerful forces" were, but he knew that if they could get inside the FBI and set him up in such a professional way, they were not to be discounted. O'Shea was in real trouble here, and he knew it.

O'Shea felt he needed to explain a basic fact to Ross—that the president is the Commander in Chief and makes his own decisions. "The president doesn't do what I say. You understand that, right?"

"Well, in this case you better hope he does."

Between a rock and a very hard place, O'Shea decided he had no choice but to play for time. He'd agree to this outlandish demand and figure out how to fix it later. He had no other choice.

"Ok," he said simply. "I'll do what I can."

"Good choice." Holding up the vial and the arrest report, he said, "I'll keep these in a safe place. If you succeed you'll get them back. And if you fail…" Ross let that last sentence dangle.

O'Shea had heard enough. "Take me back to my car."

CHAPTER 20

Downtown YMCA
Washington, D.C.
9:15 p.m., October 7, 1964

A tipsy Walter Jenkins stumbled down the stairs to the basement of the YMCA. He'd just been to a party celebrating the opening of *Newsweek*'s new Washington office—the free booze was flowing, and he'd had more than he should have. Now he had another thirst to quench.

Jenkins was Vice President Lyndon Johnson's "indispensible aide." He'd been with Johnson since coming to Washington in 1939 and served as the treasurer of Johnson's family corporation. He was a fellow Texan and the most trusted member of the Vice President's staff.

Entering the YMCA locker room, he went to the sink and washed his hands. In the mirror he caught the eye of an older man, 62-year-old Hungarian immigrant named Andy Choka. Choka smiled back at Jenkins and winked. Without a word, Jenkins put a dime in one of the pay-toilet stalls and opened it up. He went in but left the door ajar.

By the time Choka entered the stall Jenkins was sitting on the toilet. He quickly pulled Choka toward him, undoing his belt and pulling down his pants.

Then all hell broke loose. Two plainclothes officers from the morals division had been staking out the YMCA and were watching from the showers. They suddenly yelled, "Police!" bursting into the stall. One pulled Choka out by the shirt, causing him to fall to the tile floor. The other grabbed Jenkins by the arm and pulled him roughly out, propelling him against the wall.

Placing handcuffs on Jenkins he said, "You are under arrest for disorderly conduct. You have the right to remain silent..."

The Vice President's Residence
3133 Connecticut Avenue, N.W.
Washington, D.C.
7:30 a.m., October 15, 1964

Lyndon Johnson was just finishing breakfast on his balcony on a beautiful fall morning. In Johnson's mind, living in this fully-staffed, ornate, art deco residence was the only good thing that had come out of being Kennedy's vice president. The irony of this was not lost on him—he had been literally inches away from becoming president of the United States, and instead of being the most powerful man in the free world, he was now exiled to purgatory. Fate was a fickle bitch, indeed.

Johnson had a spread of Texas newspapers in front of him from the previous day. Since becoming vice president he'd had the *Dallas Morning News, the San Antonio Express-News* and the *Houston Chronicle* flown in from Texas every day. He had a deal with American Airlines to put papers on their in-bound planes from Dallas to Washington National Airport. Johnson wanted to know what the local papers were saying about him, and as the election grew closer, it was vital that he understood how the Kennedy campaign was playing. He didn't want to get blamed for losing Texas to Nixon.

Johnson heard the phone ringing and hoped it wasn't for him. He didn't like being disturbed during his morning reading time. Thirty seconds later, however, his wife Lady Bird came out to the patio. "Lyndon, honey, the phone's for you. It's Clark Clifford."

Johnson immediately knew that something was wrong. Clifford wouldn't be calling Johnson at home on a Wednesday morning unless there was a problem. "Ah, shit," he murmured.

Lady Bird gave her husband a dirty look and handed him the phone. "Did somebody fall off a horse, Clark?"

"Ah, well, in a manner of speaking, yes. I'm at Abe Fortas' house. We're here with Walter." Fortas was a Washington lawyer who had known Johnson since the 1940s.

"Walter? What's Walter doing at Fortas' house?"

"Walter is totally distraught. His doctor has been here since last night, keeping him sedated. Abe and I learned yesterday that Walter was arrested on October 8th in the basement of the old YMCA building near the White House."

"Arrested? For what?"

Clifford drew a deep breath. "Apparently he was picked up by two morals plainclothesmen for disorderly conduct. They regularly watch the Downtown Y for lewd behavior."

"Walter being disorderly? Hell, Walter is the most orderly man I know."

"Yes, sir. But apparently Walter was arrested for… ah… a lewd act with another man in a bathroom stall."

Johnson almost dropped the receiver. "What? Walter Jenkins with another man? That can't be right!"

"Walter said that he began getting calls from reporters. Apparently, someone tipped off the *Washington Star* that there was something interesting on the DC police blotter for the night of October 7th. They sent two reporters over and found the entry for Jenkins' arrest. And to make matters worse, one of the policemen mentioned to the reporters that Walter had been arrested on a similar charge in 1959."

"Goddamnit!"

"I couldn't believe it either. Abe and I visited Newbold Noyes at the *Washington Star*, and then went to the editor at the *Washington Daily News* and Russ Wiggens at the *Washington Post*. We've asked them to sit on the story and they've agreed for the moment. But this is going to break at some point soon."

By this time Lady Bird had come out to the patio to hear what the ruckus was about. She sat down opposite her husband and waited. It sounded like their dear friend was in trouble.

"What about the RNC? Any chance they know about this?" Johnson asked, referring to the Republican National Committee.

"If they don't yet, they soon will. It's only a matter of time. I wanted to let you know so you could get ahead of this with the president."

Shit!

Johnson's stomach was in knots. This was going to be a nail in his coffin with the Kennedys. He had been told to keep his nose clean and do no harm. This was would be a potential problem for their campaign.

"What do you think I should do, Clark?"

"I think you need to get over to the White House and let the president know what's going on. This is going to be a PR nightmare and you can bet the RNC is going to use this to question the morals of the administration. It's unfortunate but true. So best thing is to get ahead of this, Lyndon."

"Ok, thanks. And thanks for the heads up. What is going to happen to Walter?"

"I think we are going to take him to the hospital. He needs help."

Johnson grunted and said goodbye to Clifford. Walter Jenkins wasn't the only one who needed help.

The Oval Office
The White House
9:00 a.m. October 16, 1964

Johnson had to wait for an hour while the president finished up a visit with the Belgium Minister of Foreign Affairs. Johnson had managed to wrangle 30 minutes of Kennedy's schedule from Mrs. Lincoln, telling her it was of vital importance that he speak with the president immediately. She looked skeptical, but finally relented.

The president was standing behind his desk when Johnson walked in, clearly trying to alleviate some of the discomfort he was feeling in his back. He looked surprised to see Johnson.

"Lyndon, do we have a meeting scheduled? If so, I must have missed it."

"We don't Mr. President but I told Mrs. Lincoln that this couldn't wait." Kennedy could tell from the look on Johnson's face that something was wrong.

"What's happened?"

"You know my aide, Walter Jenkins? The one who helped you get that little 'issue' straightened out when we were in the Senate together?" Johnson was referring to a problem that Kennedy had with a lobbyist who was under the impression that Kennedy had been having an affair with his wife and was threatening to go to the press, or worse. Jenkins was able to convince the lobbyist that access to the United States Senate would be cut off if he didn't drop the issue. Coming from the top aide of the Senate Majority Leader, the lobbyist got the hint and left Kennedy alone. It would have been an embarrassing incident for someone who already had his eye on the presidency. Johnson wanted to point out how Jenkins had helped Kennedy before breaking the news.

Kennedy had a feeling he wasn't going to like what he was about to hear. "What about him?"

Johnson decided to give it to Kennedy straight, though the words were hard for him to say. "Well, on October 7th he attended a party at *Newsweek* and afterward went to the basement of the YMCA and got himself arrested while performing a sex act on another man."

Kennedy was momentarily speechless. "Is this a joke?"

From Johnson's expression, it was clearly not a joke.

Kennedy's mind was racing, trying to make sense of what he just heard. He sat down heavily in his chair. "Lyndon, that was a week ago. Why am I just finding out about it now?"

"Because Walter kept it to himself. In fact, after he got arrested he posted a $50 bond and went back to his office to work. Clark Clifford found out about it yesterday and he and Abe Fortas have been trying to keep the press at bay."

"The press? Oh, damnit, Lyndon! That's all we need. Who knows about this now?"

"The *Sun*, the *Post*, and the Republican National Committee. Pretty much everyone, I'm afraid. Mr. President, Walter is obviously ill. Overworked. Or maybe he was set up by the Republicans. I don't know. I'm willing to say whatever you want me to say to take the heat off you."

Kennedy held his hand up, asking Johnson to stop talking. He needed to think. After a few minutes, he said, "Where is Walter now?"

"He's at the hospital in Alexandria."

Kennedy walked over to his phone and picked it up. "Mrs. Lincoln, track down my brother and get him over here as soon as possible."

Johnson sat down on the couch and decided that he had said enough. To his surprise, Kennedy sat down opposite him and said, "Look, Lyndon, this is a political problem that I think we can handle. Maybe we can say that it was a one-time thing that was the result of overwork or stress."

Johnson's shoulders slumped. "Well, that's what I thought, too. But, apparently, Walter was arrested for a similar act in 1959. I never knew about that, of course."

"Of course," Kennedy said. He believed Johnson, but was nonetheless angry that this was going to make trouble for them just three weeks before the election.

The intercom buzzed and Mrs. Lincoln announced that the Attorney General had arrived. Bobby Kennedy came in and the moment he saw Lyndon Johnson his mood visibly changed. He gave the president a look to the effect of "what's he doing here" and immediately sat down next to his brother.

Bobby Kennedy looked at his brother and then back at Johnson and then back at his brother. "Ok, I give. What's going on?"

"The vice president has a story to tell you. Go ahead, Lyndon."

Johnson recounted the story again for Bobby. As he spoke he could see him go from shocked to mad to apoplectic. By the time he was finished, Bobby was pacing the room.

The president knew that his brother was going to be mad, but he wanted to focus their discussion on a solution, rather than the problem. "Bobby, let's discuss damage control, ok?"

"Damage control? Richard Nixon's a boy scout who's going to wrap this around our necks. The RNC is going to make this an issue of morals, and you can just imagine how this will play in middle America: 'Long-time aide and close personal friend of the vice president arrested for the second time in a men's room while on his knees. And he wasn't praying.'"

"So what do we do?" the president finally asked.

"I think we have to get out in front of this. Lyndon needs to frame the issue in a press conference. He needs to say that Jenkins is in the hospital and hasn't been well, and that he has resigned his position and will be returning to Texas to recuperate."

Lyndon was afraid this was coming. "Resign? Is that necessary? That will totally crush Walter."

"I'm afraid it's necessary, Lyndon," said the president. "He needs to go somewhere far, far, away. Quietly."

"Lyndon, can you get Clark or Abe to go out to the hospital and get Walter's resignation? We need that as soon as possible," Bobby said.

"Yes."

You heartless bastard, thought Johnson.

"Good. That will give us some time to work on our story. We need to focus this on Jenkins' mental health problems and make it a story about a personal failing."

"It is a personal tragedy, not a personal failing. Walter is a good man with six kids. He's given 20 years of service to this country. He's ruined."

For a moment, Bobby was chastened. "Yes, of course it is. I didn't mean to imply it wasn't. But he got himself—and us—into this mess. He's going to have to face the music."

Johnson knew Bobby was right. In fact, Johnson was also angry with Jenkins, even as he felt sorry for him.

The president stood and said, "Ok, we know what we need to do. Lyndon, take care of the Jenkins resignation and work with Pierre and Bobby on your statement. I'll see what I can find out about what the RNC plans to do with this information."

Johnson stood up and thought to himself that this was the lull before the storm. He knew he'd pay a price for this down the road, and he knew he wouldn't see it coming. That's the way Bobby Kennedy played the game. There was always a knife to stick in someone's back. And this time it would be his.

The Vice President's Residence
3133 Connecticut Avenue, N.W.
Washington, D.C.
7:30 p.m., October 19, 1964

"Christ almighty, Bird!" Lyndon Johnson rarely yelled at his wife but this time he couldn't help himself. "What were you thinking? We have planned out the public response to this very carefully and you are ruining it!"

"Lyndon, don't you dare use that tone with me. Walter and Marjorie are members of our family, not baggage to be thrown overboard. I'm not abandoning them no matter what the White House is ordering."

Johnson took a deep breath. He knew he wouldn't get anywhere with his wife by being angry. "Ok, Bird. I understand. But did you have to make a public statement?"

That afternoon, Lady Bird Johnson had released a statement to the press:

"My heart is aching today for someone who has reached the endpoint of exhaustion in dedicated service to his country. I know our family and all of his friends, and I hope all others, pray for his recovery."

"Yes, I did. And I'm not about to let other people who don't know our Walter paint him as some sort of deviant. He's a good man. An honest man, Lyndon."

"I know he's a good man. But God, what a mess! He's got a problem, obviously. He needs to get help. But he needs to do it someplace far away from here. I'm in enough trouble as it is!"

Lady Bird Johnson looked at her husband and realized that this was not something that she and Lyndon would ever see eye to eye on. She knew this side of her husband existed—the coarse, Machiavellian schemer and power broker—but she preferred to view him as the sweet father to their two daughters and the chivalrous husband he was when they were together. That was her Lyndon. So she would pick up the slack and take care of Walter Jenkins.

Later that week, after Jenkins returned home from the hospital, Lady Bird went out to see him and Marjorie as they packed their home for the return trip to Texas. She was beyond sad for the loss of such close friends who knew the real Lyndon Johnson, and who had been an invaluable support to her husband. Life wouldn't be the same without the Jenkins' in their lives. But she knew that Walter was a shattered man, and it would be good for him to get out of the spotlight and return to a place where people didn't judge like they do in Washington. "DC is an ugly place," she always said.

And in this case she was right.

Office of the Vice President
Old Executive Office Building
Washington, D.C.
9:30 a.m., October 20, 1964

"Mr. Johnson, I have the attorney general on line two," came Juanita Roberts' metallic voice over the intercom.

Here comes the other shoe, Johnson thought to himself.

Pressing the button for line two on his phone, Johnson picked up the receiver. "This is the vice president."

"Lyndon, you are about to earn your keep."

"Excuse me?"

"You are going to get on a plane and spend the next two weeks criss-crossing that shit of a state you call home, and you are going to shake hands until your fingers ache. I want you to beg, borrow and steal every vote you can. Is that clear?"

Lyndon Johnson stood up to his full 6'3" height, as if that would intimidate Robert Kennedy over the phone. He took a deep breath before replying. "Look, Bobby, you don't have any reason to talk—"

Bobby cut him off mid-sentence. "Your homosexual aide has created a huge potential scandal for us, and I hold you personally responsible."

"The fallout from the Jenkins problem has been minimal. Nixon hasn't even used it as an issue and I don't think he will. The press has let it go. You need to let it go, too."

"I'll be the judge of that," Bobby replied tersely, "and I've just seen the latest polling in Texas. It's within the margin of error, and Nixon is spending time there and buying ad space on television in all the major markets. Texas is the whole reason you are even on the ballot. If we lose Texas, we lose the election, and you are finished in politics."

Johnson squeezed the phone so hard that his fingers turned white and he struggled to control himself. "Is the president asking me to go to Texas?"

Bobby Kennedy laughed. "Do you think I'd be calling you unless the president was on board? My brother is asking you to go to Texas. I'm not asking—I'm telling you to go and to not come back until the eve of the election. As you can imagine, the president is not going back to Texas himself. So it's up to you."

Lyndon Johnson didn't blame the president for not wanting to go back to Texas. He doubted he would ever go there again.

"Do we understand each other, Mr. Vice President?"

Johnson hung up without another word. He'd go to Texas all right, but he wasn't going to dignify that little shit Kennedy with a proper goodbye.

CHAPTER 21

The National Museum of Natural History
Washington, D.C.
2:10 p.m., October 22, 1964

A civilian-attired Patrick O'Shea stood admiring the Tyrannosaurus Rex in the Hall of Dinosaurs. He had taken his son to see this exhibit many times when Kevin was young. It brought back good memories.

"My, what big teeth you have," came a voice from behind him. O'Shea turned to see Agent Rick Ross dressed in his customary dark suit and thin black tie.

Ross' presence snapped O'Shea out of his daydream. Without a word he began to walk and Ross fell in next to him.

"Any progress, General?"

"Oh, sure. I've got the president under my thumb," O'Shea replied without looking over at Ross.

"For your sake I hope you know this is no joking matter."

"Listen, I'm doing my best," O'Shea said, half-heartedly, "but there are a lot of moving pieces and I don't have control over most of them." He was trying to manage expectations, though he wasn't sure it would do much good.

As if on cue, Ross said, "I don't think excuses are going to go over well. You are going to need to produce. Or it will get very messy."

O'Shea started to get pissed. "So you've said."

Ross decided to take another tack. "So is the president close to a decision?"

O'Shea hated divulging information like this. So he said something so innocuous as to be harmless. "He might be, but it will not be before the election. If he wins, that is." The 1964 presidential election was two weeks away.

Ross knew that the election was a wildcard: If Kennedy won, the calculation was that the president would be free to make any decision he wanted, without consideration to political pressure. That, of course, could cut both ways. If he lost he would never make a major decision like this as a lame duck. He'd leave it for Nixon. Which is why Giancana was working so hard on behalf of Kennedy's campaign. He was going to ensure he won.

"Don't worry. He'll win."

O'Shea looked at Ross for a long moment, trying to decide if this was a hint as to who was paying him. He couldn't connect the dots. "Are we done?"

"Yep," Ross said, walking back the way he had come.

The destruction was unbelievable, and Ambassador Max Taylor had to see it with his own eyes. Just after midnight, VC guerillas set up mortars within the rice paddies and palm groves outside the base and started firing. Over a 39-minute period, four U.S. servicemen were killed, 72 were injured, and 17 of the 36 B-57 aircraft stationed there were destroyed.

Taylor was livid about the attack, and it again showed that the North was working to escalate the conflict. They were taking the fight now directly to the Americans, and no longer had any reservations about killing them. This was a turning point for Taylor.

Inside Bien Hoa's secure command center, Taylor composed a cable to Washington that didn't mince words. He described the attack as a "deliberate change of the ground rules that must be met with an appropriate act of reprisal," and made specific recommendations as to which targets to hit and in what order. Taylor was again doubling down on his previous recommendation that the U.S. bomb the North to get them to the negotiating table.

Coming just two days before the U.S. presidential election, Taylor knew that getting action on this request would be futile at best. What he was hoping for is to increase the pressure on Kennedy to move on the North in the coming weeks, after what everyone expected would be a victory over Richard Nixon.

In his response to Taylor, Secretary of State Dean Rusk admitted as much, saying that the timing of the election made any kind of decisive response impossible. But Rusk also hinted that the time was nearing for some kind of decisive "get in or get out" inflection point, and that this would be the topic of conversation after the election was over. He noted that the Joint Chiefs were putting significant pressure on the president to make a decisive and sustained attack against the North, and that events like last night's attack on Bien Hoa was going to harden their position even further.

Taylor knew that the president was putting himself in a tough spot with the military. The lack of a clear decision in that face of direct attacks on U.S. forces was straining the civil-military relationship, and it was even possible that a revolt among the United States military—in the form of a very public resignation—could happen if the situation got worse. Taylor knew firsthand that Kennedy's trust in the military's leadership had been severely shaken by the Bay of Pigs disaster and the Cuban Missile Crisis, when the hawkishness of the Joint Chiefs had threatened to plunge the U.S. into a nuclear exchange with the Soviets. Over the past few years, the president had become a resident skeptic of military advice and thus took nothing at face value. But it was getting to be time for the president to make a decision, and Taylor hoped it would be soon.

The Kennedy Family Compound
Hyannis Port, Massachusetts
11:15 p.m., November 3, 1964

By tradition, the Kennedy family spent election night where they'd been every election since John first ran for Congress, at the family compound in Cape Cod. Covering six acres on the Atlantic Ocean, Joseph Kennedy had purchased the property in 1926. The main house had six bedrooms and was a white clapboard style typical of Cape Cod. It had been the gathering of many family vacations, birthdays and holidays over the years.

That evening, the president and his brother and their extended families sat in the living room of the main house and watched the election returns. By 11 p.m. Eastern Standard Time it seemed clear that the election was going to be a nail-biter.

"Well, looks like we won't know anything until tomorrow just like last time," the president's mother, Rose Kennedy, said to her son. The 1960 presidential election was so close that the result wasn't known until almost noon the next day. "I guess I'll go to bed." The 74-year-old matriarch of the family rose, kissed her son goodnight and went upstairs. Her husband was already asleep—Joe Kennedy has suffered a severe stroke in 1961 and required around-the-clock care.

President Kennedy was antsy and excused himself. "I'm going upstairs." As he neared the stairs, however, he decided to go outside onto the large wraparound porch that faced the sea. It was a cold night, and Kennedy wanted to feel the brisk air against his face. He stood leaning against the rail and stared out toward the ocean, where he could make out the blinking lights of ships headed down the Massachusetts coastline. He could sense the Secret Service agents standing in the shadows, but for the moment he was as alone outside as a president could be.

Kennedy tried to get a read on what he was feeling. He wanted to win but not for the reasons most people thought. Since Jackie's death the job had become his refuge, a way to keep busy without thinking about what he'd lost in Dallas. He'd made the job his mission, and wanted to make sure that his children felt that the sacrifice they'd made in giving their mother to the nation hadn't been in vain. It had given him the motivation to run for re-election and it would now define the next four years in office. He had now run his final campaign. There was no more glad-handing or favors to curry. Win or lose he was now a free man.

And he was also a lonely man. He had truly loved Jackie, and was thoroughly embarrassed about how he'd behaved when she was alive. The philandering and partying with movie stars—he'd taken Jackie for granted, thinking that like his father, he could do as he pleased and his wife would accept it as a hazard of marrying a Kennedy. It wasn't until she was gone that he realized how stupid he had been, and how shallow he'd allowed their relationship to become. He'd saved all the good things for others—the stories, the intimacy, the friendship. She was there to raise his kids and look good on his arm. He felt a tremendous sense of guilt.

Would he have another four years in power? And if so, what would he do with it? How would he leave his mark? He wasn't yet sure. As he looked out into the dark night he knew that whatever it was, it needed to be a legacy that his children would be proud of.

* * *

At five a.m. Bobby Kennedy knocked on his brother's door. Jack had only managed to sleep for a few hours, and was already up and getting dressed.

"Come in."

Bobby threw open the door. Beside him stood his brother Teddy and his sister Eunice.

"Congratulations, Mr. President," they said in unison.

"We won?"

"We won, Jack. They just called Illinois and Michigan."

"What was the margin in Illinois? As close as last time?" Kennedy had won Illinois by less than 9,000 votes of 4.75 million cast.

"This time you won by a landslide. 22,000 votes!"

Kennedy smiled. Clearly, the deal he struck with Giancana had been wise, because without the unions' help, he would have lost Illinois and the election. "What will be the final electoral college count?"

"271 for you and 265 for Nixon," his brother Ted said.

"Jesus, that was close."

"Close like a hand grenade, Jack. You won. That's all that matters."

Patrick O'Shea awoke the morning after the election to learn that he'd be employed for at least another four years. He turned on *The Today Show* and was shocked to see how close it had been. The president took 50.1% of the popular vote and again won a squeaker of an election. But a win is a win, as they say.

At breakfast that morning, Maddie seemed jubilant at the result. She craved the stability they had now, being in one place for the past four years had been very important as Kevin and Elizabeth neared adulthood. All the moves over the years made it hard for the kids to make consistent connections, and being in Alexandria had been a great benefit.

In truth, Patrick was ambivalent about Kennedy's win. As much as he needed the job, he was constantly looking over his shoulder, waiting for the drug bust to rear its head. He didn't know how it would happen— an anonymous leak to the *Washington Post*, a letter to Robert Kennedy, a visit from the Alexandria police at home with an arrest warrant in hand. But he was certain it would come unless Kennedy chose not to abandon South Vietnam. He considered telling the president what had happened and why. He knew the president trusted him and would believe his story. But he also knew that it would put Kennedy in an impossible situation. Once Kennedy was aware of the arrest he'd be in in a bind. He could put pressure on the FBI and the Alexandria police to make the arrest go away, but that was dangerous as there were too many people who could leak the arrest to the papers, and if it came out that Kennedy had known about it and covered it up, he'd be in serious political trouble. It was just too dangerous.

So, O'Shea was on his own with an impossible task—to try and get the most powerful man in the world to do the opposite of what O'Shea desperately wanted him to do.

CHAPTER 22

Outside the Village of Tay Ninh
Republic of South Vietnam
1:20 a.m., November 21, 1964

Rock Francisci had been packed and ready to go for the better part of a week. That's when he heard from the Guerinis that two of the Union Corse's men had been kidnapped and tortured by ARVN units loyal to General Khanh, their mutilated bodies dropped outside of the French Embassy in Saigon. It was only the start—other members of the Saigon underworld involved in the passage of opium and heroin were being systematically arrested, and many died under mysterious circumstances while in custody.

Francisci could see a clear pattern. Since the U.S. presidential election, something fundamental had shifted with the Americans. He had initially turned to Conein for protection, but when he did Conein made clear that the CIA had lost its motivation to intervene to keep the flow of opium moving and there was nothing that could be done for Francisci. The Union Corse's control of the opium trade had been squashed, and with it the lucrative links to Sam Giancana and the American market. The clock was ticking and Rock Francisci had to get out of Vietnam.

That was easier said than done. Khanh had tightened security around the Ton Sun Nhut airport and the Air Laos Commericale offices were now under 24-hour surveillance. He couldn't get near. Three of his planes had been seized and the offices searched. There was nothing left for him there. Fortunately, two of his company's Beechcraft C-45 aircraft had been out of the country during the seizures and Francisci had managed to keep them squirreled away at a remote airstrip in Laos. That would still allow him to stay in business, and it might even save his life.

At that moment he was crouched in a ditch outside of a small airstrip six miles outside the city of Tay Ninh. He was awaiting the arrival of one of his planes from Laos, which was supposed to land just long enough to pick him up. The ground was muddy and he had ruined his favorite leather shoes he had bought in Paris. They'd cost him more than 100 Francs.

"Shit," he muttered under his breath.

Because the airstrip was unlit, he had brought a flashlight to signal the plane when it got near. The instructions to the pilot were to buzz the field at 100 feet and if Francisci was there, he'd signal the pilot with the light. He'd been waiting there for more than an hour when the distinctive sound of the Beech's dual Pratt & Whitney R-985 Wasp Junior engines could be heard. Putting out more than 450 horsepower each, the engines were powerful enough to carry more than 5 tons of cargo over the mountainous terrain of Vietnam and Laos.

Francisci listened intently in the darkness as the Beechcraft approached, dropping quickly down out of the sky and racing down the length of the airfield at less than 100 feet. As the plane passed, Francisci turned on his flashlight and waved it over his head. He had no idea if the pilot had seen him. The arrangement was for the pilot to make two passes. If he didn't see him after the second time, the pilot would be gone and so would Francisci's chance at freedom.

Fortunately, the pilot did see Francisci's light and on the second pass made a perfect landing on the dirt strip, reversing thrust on the engines as quickly as possible to minimize the post-landing roll. The pilot wanted to be in and out as quickly as possible.

Spinning around, Francisci stood up with his bag and began running toward the plane which had now slowed to a crawl. Just then, headlights appeared at the foot of the runway, and two military jeeps appeared, racing down the runway at full speed.

The Beech C-45 is a "tail dragger," meaning it has a wheel on the tail and when on the ground sits at a steep angle. The co-pilot of the plane had opened the door and dropped the stairs, which just skimmed the surface of the runway as the plane continued to move. As Francisci got closer to the door, he managed to throw his bag up the stairs, which hit the co-pilot in the chest and knocked him backward and on to his rear end. Francisci then lunged for the stairs, catching his foot on the lowest rung and hitting his face on the top step, breaking his nose and causing it to bleed all over his clothes. By this time the co-pilot had returned to the doorway and managed to pull Francisci fully into the plane, grabbing the stairs at the same time and bringing them to a close.

"Go! Go!"

The pursuing Jeeps had covered more than half the runway and were headed right for the plane. The pilot immediately spun the plane around and put both throttles to maximum power, and the plane, empty, save for the pilots, Francisci, and his bag, hurtled forward. The pilot, a former French Air Force fighter pilot, pointed the plane right down the centerline in a game of chicken. He knew that the law of physics was on his side given the power and weight of the plane, and so he was betting that the drivers of the jeeps would blink first.

He was right, but not in the way he expected. One of the jeeps immediately peeled off and stopped at the side of the runway, and two soldiers got out and started firing their M16s. At first the fire was wild, but gradually they got their range and as the Beechcraft approached, stitched a line of bullets across the fuselage. Inside, Francisci was glued to the floor of the

cargo area, hoping that he would be out of the field of fire. His nose continued to bleed and hurt like a son-of-a-bitch. He didn't need to get shot, too.

Fortunately for Francisci and the pilots, the ARVN soldiers proved
to be very poor shots, and the Beechcraft managed to lift off just 100
feet from the other jeep that, much to the pilot's relief had slammed
on his breaks as he realized that the plane was not going to stop. The
plane's landing gear just missed the top of the Jeep's aerial.

At the rear of the plane, Francisci lay against the fuselage, sweating
profusely. He had never been so scared in his life. He was not used to getting shot at—he was a gambler but not a fool, and he had found success in
life by playing odds that fell in his favor. He now hoped that getting out of
Vietnam would allow him to build new routes from Laos into Thailand, and
improve his odds of keeping a good relationship with the Guerini brothers.

The Winter White House
Palm Beach, Florida
2:20 p.m., December 9, 1964

"Daddy, I miss Mommy," Caroline said, as she and her dad played together in the pool. Caroline's brother, John Jr. was sitting on the lap
of Kenny O'Donnell, who was sipping a Coca Cola at a poolside table.
All of Kennedy's political aides doubled as babysitters and child-care
workers. It was now part of the job.

"I miss her too, sweetheart. Mommy is in heaven watching over you.
She can see you right now." Jack looked up into the bright afternoon
sky. Caroline did too, and waved.

"Hi Mommy! I love you."

God this is hard, thought Kennedy.

O'Donnell watched the conversation between his boss and Caroline and
winced. There was nothing to be said or done, which made those who spent
their lives supporting Kennedy terribly frustrated. For all the activity during

the daytime, they couldn't do anything about the evenings and the weekends, or the vacations, where the absence of the kids' mother was so apparent.

Kennedy loved the Palm Beach house. His father had bought the estate in 1926 and the Kennedy family spent many Thanksgivings there. Mediterranean style, with a pool that faced the Atlantic Ocean, Kennedy found it peaceful in a way that Hyannis Port was not. The property abutted the beach where a large concrete retaining wall made a perfect perch to watch the kids play in the sand. When Bobby's family was there it was a veritable summer camp. But for most of this week, only Jack and the kids, along with the normal complement of staff, were in residence.

That changed with the arrival of Patrick O'Shea, who had flown down on an Air Force plane to Cape Canaveral Air Force Station in Brevard County, then making the four-hour drive to Palm Beach in a government sedan. O'Shea normally enjoyed the drive along coastal A-1A, but not today.

The ostensible reason for his visit was to prep the president for a series of national security meetings that were planned for mid-December, where O'Shea knew that critical decisions on Vietnam were going to come up. Up until his little run-in with the FBI in Georgetown, this was to be the first salvo in his attempt to help George Ball move Kennedy toward the "get the hell out" position on Vietnam.

However, with his arrest and the visit he'd had from the FBI that had now changed. For the past week he'd been doing as he was told—preparing an alternate argument for the president that was designed to keep the U.S. engaged in Vietnam as long as possible. He'd taken MACV and the Pentagon's rosiest assessments of progress and compiled them into a cohesive argument as to why they needed to continue forward. He believed almost nothing of what he'd written, but he'd written it anyway, and was prepared to deliver it as convincingly as he could.

On the long drive South he thought about his father.

Once, when he and his brother Tim were young, they had been caught shoplifting candy from the neighborhood market. The shopkeeper had given them a pass, knowing that they were the sons of a police officer. His brother was ecstatic at having avoided what would certainly have been a stinging punishment from their father, but Patrick was troubled. He'd known he had been caught doing something wrong, and somehow not being punished disturbed the natural order of things. He had been taught to tell the truth even if the consequences were bad, and had come to believe that taking your punishment was the only way you could truly put something behind you. Unlike his brother, Patrick felt no victory in escaping his father's wrath.

So, when his father got home that night he promptly ratted himself out. He managed to avoid implicating Tim—his brother needed to deal with that moral struggle on his own terms. When his father heard the story he was upset but not angry. Patrick's punishment was harsh—three weeks of extra chores, no weekend movies and no baseball—but not nearly as harsh as it would have been had he not confessed. That was vividly borne out a week later, when his dad heard from the shopkeeper that Tim was also involved. Tim, for his lack of honesty, got punished severely.

That was a lesson that O'Shea thought about often. It seemed particularly appropriate for today.

Was he going to lie to the president to save himself?

By the time O'Shea arrived in Palm Beach, Kennedy and the kids were out of the pool and the president was relaxing at a table, shielded from the sun by a large blue umbrella. "Patrick, welcome to sunny Florida," the president said. O'Shea took a seat and placed his briefcase on the ground next to him. He wore his Class "A" green uniform with black tie, and immediately began to sweat.

"I know I can't order you to take off your coat and tie, because it would be against regulation and I'd hate to get you in trouble," Kennedy joked.

"I'll be fine, sir. It's a lot cooler here than in the jungle, that's for sure."

The president knew this was a veiled reference to the mission into

Laos. "Speaking of the jungle," Kennedy reached into a folder that sat on the chair next to him and pulled out a letter written on yellow paper. "I'd like you to read this," he said, handing it to O'Shea.

O'Shea took the letter and unfolded it. At the top it said "Telegram," but it was clearly typewritten. At the bottom was the signature of Ho Chi Minh. O'Shea looked at Kennedy with wide eyes.

"This is the response to that delivery you made for me."

```
President Kennedy:

Your letter was most appreciated.  I regret that the
opportunity for cooperation has now passed.  My letter
to President Truman so long ago came at a different
time.  Our National Liberation Front is now committed to
one Vietnam, united in its independence.  We will not
negotiate away the liberty of our peoples, and will not
rest until the brothers and sisters of north and south
are once again part of a unified nation.
```

Ho Chi Minh

```
Ho Chi Minh
```

Though O'Shea hadn't read Kennedy's initial letter to Minh, it was clear from this response that Kennedy had made an offer to meet with him to talk peace, and to welcome North Vietnam into the community of nations if he agreed to cease infiltration into the South.

Kennedy looked at O'Shea and waited for a reaction. Getting none, he said, "I hope you can see now why I sent you into Laos."

"Yes, sir."

Kennedy sighed. "I wish I could have done it differently, and I know I put you in harm's way. It's unfortunate to be in a position that I can't trust my own government to play things straight. But I knew that had I used normal diplomatic channels, the letter would have leaked and created a firestorm, and I'd have spent all my time doing damage control with McNamara and Bundy. I wanted to see if there was an opening before dealing with all that crap."

O'Shea, who was well aware of the power of entrenched interests inside of government, replied, "Of course, Mr. President."

"And so now we know."

O'Shea looked down at the letter again. "Yes, sir. I guess we do."

Just then a white-jacketed mess steward appeared and asked O'Shea if he wanted a drink. "Coke, please," said O'Shea.

The president, pointing to his still full drink said, "I'm fine, Manuelo, thank you."

"The navy really knows how to do food service, Patrick. You have to admit that we've got the Army beat on that front."

O'Shea laughed. "I'll give you that one, Mr. President. The navy does a fine job with canapés."

"We had a good night last week," the president said, an oblique reference to the results of the election. Kennedy knew that O'Shea's career had hung in the balance and that beating Nixon was personally important to him.

"Yes, sir. By the way, congratulations on the win."

"I didn't make it look easy, did I? Glad I can't run again. Don't think I'd survive a third time."

Manuelo dropped off O'Shea's Coke and put down a bowl of mixed nuts.

Kennedy then asked seemingly out of the blue, "When you were wounded in Korea, did you think you were going to live?"

O'Shea was surprised by this question. "Honestly, I didn't have much time to think about it. We were cold and just trying to stay alive. I was too busy worrying about my men."

Kennedy thought for a moment. "Funny, because when PT 109 was cut in half by that Jap destroyer, I had the same reaction. The only thing

I cared about was getting the eleven men on my boat safely off that deserted island we ended up on."

"That's because we fight for each other."

"I'm not sure those who haven't been in the military—or in combat—understand that. Even as Commander in Chief I still feel that way—especially so."

O'Shea thought he understood what the president was driving at. He still saw himself as a commander of men who were depending on him to take care of them and to do the right thing. It was a very heavy burden to bear.

"All of which makes the next few weeks so critical. We have a series of National Security Council Meetings coming up and I have told McNamara, Rusk and Bundy that it is my intention to figure out what we are going to do in Vietnam in 1965. I want you to know my thinking at this point is that all options are on the table."

"Yes, sir."

"The good news is that winning re-election has freed me from the politics of all this. So let's get to work. Where should we start?"

O'Shea took a deep breath and pulled out a pair of folders. One of them contained the argument he'd compiled to argue for escalation. The other was the memo he and George Ball put together, arguing forcefully for the opposite.

Two gates the silent house of sleep adorn...

This was his moment of truth. "Mr. President, I've prepared a number of reports for you, but what I want to start with is..." O'Shea didn't finish his sentence. He sat staring at the president. He couldn't stop thinking about his father.

After a long moment the president said, "Patrick?"

"What I want to start with is a memo put together by George Ball."

He couldn't do it. He put his own folder back in his briefcase. He'd take his punishment.

"Well, I know what position this is going to take," Kennedy said, chuckling.

O'Shea smiled. "Well, yes, sir. Secretary Ball is not shy about his position. But I think you will find this very enlightening," he said, handing the memo to Kennedy. It was entitled, *"Validity of the Assumptions Underlying our Vietnam Policies"* and dated October 5, 1964.

"This was written over two months ago. Why didn't I see this sooner?"

"As I understand it, Mr. President, the memo was withheld from you by Secretaries Rusk and McNamara. I can't say why."

The president shook his head. He knew why. The president looked down at the papers in front of him. The summary that O'Shea and Ball had put together at their clandestine meeting at the State Department was on top.

Kennedy read the summary carefully, focusing on its final paragraph:

As I see it, we have essentially four options in front of us now in Vietnam:

Continue with the present policy. This approach would lead to more of the same: gradual failure and deterioration of our position.

Send U.S. troops to South Vietnam. This would result in the worst of both worlds: high U.S. casualties and a prolonged quagmire in Vietnam's rice paddies and jungles.

Bomb the North. Clearly preferable to b) above, but still a holding action which forestalls further decisions to come, and invites greater offensive response from the North.

Negotiate a political settlement. This is the preferred approach to our policy, ensuring a coalition settlement that would enable us, as in Laos in 1961, to extricate the U.S. without further American casualties.[1]

---

1 Halberstam, *The Best and The Brightest,* 491–499.

The president looked up from the memo. "So I gather you support these findings?"

In for a penny, in for a pound, thought O'Shea.

"Sir, in full transparency, I helped Secretary Ball write that summary."

"Really? Now that's interesting. I hope that Secretary McNamara didn't see you heading into the State Department."

"No chance of that, Mr. President. I was careful."

The president nodded and thumbed through Ball's 67-page memo. He returned to the summary page and read out loud a sentence that stuck out: "And once on a tiger's back we cannot be sure of picking the place to dismount." He looked at O'Shea and said, "George has a way with words. That's a powerful image."

"It is, Mr. President. I think it's spot-on."

The president took off his Ray Ban sunglasses and cleaned them with his napkin. "I hate communism, Patrick. I truly do. It's anathema to all the values I hold. I pledged when I was first elected to bear any burden to further the cause of freedom. I still feel that way. I'm going to have a hell of a time explaining to the American people why this isn't a burden we should bear."

O'Shea felt comfortable enough with the president to say what was really on his mind. "Maybe. But if George Ball is right, you will have to explain to the American people how you got us mired into an intractable war that can't be won that will cost the lives of many Americans."

Kennedy thought for a moment. "But what if you and Ball are wrong? What if this is the first domino to fall? What if this leads to hundreds of millions of people being subjugated under communist rule?"

O'Shea shrugged. "That's why they pay you the big bucks, Mr. President."

"Whatever they are paying me it's not enough. This fucking job has cost me a lot more than money."

"I know."

After a moment, Kennedy drained the last of his drink. "Ok. Let's review what arguments we are likely to hear next week when we convene the NSC. I want to be prepared for the options I'm going to hear."

O'Shea dipped into his briefcase and came out with a stack of notes. "Ok, let's start with the Joint Chiefs of Staff…"

The Office of Clark Clifford
President's Foreign Intelligence Advisory Board
Old Executive Office Building
Washington, D.C.
2:00 p.m., December 11, 1964

"Mr. Clifford, I have Secretary Ball on two."

Picking up his phone and punching line two, Clifford said, "Hello, George. I figured I'd be hearing from you this week."

"Well, we have the seventh game of the World Series happening in two days' time and it's the bottom of the ninth and we're down by two." Ball was an inveterate baseball fan and loved to use sport analogies. "We need our cleanup hitter at the plate."

"And whom might that be?"

"Babe Ruth Clifford." Ball laughed.

"You should know, George, that football was my sport, but I get your point. You want me to argue the case for getting out."

"I do, and so does the president's military advisor, Brigadier General O'Shea. He and I have been working on a brief that I'm going to send over to you today. I think it will help to clarify our—your—arguments."

"But wouldn't it be more convincing coming from you, George? You are number two at State. And you know this issue cold."

"Clark, I've been arguing this position now long enough that my words have lost impact. It's expected of me and I've become something of the house pessimist. We need a fresh voice with some clout, and yours is it."

"Send over the brief and I'll have a look. I'll call you if I have questions."

"Clark, I appreciate this. More than you know." Ball said this with emotion, and it wasn't lost on Clifford.

"I do know, Mr. Secretary. We'll give it all we've got," Clifford said with emotion of his own.

As Clark Clifford entered the Cabinet Room, President Kennedy smiled and waved him to an empty seat at the table. As the Chair of the President's Foreign Intelligence Advisory Board, Clifford was a regular attendee of senior foreign policy meetings. He looked around the room and realized that this was indeed the "World Series" of meetings—the entire national security establishment was present. And seated along the wall behind the president was Patrick O'Shea.

Clifford had prepared his brief as any good lawyer would, and knew it cold. But he was under no illusion that the argument would be well-received by this audience. The men at this table were deep believers in American power and primacy, and had taken away from the success of the Cuban Missile Crisis that they could use power in a controlled way to achieve political ends. If they could stare down the Soviets, they certainly could force North Vietnam to do what they wanted. This was not a group inclined to retreat.

The president opened the meeting by reviewing the series of recommendations he had in front of him from the Pentagon, all of which included one form of escalation or another, each starting with an intensified bombing campaign against North Vietnam. Putting the papers down in front of him, he turned to George Ball and asked for his views.

Ball stole a glance at Clifford and realized that he couldn't pass the baton after the president asked for his opinion. So he dove in.

"Escalating is exactly the wrong response. We can't win. The war will be long and protracted, with heavy casualties. The most we can hope for is a messy conclusion. We must measure this long-term price against the short-term loss that would result from withdrawal."

The room was silent and Ball, now with a head of steam, continued. Uncovering a chart that correlated public opinion with American casualties in Korea, Ball predicted that the American people would not support a long and inconclusive war. "World opinion would also turn against us. I know that withdrawal is difficult for any president, but any great captain in history at some time in his career has had to make a tactical withdrawal when conditions were unfavorable. This is like a cancer patient on chemotherapy. You might keep the patient alive longer, but he would be fatally weakened in the long run."

Clifford thought that Ball had done himself proud. Looking at Kennedy, he could see the president cogitating on Ball's argument.

Finally, the president said, "George, wouldn't all those countries—Korea, Thailand, Western Europe—say that the United States is a paper tiger? Would we lose credibility by breaking the word of two presidents if we give up as you propose? Everyone has been telling me that it would be an irreparable blow."

"Mr. President, I most definitely disagree. In fact, I believe that most of the places you mentioned think that South Vietnam isn't worth saving because it has a corrupt, unstable government."

Kennedy nodded and then went around the room. One by one the senior national security establishment lined up against Ball, making the familiar argument that abandoning South Vietnam would be a radical turn-about after all the U.S. had done and to make it an independent nation and a bulwark against communism.

Clifford took careful notes, but never had the opportunity to speak up. He'd have to find another venue to argue his case to Kennedy. After two hours the meeting broke up, with the president thanking everyone and telling them that he was heading to Camp David for the weekend to review his options.

As Clifford passed Ball in the hall, he gave him a thumbs-up and whispered, "You hit that ball pretty well, George."

To which Ball said, "I'm not sure it got out of the park."

* * *

Just as Clifford was preparing to leave the White House, a Secret Service agent found him at the West Portico waiting for his car. He told Clifford that the president wanted to see him in the Oval Office.

The president was debriefing with his brother when Clifford walked in. "Clark, sorry you didn't get to chime in today. I do want to know what you think. Would you and your wife Marny want to come up to Camp David on Saturday? Bob and Margie McNamara will be there as well. We would get a chance to relax and have some private talk about Vietnam."

Knowing that George Ball would see this as the opportunity to argue their case opposite the chief prosecutor of the opposing side, Bob McNamara, Clifford immediately accepted.

The East Room
The White House
11:00 a.m., December 17, 1964

Patrick O'Shea and Colonel Ed Summers stood to the side of the stage beaming as they watched President John Kennedy approach the podium. Standing at attention behind him, flanked by a color guard and the flags of the three branches of the U.S. military, was Captain Roger Donlon.

"Ladies and Gentlemen, distinguished guests and members of our armed forces. I am pleased to have this opportunity to present our nation's highest award for valor, the Medal of Honor, to Captain Roger Donlon, U.S. Army, for actions in South Vietnam on the night and early morning of July 5 and 6th, 1964. Serving as the commanding officer of the U.S. Army Special Forces Detachment A-726 at Camp

Nam Dong, Captain Donlon distinguished himself with courage above and beyond the call of duty when a reinforced Viet Cong battalion suddenly launched a full-scale, predawn attack on the camp. Over a period of six hours, Captain Donlon repeatedly risked his life rallying the troops under his command, and coordinating the camp's defense while being wounded several times by enemy fire. Because of Captain Donlon's gallantry, intrepidity and dedication to his men, Camp Nam Dong was prevented from being completely overrun, and the lives of more than 450 men under his command were saved.

"I want to also note that this is the first Medal of Honor awarded since the end of the Korean War more than ten years ago. Its award today to Captain Donlon represents not only one man's heroism, but the hard work that our brave Special Forces community is doing in Vietnam against the communist incursion, and is a fine example of the capabilities that the Green Berets bring to the battlefield."

With that, President Kennedy turned and draped the star-shaped medal with the blue and white starred sash around the neck of a clearly embarrassed Roger Donlon. After shaking Donlon's hand, Kennedy started applauding and soon the whole room was giving Donlon a standing ovation.

CHAPTER 23

Camp David
Catoctin Mountain Park, Maryland
1:00 p.m., December 19, 1964

It was a short 25-minute flight to Camp David from the White House aboard the presidential helicopter, a Sikorsky VH-3 Sea King. Clark Clifford and his wife Marny shared the helicopter with Robert and Margie McNamara and their son Craig. Also on board was Patrick O'Shea and presidential aides Kenny O'Donnell and Larry O'Brien. The president and his children, along with Bobby Kennedy, had flown up the previous day.

Camp David was originally built in 1935 during the New Deal as a recreation camp for federal employees and their families. During World War II, Franklin Roosevelt began using the camp as a presidential retreat, taking advantage of the altitude and clean air as a tonic to his ailing health. Roosevelt issued a set of instructions on how the buildings should be remodeled and asking for the construction of what became

Aspen Lodge, which resembled the Roosevelt winter vacation home in Warm Springs, Georgia. The camp was renamed the USS *Shangri La*, until Dwight Eisenhower christened it "Camp David" after his grandson, and the name stuck.

Clark and Margy Clifford unpacked their overnight bags inside Birch Cabin, one of the many scattered private cabins on the Camp David grounds. They had a few hours to relax before dinner, and they took a stroll around the wooded grounds, bundled in jackets and scarves in the 40-degree weather. The McNamara's were in nearby Dogwood Cabin, while the president stayed as usual, in Aspen Lodge. His children stayed in Witch Hazel Cabin which had a nursery and caretaker quarters for the children's nanny and was adjacent to Aspen.

Walking along the trails, Clifford went over the argument he was going to make to the president, and prepared himself to rebut the points that he was certain McNamara would bring up. The lines seemed pretty clear at that point and he didn't expect much new information to be introduced. Clifford's main question now was whether the president truly remained open to persuasion. Would any argument on either side make a difference at this point? George Ball certainly hoped it could, but no one was really certain. The president largely kept his own counsel when it came to Vietnam. All Clifford could do was argue his brief and hope that the judge and jury sided with him.

* * *

The meeting Clifford had been waiting for took place just after dinner in the Aspen Lodge. The president, dressed in khakis and a blue sweater, sat at the head of the dining room table. Clifford sat to the president's left and directly across from McNamara, and Patrick O'Shea sat next to Clifford. The Filipino stewards who staffed Camp David brought coffee and some after-dinner chocolates and set them in the center of the long mahogany table. Aspen Lodge was more like a hunting lodge than a five-star hotel, but it was comfortable and offered an opportunity for the president to focus on the very important issue at hand.

"I've asked you both up here because we are on the precipice of a major decision on Vietnam. The situation in Saigon continues to deteriorate and it is now clear to me that we are at a turning point in our commitment. If we are to stay we will need to dramatically escalate our military support of South Vietnam, including taking offensive actions against the North. If we are not to take those steps, then we must get out—hopefully in a way that both preserves the lives of our military and maintains as much of our honor as possible." The president stopped and looked at both men. "Do you both agree with this assessment?"

Both Clifford and McNamara said in unison, "Yes, sir."

"Good. You both agree on something," the president said, trying to break the tension. Clifford smiled at the joke, but McNamara remained stone-faced. He had clearly come for a fight.

"Clark," the president said, "we've known each other a long time and I want to hear your views. You are one of the few people I trust to give it to me straight because you are not tainted by past decisions and have no dog in this fight."

Clifford dove right in. "Mr. President. I hate this war. I do not believe we can win. If we send in 100,000 men, the North Vietnamese will match us. If the North runs out of men, the Chinese will send in 'volunteers.' Russia and China don't intend for us to win this war." Clifford paused, composing his thoughts. "And what if we did win? What then? We would face a long occupation with constant trouble. And if we don't win after a huge build-up and escalation, it will be an even bigger catastrophe. The stakes of losing grow precipitously with every increase in our commitment. We could lose more than 50,000 men in Vietnam. It will ruin us. Five years, 50,000 men killed, billions of dollars—it is just not for us."

The president listened with great interest. Clifford was more passionate and emotionally charged than Kennedy had ever seen him before, and it was clear that these were very deeply held beliefs.

Clifford continued, "Mr. President, you just won a great victory and have more political capital than you will ever have again. Use this political capital to make a bold move to get out of this unwinnable war. Let the best minds in your administration quietly search with other countries for an honorable way out. Let us immediately moderate our public position in order to do so—lower our sights, as well as the expectations of the American people. Now is the time to spend your capital. If you don't, I can't see anything but catastrophe for our country." [1]

"Thanks, Clark. Bob?"

"Mr. President, as I did the other day in refuting George Ball's arguments, I disagree with the fundamental premise of Clark's position—that we have no chance of success in Vietnam. Based on my statistical analysis of the progress we've been making in the countryside, I think there is ample evidence that we can force the North to stop its incursion in the South, irrespective of the stability of the South Vietnamese government—"

"But Bob," the president interrupted, "if you are arguing this is irrespective of a stable partner in Saigon, then do you mean we would be picking up the slack with more forces? Not just bombing, but an active ground-combat campaign?"

McNamara took a breath and answered. "Based on Ambassador Taylor's recommendations and in consultation with the Joint Chiefs, we feel that we'll need between 50,000 and 100,000 troops on the ground by the end of 1965. These troops will provide base security for our air operations and mount active hamlet and village security plans to protect the population in the countryside."

"That number sounds low to me," said Clifford. "Based on the review of intelligence, even hamlet security in a nation the size of South Vietnam will be very troop-intensive. What is the upper-end of the commitment we might have to make in terms of troop numbers?"

---

1 Clark Clifford, *Counsel to the President*, 419.

"It depends, of course, on events on the ground. Our projections are that we may need upwards of 300,000 men in country to fully accomplish the goals we've laid out. Not all at once, mind you, but over the next several years."

This was the clearest recitation of the Pentagon's plan that Kennedy had ever heard. He was amazed at the size of the future commitment, even as he was appreciative of the candor. "Thanks, Bob, for finally laying it all out."

"Mr. President, I understand that this is a huge commitment. But the stakes warrant it. Our reputation in the world is on the line and we must not falter."

Clifford was aching to cross-examine McNamara on every point he had made, but never had the chance. The president was now lost in thought and decided he'd had enough for the night. Clifford and McNamara returned to their respective cabins, but the president went walking for more than an hour, trailed by a Secret Service agent even in the relative security of the well-guarded camp. It was clear to Clifford that the president was engaged in an intense internal debate, and which side came out on top was anyone's guess.

CHAPTER 24

The Salvatore "Sam" Giancana Residence
1147 S. Wenonah Avenue
Oak Park, Illinois
2:10 p.m., December 21, 1964

Frank Nitti and Underboss Tony Accardo sat tensely at a kitchen table littered with newspapers. Sam Giancana was a news junkie and spent every morning pouring over the *Chicago Tribune* and *Herald*, as well as the *New York Times* and the *Wall Street Journal.*

At that moment Giancana was pacing back and forth across the linoleum tile floor, a cigarette dangling from his thin lips. Even for someone who spent most of his life irritated, Nitti could tell that the boss was especially angry this morning. Word had come late the previous evening that the opium lines had been totally cut in Laos, and that the Union Corse's heroin production had ground to a halt.

"We are going to hurt that SOB. And I mean h-u-r-t." he said at last.

Nitti looked confused. "Sinatra you mean?"

"I wouldn't waste a bullet on Francis. No, I mean the fucking president."

"Boss, you know me—I'm all for putting the hurt on anyone who wrongs us," said Nitti, "but Kennedy? He's impossible to get to. Since the assassination attempt the Feds have doubled his protection. We can't get within a mile of the guy."

Giancana sighed. "There are many ways to hurt Kennedy. We don't have to make a frontal assault. No, we're going to hurt someone close to the president. Not family—that's too risky."

"Who then?" asked Accardo.

"Someone the president has come to rely upon, and who offers the added bonus of being part of how he screwed us in Vietnam."

Nitti grinned. "That Mick general? What's his name? O'Shaughnessy?"

"It's O'Shea. Patrick fucking O'Shea who was supposed to keep us in Vietnam. He failed."

"Technically the U.S. is still in Vietnam. So he hasn't really failed," said Accardo. Only the Underboss had the stature to contradict Sam Giancana and not take a bullet to the head.

"You want to split fucking hairs, Tony? As far as I'm concerned we are out of Vietnam. And that's close enough for me," Giancana said.

Accardo shrugged. "Ok, Sam."

Nitti was now excited. "So you want me to tell Ross to open up the drug case and have O'Shea arrested?"

Giancana sat down and lit another cigarette. "I want you to call Ross, alright. Tell him I have a job for him."

When tanks began rumbling through the streets of Saigon, South Vietnamese President Phan Kac Suu knew there was trouble brewing. Over the past several months Khanh and his military junta had been working to sideline the 17-member High National Council (HNC), an appointed body that Khanh himself had created under pressure from the Americans to provide Vietnam with a semblance of civilian rule. Under Suu's leadership, the HNC had begun to assert more power than Khanh was comfortable with. The last straw was when the HNC denied Khanh's request to retire many of the older generation of senior military officers in the ARVN, making room for the Young Turks that he wanted to appoint to positions of power.

Holed up in the HNC offices, Suu received a formal announcement that the HNC was being disbanded, and that all members of the Council were going to be arrested. Khanh flooded the city with troops and the Army-controlled National Police, and before dawn they had arrested five of the HNC members, dozens of other politicians and hundreds of civilian protestors. Khanh and his generals had put an abrupt end to the civilian government in Vietnam, and Saigon was again in chaos.

Office of the U.S. Ambassador
U.S. Embassy, Saigon
8:30 a.m., December 23, 1964

"Goddamn those amateurs! I had better discipline from the cadets at West Point!" exclaimed Ambassador Maxwell Taylor when he got the news of the HNC's dissolution and the chaos in the streets of Saigon. Over the past several months, it had been Taylor's personal mission to create a semblance of civilian control in the South Vietnamese government, knowing that Khanh was a serious liability and believing that a legitimate civilian government could gradually take on power from the military.

Taylor had been increasingly frustrated by Khanh and was at the end of his patience. He had warned them many times about the problems that South Vietnamese instability was creating for the American effort and wanted the coups to stop. Apparently, they hadn't gotten the message.

By 10 a.m. Taylor had the Young Turks, minus General Khanh, in his office and they bore the brunt of his rage. Not allowing them to sit down, he treated them to a dressing down that befitted the way he saw them—as junior officers in a kid's army.

"Do all of you understand English?" Taylor asked. When they nodded yes, he went on. "I told you all clearly that we Americans were tired of coups. Apparently I wasted my words." Taylor then decried the removal of the HNC as "totally illegal." "You have made a real mess. We cannot carry you forever if you do things like this."

Pausing for effect, Taylor went on, pacing in front of the uniformed South Vietnamese generals. "The HNC is an integral part of the country's governance and it needs to be restored. Civilian legitimacy is essential in a democracy. If you do not restore the HNC or transfer powers to a similar civilian entity, then aid will be withheld. The American people will not continue to support a two-bit military dictatorship."

By the looks on their faces it was obvious that the generals were shocked at how Taylor was speaking to them. In deference to Khanh, they chose to say little other than to provide some general reasoning as to why the HNC had to be disbanded.

Taylor was unimpressed with their reasoning. "I don't know whether we will continue to support you after this. You people have broken a lot of dishes and now we have to see how we can straighten out this mess. You are dismissed."

With that Ambassador Taylor signaled his aide to escort the Young Turks from the building.

* * *

The next day, Taylor went to see General Khanh at his office at ARVN Headquarters, located on the outskirts of the Ton Sun Nhut airbase. Khanh received him in his opulent office, ringed by the flags of various ARVN units. He sat behind his big desk, didn't rise when Taylor entered and didn't offer the Ambassador anything to drink.

Taylor was also all business. He repeated the scolding he had given the Young Turks, telling Khanh that the dissolution of the HNC was not in keeping with the alliance they had developed and the loyalty that Washington expected of Saigon.

"Mr. Ambassador," Khanh responded, "my nation is not a satellite of the United States. And when you speak of loyalty, do you mean like the way the United States supported the overthrow of President Diem? That did not show much loyalty to Vietnam. Loyalty must go both ways."

Taylor struggled to keep his temper in check. "General, I must say that I have lost confidence in your leadership. And as a result, military supplies being shipped to Vietnam will be withheld after arriving at Saigon, and American help in planning and advising ARVN military operations will be suspended."

Khanh's face reddened. "You should keep to your place as ambassador. It is really not appropriate for you to be dealing in this way with the commander-in-chief of the Armed Forces of South Vietnam, nor was it appropriate for you to have summoned some of my generals to the embassy yesterday. In fact, I am considering having you expelled from my country."

Taylor laughed. "I can assure you that if you move to have me expelled, General, the United States will immediately cease all support of South Vietnam and you will be left to fend for yourself."

"Yes, well, we shall see about that. My feeling is that you are too deep into this commitment to back out like that, Mr. Ambassador. I don't believe that your President Kennedy will suddenly cut and run because I send one of his hired hands home."

Taylor wanted to pin this little man against the wall by his neck and pummel him with his fists. If he were to be expelled, he'd prefer to go out in a blaze of glory and take this corrupt piece of crap out of action. After taking a few breaths, reason prevailed. Taylor knew that such an action in Khanh's office would make him vulnerable to arrest, even if he had diplomatic immunity.

"I think we are done here, General Khanh."

The Residence
U.S. Embassy, Saigon
8:00 p.m., December 23, 1964

Ambassador Max Taylor and his wife Lydia were just sitting down to dinner inside the Embassy residence when the floor shook beneath them, violently enough to spill water from their glasses.

"Max, what is that?"

"Felt like an earthquake." Just as Taylor got up to look out the window, a blinding flash and huge explosion threw him to the floor. He instinctively reached up and pulled his wife down toward him, and they took refuge under the table. Two more explosions happened in quick succession, and then it became quiet.

Taylor looked at his wife and said, "Those are mortars. I want you to get down to the basement bunker. Go!"

Lydia crawled out from under the table and ran to the door. She paused for a moment and looked back at her husband, who was already on the phone to the head of the Embassy's security detail. Then, without another word, she slipped quietly through the door and was gone.

Over the next ten minutes, Taylor made a series of calls. He first ordered MACV units to create a cordon around the embassy. While the mortar fire was scary and could cause casualties, the real threat was ARVN rolling their tanks through the Embassy gates. After the confrontation with Khanh earlier in the day, Taylor couldn't be sure that this wasn't a precursor to a full-scale attack. He wasn't going to take any chances.

His second call was to the Situation Room at the White House, where he made it clear that the situation in Saigon was quickly deteriorating and that a decision must be made as soon as possible on how to respond to the Khanh's government latest aggression against U.S. interests.

The Situation Room
The White House
8:45 a.m., December 24, 1964

For those in the Pentagon who desperately sought escalation in Vietnam, the news of the dissolution of the HNC, the deteriorating relationship between Khanh and Taylor and the mortar attack on the U.S. Embassy couldn't have come at a worse time. With the entire national security apparatus awaiting Kennedy's decision on next steps, the Pentagon was looking for stability in Saigon upon to which to build a comprehensive action plan for air and ground combat. Having the American ambassador under attack and worrying about expulsion was not the way to start a successful military campaign—especially when that ambassador is himself a former chair of the Joint Chiefs of Staff, and largely in charge of the American effort in Vietnam.

Patrick O'Shea stood next to Deputy Secretary of Defense Cyrus Vance and listened as Roger Hilsman gave an update.

"Taylor just called and said that the U.S. Embassy is under mortar attack and that he has ordered all civilian personnel into the Embassy bunker. It is unclear whether this is an isolated incident or whether it's a prelude to a larger attack."

"Jesus!" Vance responded.

Hilsman said, "The situation is now untenable. Taylor has lost his ability to influence Khanh. And we have no idea if Khanh has ordered this attack or not. For all we know this may be the start of yet another coup. That is going to make it more difficult for us if we decide to go in deeper."

"I'm heading up to see the president. Care to join me?" Hilsman said, looking at O'Shea.

Grabbing his bag, O'Shea joined Hilsman and headed toward the elevator leaving Cyrus Vance to contemplate the Defense Department's next move.

The White House
Washington, D.C.
9:30 a.m., December 24, 1964

When O'Shea and Hilsman arrived at the Oval Office they were told that the president had just gotten off the phone with Senator Richard Russell of Georgia, Chairman of the powerful Senate Armed Services Committee.

Looking at Hilsman, the president said, "I just updated Russell on Vietnam. You know what he said?" In an exaggerated southern twang Kennedy said, "Be careful of falling into the rabbit hole in Viet-Nam, Mistuh President. It's a might dark down there, and you may not find your way back out again."

Hilsman laughed. "He does have a way with words."

Kennedy said, "So Roger what are we hearing from Taylor?"

"Sir, Taylor called 20 minutes ago to tell us that the Embassy has come under mortar attack. Damage has been minimal. Taylor assumes the attack came from Khanh's forces, but that hasn't been confirmed. This comes on the heels of Khanh threatening to expel Taylor, and it is Taylor's view that South Vietnam is headed toward another coup. The Young Turks are plotting against him, and it is clear that they are not going to restore the High National Council," said Hilsman.

The president looked at O'Shea in disbelief. "Those fuckers are now shooting at us?"

O'Shea nodded.

Kennedy stood up suddenly and winced in pain. He walked to the window behind his desk. Facing the Rose Garden, he said, "I've been thinking a lot about the impromptu meeting I had in Normandy with Eisenhower and De Gaulle. The last thing that De Gaulle said to me was that I should find an event that you can point to which proves to the American people that Vietnam is not worth saving."

O'Shea looked at Hilsman and raised an eyebrow. "Sir?"

Hilsman had clearly taken the president's meaning. "Shall we convene the Security Council Mr. President?"

Office of the U.S. Ambassador
U.S. Embassy, Saigon
3:00 p.m., December 24, 1964

"Can you believe this shit?" Taylor exclaimed to the embassy's chief consular officer. He stood at his desk stooped over the afternoon edition of the *New York Herald Tribune* and read aloud. "If General Taylor did not act more intelligently, Southeast Asia would be lost, and that the US could not expect to succeed by modeling South Vietnam on American norms. Taylor's attitude during the last 48 hours has been beyond imagination."[1]

"This is unbelievable!" said the consular officer, genuinely angry.

Pressing the intercom on his desk, Taylor said to his secretary, "Call a press conference."

* * *

Approaching the podium at the Embassy pressroom, Taylor looked angry. He wore a tan suit with a red tie, and a small combat infantry badge pinned to his lapel. For the military, this was the one badge that clearly told others that you'd been in actual combat. It was a sign of the warrior class.

"Ladies and gentlemen. I have a short statement to make. Over the past two weeks the Government of General Khanh has been acting in

---

1 *New York Herald Tribune*, December 24, 1963.

a way that is contrary to the expectations of the United States government. Khanh has sanctioned a military attack upon the sovereign U.S. Embassy and has participated in improper interference into the purview of civilian government by disbanding the High National Council. The HNC is an essential element of democratic government in South Vietnam, and it is essential that it be reinstated. Failure to do so will lead to the United States cutting its aid and support to the government of South Vietnam. Thank you."

The Residence
U.S. Embassy, Saigon
8:00 p.m., December 24, 1964

The telephone rang as Taylor and his wife were trying to enjoy what remained of their Christmas Eve. They were sipping spiced eggnog and listening to Christmas music on the Armed Forces Radio Network. It was Taylor's political attaché calling.

"Sir, sorry to bother you on Christmas Eve. I have two pieces of information that you need to hear. First, Khanh went on television about an hour ago. My team did an analysis of his speech. Shall I bring it up?"

"Can you just read it to me?"

"Yes, sir. General Khanh has issued a 'Declaration of Independence' from foreign manipulation and American colonialism, stating that the time had come for Vietnam to set its own destiny. And I quote: 'We must ask the colonial powers to leave now, as we did in 1954 when we expelled the French from our country. Now it is time for the Americans to follow.'"

"God damn that asshole!"

"Max!" Taylor's wife exclaimed, not liking the foul language. He looked at her and mouthed, "Sorry."

"What's the second piece of information?" asked Taylor.

"The CIA station chief in Saigon says that Khanh has been secretly negotiating with the communists on a peace deal that would enable them to expel the United States from Vietnam.

They aren't sure of the progress of these talks, but back-channel communications were going on in an effort to set an agreement."

At this, Taylor started to laugh. "You can't make this sh-- ah, stuff up! Ok, thanks for the update. I'll contact Washington," Taylor said and hung up the phone.

In truth Taylor was no longer angry. He was resigned now to the reality that the Khanh government was not salvageable, and that the U.S. must be prepared to either go it alone in Vietnam or get out. Either way, the time for temporizing was over. A "go, no-go" decision was at hand. There were no more half step, dip-a-toe-in-the-water options.

It was now or never.

The Oval Office
The White House
Washington, D.C.
10:30 a.m., December 25, 1964

It was unusual for President Kennedy to be working in the Oval on Christmas day. But there would be no going to the Winter White House in Florida for Christmas this year: Duty was calling. He had sent Caroline and John Jr. off to Hickory Hill so they could enjoy Christmas with Bobby's kids.

He had spoken to Maxwell Taylor earlier in the day. It was clear that the time for deciding was upon him.

After the Bay of Pigs, Kennedy had taken responsibility for the fiasco by joking that "success has many fathers but failure is an orphan." Yet at this moment, standing in the Oval Office on a cold Christmas morning, Kennedy felt anything but alone. He could feel Jackie's presence, and the comfort that provided him was immense. He felt like the freest man in Washington—unshackled by electoral politics and wholly unconcerned with the kind of political calculations that led smart men to do stupid things in the interest of expediency.

He picked up his phone. "Evelyn, please ask Pierre to come see me as soon as he can."

"Yes, sir."

Ten minutes later, Press Secretary Pierre Salinger came in. "Pierre, can you alert the networks that I would like a 15-minute time slot tonight at 9 p.m. EST. It will be a talk given from here in the Oval."

"Sir?" Salinger said, obviously surprised. It was unusual for a president to address the nation on such short notice, and on Christmas Day, no less. "What should I tell them the subject is?"

"Tell them it's a foreign policy speech on a subject of national importance."

That wasn't much to go on, but Salinger said simply, "Ok, Mr. President. You want 15 minutes. What about the speech? Do you want me to get Ted Sorensen on it?"

"Have Ted stand by. I hate to ruin his Christmas, but I'm not sure this can wait. I'm going to work on some notes first. I may or may not need him."

"Yes, Mr. President."

"Oh, and one other thing Pierre. Can you ask Mrs. Lincoln to get General O'Shea on the phone? I'm going to need him tonight."

The Oval Office
The White House
Washington, D.C.
9:00 p.m., December 25, 1964

President Kennedy, in a blue suit and red tie, sat behind the Resolute desk and stared straight into the camera in front of him. The speech he had written himself had just been loaded into the screen below the camera, and would scroll as he spoke. As a backup, he had a typewritten copy of the speech before him. Standing along the back wall were Bobby Kennedy, Pierre Salinger and Roger Hilsman. Most of the White House staff was off for Christmas, so the West Wing and the residence had an eerily quiet feel.

At precisely 9 p.m., the producer began the countdown, "Three… two… one" and the red light on the camera went on. The President of the United States was addressing the nation on all three networks simultaneously.

"Ladies and Gentlemen, good evening from the Oval Office. I speak to you tonight, on the holy day of Christmas on a matter of great national importance…"

CHAPTER 25

The Pentagon
Washington, D.C.
9:00 p.m., January 22, 1965

Brigadier General Patrick O'Shea walked quickly down an E-ring corridor in search of the nearest exit. He had been at the Pentagon at the request of the president. Since "the speech"—the term now universally applied to the president's Christmas night address—O'Shea had a target on his back, and the Pentagon was now unfriendly territory.

Today's meeting concerned final logistics for which U.S. military forces would remain in country once the MACV headquarters was finally closed. There remained only 3,000 U.S. military personnel in country, and they had been leaving at a rate of 250 a day. Kennedy knew that his decision on Vietnam had been like salt on an open wound to both McNamara and the JCS, and he wanted to ensure that they weren't cutting corners or otherwise dragging their feet. Huge bureaucracies had a way of slow-walking unpopular directives, and O'Shea had become Kennedy's insurance that this wouldn't happen.

Any hope O'Shea had maintained that he could salvage his military career after "the speech" had been quickly dashed—in the eyes of the Pentagon, his complicity in the president's decision to stand down in Vietnam had permanently branded him a Judas. He would receive no grace. He had come to rely on a handful of junior officers to keep him informed as to when and where meetings were taking place in the huge Pentagon labyrinth. While the president had ordered the Joint Chiefs to inform O'Shea when key meetings on Vietnam were taking place, it seemed to never fail that a last minute room change was required. More than once O'Shea showed up at a meeting breathing heavily from a half-mile sprint, having gone to the original meeting location only to find that it had been rescheduled at the other end of the building. Such were the petty games of scorned senior officers.

By the time O'Shea reached his car in the sprawling, poorly lit Pentagon parking lot, it was dark. The temperature was near freezing, and he fumbled with his keys to unlock the driver's side door of the Plymouth sedan. Once inside, he quickly placed his uniform cap and briefcase on the passenger seat and started the car, turning the heater on high and revving the engine to ensure it wouldn't stall. It was only when he put the car in reverse and turned to back out of the parking space that he saw the .45 automatic pointed at him from the back seat. O'Shea slammed on the brakes.

"Keep your hands on the wheel and look straight ahead," FBI agent Rick Ross said calmly.

O'Shea did as he was told. He was suddenly no longer cold. In fact, he could feel sweat starting to form in the middle of his back.

"Ross, what the hell—"

"Shut the fuck up and listen to me. I want you to drive as if your life depends on it. Nice and easy. Go out the gate and head toward Gravelly Point. You know where that is?"

O'Shea nodded. Gravelly Point was a marshy area on the Potomac River just across from the Pentagon and in the flight path of Washington National Airport.

O'Shea backed the Plymouth out of the parking space and headed toward the exit. He drove slowly trying to buy himself more time to think through his options. Ross was now directly behind him, angled so that O'Shea couldn't see him from the rearview mirror. He'd obviously had a lot of practice at this.

O'Shea reached the Pentagon parking exit and contemplated alerting the guard standing just inside the gate, but he then felt the gun through his seat, poking into his back, and thought twice. He looked at the guard as he passed, hoping he'd notice the terror in his eyes. Instead, the guard crisply saluted and waved the car through.

Having now turned onto George Washington Memorial Parkway, O'Shea headed toward the river.

"Why are we going to Gravelly Point?"

After a pause, Ross said, "You didn't do your job."

Now O'Shea was really panicked. This made no sense. He was expecting Ross to send the drug case to the police. Why was he doing this?

As O'Shea drove onto Gravelly Point, Ross told him to pull up to a small patch of dirt that abutted the marsh.

"Ok. Stop here."

For a very long minute they sat in silence. Ross waited patiently to see if anyone was coming down Mount Vernon Trail—it was popular with dog-walkers but desolate this time of year. Just then a passenger plane from Washington National Airport lumbered overhead, shaking the ground as it passed. O'Shea struggled to calm himself.

O'Shea said, "Why don't we head to the Arlington police? You can turn me in—"

Before O'Shea could finish his sentence another jet roared overhead. An observant passenger looking out the window might have noticed several flashes of light in quick succession emanating from a vast expanse of black. Probably someone out for a stroll carrying a flashlight, they might have thought.

This novel blends fantasy and history together. While it is impossible to know exactly how John Kennedy would have dealt with Vietnam had he survived Dallas, I've inserted him into the narrative as if he had lived—substituting Kennedy for Lyndon Johnson in the real debate over escalation during 1964. All of the characters involved in the discussions on Vietnam are real, and much of the dialogue is taken from first and secondhand accounts of meetings as described by many of those who participated. I've included a bibliography here of the sources I used to recount the historical record.

Other elements of the story are also rooted in history. Lucien Conein was a CIA agent in Saigon during the early 1960s and participated in the coup that toppled the Diem regime. Rock Francisci and the Guerini brothers were active in the opium-heroin trade during this period and ran a vast drug smuggling operation in Laos during the 1960s and 1970s that was supported by the CIA. Sam Giancana, Frank Nitti and Frank Sinatra all played a role in the 1960 presidential campaign, and influenced Kennedy's victory. And Captain Roger Donlon did in fact win the first Medal of Honor in the Vietnam for his heroism at Nam Dong, a battle that I tried to faithfully describe in this book.

On the Kennedy Assassination

Beschloss, Michael R. *Taking Charge: The Johnson White House Tapes, 1963-1964.* New York: Simon & Schuster, 1997.

Holland, Max. *The Kennedy Assassination Tapes.* New York: Knopf, 2004.

Manchester, William. *The Death of a President, November 20 – November 25, 1963.* New York: Little, Brown, 2013.

On Kennedy, Johnson and Vietnam

Berman, Larry. *Planning a Tragedy: The Americanization of the War in Vietnam.* New York: W. W. Norton & Company, 1983.

Clifford, Clark M. and Richard Holbrooke. *Counsel to the President: A Memoir.* New York: Random House, 1991.

Fitzgerald, Francis. *Fire in the Lake: The Vietnamese and the Americans in Vietnam.* New York: Back Bay Books, 2002.

Halberstam, David. *The Best and the Brightest*, 20th ed. New York: Modern Library, 2002.

Herring, George C. *America's Longest War: The United States and Vietnam, 1950-1975.* 4th ed. Columbus: McGraw-Hill Humanities/ Social Sciences/Languages, 2001.

McMaster, H.R. *Dereliction of Duty: Johnson, McNamara, the Joint Chiefs of Staff and the lies that led to Vietnam.* New York: Harper Perennial, 1998.

New York Herald Tribune, December 24, 1963.

The Pentagon Papers: United States – Vietnam Relations, 1945–1967: A

Study Prepared by the Department of Defense. 12 vols., Washington D.C.: Office of the Secretary of Defense, 1971.

Sheehan, Neil. *A Bright Shining Lie: John Paul Vann and America in Vietnam*. New York: Vintage Books, 2009.

On Bobby Kennedy

Schlessinger, Robert. *Robert Kennedy and His Times*. New York: Mariner Books, 2012.

Thomas, Evan. *Robert Kennedy: His Life*. New York: Simon & Schuster, 2013.

On Lyndon Johnson

Caro, Robert. *The Passage of Power: The Years of Lyndon Johnson*. New York: Vintage Books, 2012.

Goodwin, Doris Kearns. *Lyndon Johnson and the American Dream*. New York: Open Road Media, 2015.

On The Opium Trade

McCoy, Alfred W. *The Politics of Heroin: CIA Complicity in the Global Drug Trade*. Chicago: Lawrence Hill Books, 1972.

On the Chicago Mob

Federal Bureau of Investigation. *Sam Giancana – The FBI Files*. Washington, D.C.: The Federal Bureau of Investigation, 2009.

Giancana, Chuck: *Double Cross: The Explosive Inside Story of the Mobster Who Controlled America*. New York: Skyhorse, 2010.

Ken Davenport is an entrepreneur and novelist based in San Diego, California. He has taught courses on Vietnam and political science at Colorado State and Chapman University, and is fascinated by how major historical events often hinge on fate's fickle hand.

Ken's built multiple businesses, lived in Switzerland as a kid, did his graduate work in London, spent a nomadic year in Tokyo, where he learned Japanese (or tried), and now spends much of his free time helping military veterans transition to the civilian world.

To learn more about Ken, his current and upcoming novels, news and updates, go to www.kendavenport.net.

Made in the USA
Columbia, SC
18 February 2018